THE COURT AT CASTLE CHANSANY

CHARLOTTE E. ENGLISH

SPELLBOUNDE PRESS

The Court at Castle Chansany (Castle Chansany Omnibus)

by Charlotte E. English

Published by SpellBounde Press
Copyright © 2023 by Charlotte E. English

Cover design and interior art by Holly Dunn

www.spellbounde.com

Ebook ISBN: 978-4-92824-68-4

Paperback ISBN: 978-9-492824-67-7
Hardback ISBN: 978-9-492824-66-0

This collection is dedicated, with my love and gratitude, to my own court of oddities and eccentrics. There's no family like found family. Thank you for being you, and for being here.

<3

DRAGONSKIN

Sorting through Wizard Garstang's Potionery one airy, improbably-coloured bottle at a time, Jessamine went through what seemed an infinite number before happening upon the one she sought (and too many of these ended up splashed over the rosewood floor, alas, or would have, were it not for the ever-ready sylphs catching them up and sweeping them to safety before they could fall).

The chosen phial bore no obvious signs of difference from its fellows, Wizard Garstang being the meticulous type, and preferring the contents of his Potionery to match exactly. It was six inches tall like the rest, bulbous in the body and graceful about the neck, and tightly stoppered with some porous material ("So that they can breathe," Wizard Garstang had answered upon enquiry, without specifying who or what or how).

Jessamine knew this bottle (a clear glass, just faintly tinted with emerald) for the one she sought by the great eye that slowly opened within, blinked once at her, and then slid sleepily closed. Emerald like the glass was this eye, only a thousand times more vivid, with a slit, black pupil. The wisdoms, glories and resentments of uncountable years glittered in the depths of that eye, and Jessamine was not sorry that it did not open again.

She put the bottle into her velvet potion-bag, and carefully tied the string. This she hung (securely!) from the belt of her mustard-yellow gown (a colour no one would have chosen, for its hue reeked of seedy magics and bile; but Jessamine was grateful for the luxury of the fabric, and she liked besides the way its skirt swirled over her hips).

'You have got it?' asked a gossamer voice, floating somewhere above her left ear.

'Safe and sound,' said Jessamine. 'As you have kept those I elsewise would have ruined. Stars! I swear the poxy things throw *themselves* off the shelves.'

'Why, but they do,' said the voice.

'I hope the Wizard pays you well for your service, then, or he'd have nothing of his Potionery left.' She wondered as she spoke what a sylph might want by way of currency, for their lives in Castle Chansany must be simpler than most of its residents. Did they wear clothes, or require sustenance? Jessamine had never seen a sylph, not possessing the requisite eyes, but she thought not.

'Does he pay *you* well,' said the sylph, 'to fetch his trinkets?'

'He pays me in knowledge,' said Jessamine gravely, for it was true, though her secret heart wished for some halcyon day when she might, against all odds, advance beyond the lowly status of Apprentice Potioner. Then might she not command fees of her own? She could choose how she lived, and where—and the colour (and fit) of her gown would be her own to determine.

Frivolity to think it at all, and the Wizard, were he to hear of it, would raise that terrible, satirical brow, and send her at once to clean the Mixery. But Jessamine, half a fairy and half a human, with all the uglinesses of both, had no other beauties to enjoy. Might she not, someday, aspire to a ribbon or two?

'They need not even be silk,' she said, thinking of ribbons.

But the sylph thought still of knowledge. 'Do they, then, craft books out of silk?' said the sylph, intrigued. 'I hadn't thought it so.'

'The Wizard would have such an oddity,' said Jessamine. 'He has one of everything somewhere, I'm sure of it.'

Including a sleeping and fearsome old power stopped up in a bottle, on the topic of which, she ought by now to be halfway to the Dispensary with it.

With a bob of a curtsey for the sylphs—it never hurt to be polite, with ethereal things—Jessamine hurried out of the glittering, colour-drenched Potionery, closing the door upon its old oak shelves and bottled secrets.

Her lithe little feet carried her post-haste down the three passages that divided the Potionery from the Dispensary, one hand cupped protectively around her velvet potion-bag as she went.

Wizard Garstang sat ensconced in the best-of-all-chairs, the thing having taken up a station in the shadowiest corner of the Dispensary. It did not belong in there, of course; there was scant room for so oversized an article, and its jewel-coloured upholstery and curlicued conceits were ill-matched with the scrubbed, dark wood of the walls and floors. But the chair, like most of Castle Chansany, obeyed the Wizard's bidding; where it was wanted, it was wont to appear.

The Wizard wore an embroidered surcoat and a velvet mantle, as befit his status. It wasn't called frivolity when a man wore finery, Jessamine knew; perhaps because there were no ribbons. The jewels adorning his fingers, and the curls to the toes of his shoes, didn't count.

Wizard Garstang's swarthy countenance lit with something upon seeing Jessamine; was it relief? 'Ah! You have it,' he said, leaping lightly out of his chair.

'Of course,' said Jessamine, a touch crossly, for did he have no faith in her at all? (Or in the sylphs, at any rate; she need not mention how many bottles they had saved from a messy demise). Untying the emerald-tinted bottle from her girdle, she offered it to the Wizard. He did not take it with his own hands, but instead wafted the phial aloft on a stray wisp of mist. The sleeper did not wake; all that stirred within was a low glimmer, as of a dying fire.

'There, shall that do?' said Wizard Garstang, but not to Jessamine. She had not seen the person into whose care he intended to consign the bottle; as far as her eyes could tell her, he was alone.

'Admirably,' said a hissing voice, and what had appeared to be a darkened sconce upon the wall writhed about, shedding its iron-wrought semblance and becoming a boggle. The boggle, pale as milk and a little greenish, but clad in fine Court attire, clambered down the wall and righted himself upon the floor; then, bowing to the Wizard, he plucked the proffered bottle from the air, pulled out the stopper with a swift, deft movement, and downed the contents in one swallow.

'But—!' said Jessamine, appalled, for *something* had been imprisoned within. Something alive.

The boggle looked at her. 'Treganda's daughter, are not you? My regards to your mother.' Then, after belching out a gout of emerald-coloured flame, he sauntered to the Dispensary door and out into the passage, leaving Jessamine staring after him.

'He didn't *pay*?' she said, in great indignation.

'Payment is coming,' said Wizard Garstang, with a look of unholy amusement. Jessamine knew that look. It meant the Wizard was up to something.

A suspicious glare, however, failed to elicit an explanation, and she knew better than to ask. The eyebrow would go up, his dark eyes would fix her with a gimlet glare, and he would instantly find more work for her to do.

'He knows my mother,' she said instead.

'I fail to see the relevance.'

'I hope you won't incinerate him completely, if he is a friend of hers.'

'Only a little bit? Would that be permissible?' Up went the eyebrow.

'About the edges, perhaps,' said Jessamine. She had not yet ceased to pity the sleeping creature with the unsettling eye, greedily gobbled down, as though it were a stomach-settling draught, or a headache remedy.

Wizard Garstang did not reply, nor did he move. He stood frozen, head lifted, as though awaiting something.

'He seemed awfully pleased about something,' Jessamine suggested.

'He is to be disappointed,' said the Wizard.

A crashing sound split the silence, and the sudden roar of a ferocious inferno.

The Wizard began to smile, and then to grin; and when, moments later, the Dispensary-door opened again, and a thing of living flame wandered in, the grin became positively gleeful.

The flame-thing spat in disgust, spraying globs of white flame about the floor. 'Something tastier, I believe I said?'—uttered with the suppressed tumult of a forest fire, and laced with flam- ing crackle.

'You object to boggle?' said Wizard Garstang. 'But seasoned liberally with baseless arrogance! And, I believe, more than a hint of foolhardy ambition?'

'Succulent enough, I grant you,' said the fire-thing. Jessamine expected more, but it did not speak again. It looked up at the Wizard, licking its flaming jaws, and the bursts of fire wreathing its slender body, tapering tail and three, scaly legs dimmed a little.

Wizard Garstang permitted the emptied bottle to float to the dragon's feet, and with a further grumbled curse, uttered in syllables incomprehensible to Jessamine, it slithered over and poured itself down the neck, neatly bottling itself once more.

The emerald eye stared hard at Jessamine, in its depths lurking a twinkle of... satisfaction? Amusement?

Then the eye closed, and vanished.

'That dragon has only three legs,' said Jessamine after a while.

'The fourth was lost.'

'How?'

'I haven't asked.'

'I suppose it would be rude.'

'The wise are not rude to dragons, as a rule,' agreed the Wizard.

Jessamine only nodded.

'You are not going to ask me why I have fed your mother's friend to a dragon?'

'I should suppose he deserved it.'

'Perhaps it's only that Dragonfly was hungry, and I am a tyrant.'

'Naturally you are a tyrant,' said Jessamine. 'You're a *Wizard.*'

He smiled.

'Besides, he appears to have fed himself to the dragon.'

'So he did.'

'Expecting a different outcome, was he?'

'He imagined himself worthy of one.'

Having no further interest in the matter, Jessamine made him her graceless curtsey by way of farewell; it didn't hurt to be (passingly) polite to Wizards. 'I'll return Dragonfly, shall I?'

Wizard Garstang gave her back the bottle, this time with his own hands, which were warm and oddly roughened. *Hers* were so, and no wonder, with all the scrubbing she did; but what business had a grand Court Wizard with callused fingers? A puzzle, and Jessamine made the mistake of looking up, startled, into his face, as though the answer might be found there.

He was laughing at her. 'Carefully now, Jess-o'-mine. If you break Dragonfly's bottle, you will be the next delicacy in his banquet.'

Jessamine clutched the bottle close, thankful she had not run through the winding passages between the Potionery and the Dispensary. 'He wouldn't find me at all delectable. Perhaps one of the Court ladies, by preference.'

Wizard Garstang's glinting grin reappeared. 'I should like to feed every one of them to Dragonfly. Go,' he said, flicking his fingers towards the door. 'And *do* be careful.'

Outside, Jessamine found a display of scorch-marks streaking the cool stone some halfway down the passage. As she passed by, they shimmered silver, and melted away, leaving no trace of the boggle or his unhappy fate.

Save for one jewel: a small ruby, whose fire-licked depths offered some hint as to how it had survived the incineration of every other of the boggle's effects. Jessamine put it into her velvet potion-bag, next to Dragonfly's bottle, and went on to the Potionery.

A gale greeted her upon crossing the threshold—tore the hapless door out of her hands entirely, and sent it slamming wildly against the wall. A revolt in full swing, she quickly saw: the deep shelves, labelled in Wizard Garstang's own looping script, stood empty, their contents ferociously a-whirl above Jessamine's head.

'Shut the door!' called three airy voices at once, not so gently-wafting as before, now more of a howling cyclone in triplicate.

Jessamine tried, but the winds fought her, and she, small and spindly as she had always been, had not the strength to overcome them.

'*You* must shut the door!' she cried, and this command being more promptly attended to than she had expected, she took a vast leap back over the threshold and into the passage, just in time to save herself being brained by the flying door.

Two potions tore out after her. A common Toading Draught she caught in her quick hands before it had flown far; but the Wizard's signature mix, a Wishful Elixir, made it almost as far as the Mixery before she snatched it up. Feathery wings sprouted beneath her fingers, and she winced as the sharp pinions stabbed at her hands.

'Stop that,' she grumbled, squeezing both bottles as hard as she dared. It would not do to shatter the glass, but she *was* displeased. 'And so will the Wizard be, when he hears of this!' she admonished.

The Wishful Elixir quieted, its roil of colours fading to a dull, sulky grey.

She could not leave Dragonfly in the midst of such chaos. He would be shattered to bits in seconds, and then what? He appeared to like his bottle, having slithered back into it with apparent alacrity. What might a boggle-eating fire-licker do to a mere Jessamine, if she smashed his house?

All three potions found a place upon a high shelf in the Mixery, Dragonfly's bottle separated from the rest by a clear four feet, and the Mixery door firmly locked.

Later, standing with her arms elbow-deep in the stone sink of the Mixery-Room, scrubbing away the remains of a Purging Draught, Jessamine heard the one sound she had dreaded all morning through: a shattering and a splintering, as of glass rendered abruptly into dust.

'Stars alive, can a fairy not work in peace?' she roared, terror emerging as fury. The lingering vestiges of Purging-Draught went everywhere as she wrested her arms free of the muck, and tore across the room.

It was not Dragonfly's bottle: that fact alone could (to some degree) quiet her racing heart, and soothe her anger. The emerald-tinted phial stood, meek and quiet, at its separate end of the shelf, half-hidden in shadows and the draping lace of a cobweb.

Nor was it the Toading Draught, which sat like a mud-coloured rock at the other end, peacefully bubbling.

'Twas the Wishful,' sighed Jessamine. 'It would be, of course,' that being the next-most horrible possibility. The bottle lay in a thousand pieces, having shattered so heartily as to leave traces of itself sprayed all over the floor. The contents were grey no longer. Purple and periwinkle, turquoise and moss, and the strange, indeterminate colours of heartache: the myriad colours were racing down the shelf, pouring over the edge, and generally making another great mess which Jessamine would be obliged to dispose of.

Intent as she was upon this fresh calamity, only belatedly did Jessamine observe that the Wishful had run a long way down the long, oaken board, and before she could prevent it, the miserable stuff engulfed Dragonfly's bulbous little house.

'No—!' she started, hurling herself after it, but too late. All the colours merged into the emerald-tinted glass, which began to smell, unaccountably, of berry-pie.

'Drink me,' said Dragonfly.

Jessamine stopped. 'What?'

'*Drink me.*' It could only be Dragonfly speaking, what with the crackle of flames all in the words.

'I certainly shan't,' said Jessamine.

'Why not?'

'You'd devour me,' Jessamine said, folding her arms, and backing a pace or two away from the compromised shelf. 'Burn me all up, like that foolish boggle. And what have I ever done to you to deserve it, I ask you?'

'Maybe I wouldn't,' whispered Dragonfly, oddly seductive. 'Maybe you would devour *me.*'

'I do not wish to!'

'I wish somebody would.' The voice was mournful now, almost weeping.

'You aren't making any sense,' said Jessamine, beginning to feel cross again. 'And I have cleaning to do.'

'*Drink me!*' roared Dragonfly. '*I command it!*'

'I answer only to the Wizard's commands,' said Jessamine, and with a sniff of disdain turned her back upon the too-colourful bottle and returned to the sink.

There followed a quantity of inarticulate snarling, and a sensation of intense heat against her skin. She did not turn again. If she did, she would witness Dragonfly, out of his house again, and trying with all his might to terrify her into obedience. And there was no saying but that he *might*, for a Jessamine was a small, weak thing, no match for fire-lickers.

When the snarling had quieted, she said, without turning her head: 'Perhaps if you were to explain, instead of roaring?'

'*Explain*?' spluttered Dragonfly.

'Why you would wish to be imbibed. It's a strange request, you must allow.'

After an indignant silence, which lasted a full minute at least, Dragonfly said: 'It's my Dragonskin.'

'Your... your *skin*?' Startled, she turned her head, and beheld a formless inferno occupying the darkest corner of the Mixery. 'Have you got any, under all that flame?'

'Yes,' said Dragonfly bitterly. 'And you don't want it, do you? No one does.'

Picturing the lifeless hide of a dragon, deprived of its innards, and draped all over the shelf, Jessamine was silent with horror.

'I thought the boggle might do,' said the dragon, heedless of the effect of his words. 'But it's no good. There wasn't enough of him.'

'Then why ask me?' Jessamine squeaked. 'I'm no taller!'

'What has height to do with anything?'

Jessamine began to answer, but finding herself incapable of a sensible response, gave up the point. What *had* height to do with anything, indeed? 'What is it I am to do with your Dragonskin, supposing there's enough of me?' she said instead.

'Why, wear it! What else would one do with it?'

The Wizard, she thought, would drape it over his best-of-all-chairs, and sit on it. Perhaps that was why Dragonfly had not plagued *him* with his peculiar request.

She asked anyway. 'Did the Wizard decline?'

'I haven't asked him, and I shan't,' said Dragonfly. 'What a preposterous dragon he'd make!'

True, reflected Jessamine. There had not been enough of the boggle to make even a halfway dragon (and upon reflection she could see that there was not; strange that it had escaped the Wizard), but there was far too much of Wizard Garstang. He would burst his bounds, like a swollen river, and his *Wizardliness* would go cascading all over.

Probably Jessamine would have to clean it up.

'So I'm to be dragoned, then?' said Jessamine. 'I am sorry, but I'm no clearer about the business than I was before. Why should you wish to give up your Dragonskin?'

'I am tired,' breathed Dragonfly, and the searing heat, mercifully, lessened. 'For all that I'm only a potion, I'm a potent one, and I've been much employed.'

How long the dragon-potion had lurked upon the shelves of the Potionery, Jessamine could hardly say. Certainly she had not seen him before, but she had been the Wizard's Apprentice for less than a year.

'You would not have to clean the Mixery,' Dragonfly said, and Jessamine stopped scrubbing, arrested.

'Or the Dispensary,' he went on. 'Or the Potionery, either.'

Jessamine dropped her scrubbing-brush. It fell into the soapy, grimy water with a splash, wetting her apron and, underneath it, her gown.

'I see I have your attention,' said the dragon.

'You do,' she allowed.

'Well then, let me see!' Restored, by hope, to high good humour, Dragonfly obligingly ceased to burn her at all. 'What else do you want? There is not much you could not have.'

'Living in a glass bottle, pouring myself down other people's guts all day?' Jessamine narrowed her eyes. 'You have funny notions of freedom, sir.'

'No, no! That isn't at all how it would be. What is it that you want?'

'A ribbon,' said Jessamine.

'A ribbon?'

'Silk, and the colour of the sky in summer.'

Dragonfly was silent a moment. 'Is that all?'

'Yes.'

'It can't be.'

'It is.'

He scoffed. 'I thought you a weightier sort of person.'

'Then there cannot be enough of me, can there? You had better ask someone else.' She resumed scrubbing.

Dragonfly, ruminating, did not answer. At length he said, slyly, 'When I was younger, I used to go all about the Castle. With the Wizard Baldringa. She did nothing but that she asked for my counsel.'

'I thought you said you were only a potion.'

'And you are only a girl.'

'You make an excellent point.'

'So you'll do it?' The flames erupted again, bright with hope.

'I'll *think* about it.' Jessamine returned to her scrubbing, and this time Dragonfly did not interrupt her.

After all, would it be so very bad if she failed, like the boggle, and became dragon-food? The Wizard would soon find someone else to clean his Mixery, and she had never excelled at the Wizardly arts herself. Even *he* agreed that she never would.

She was here only because of Mother. The fairy half of her heritage came from Treganda; a famous Court beauty some twenty years ago, Treganda was as ravishingly beautiful as she was difficult of temperament. Jessamine's utter failure to inherit either of these qualities had been an eternal source of disappointment to Treganda (who did not imagine herself difficult so much as charmingly wilful); so when the Wizard Garstang, somewhat the worse (or the better) for the Queen's honey wine, had offered her an Intolerable Insult, and subsequently a forfeit in recompense, the beauty had been quick to demand an apprenticeship for her gawky, impossible child. The fact that Jessamine had neither aptitude for nor interest in Wizardry had been nothing to her.

Why the Wizard had agreed to such a forfeit in the first place, or kept her on afterwards, remained a source of mystification to Jessamine.

As did the nature of the Intolerable Insult, which neither Treganda nor the Wizard would ever tell her.

She'd stayed because she recognised in her mother's manoeuvrings a desire to be rid of her obligations to so strange a child; and being fed and clothed in the service of so magnificent a character as the Court Wizard rather beat scrubbing pots in the scullery.

An alternative future for her daughter as the resident Court Dragon might please Treganda just as much. And there was considerable beauty about Dragonfly. It was not the beauty of silken wings and tresses, like her mother's, nor that of velvet gowns and ribbons, such as she craved in her secret heart. It was the beauty of strange and ancient magics, of elements and nature and power and myth, and Jessamine gave the possibility serious thought—at least until she had finished cleaning the Mixery.

'Well?' rasped Dragonfly from his bottle, as she staggered back over the threshold with her burden of buckets and mops.

'I am sorry, Dragonfly, but I believe I cannot,' she said, setting the buckets down for a moment. 'You see, you make a strong case for Dragonhood, but that isn't what I am. I am a creature of four plain limbs and shivering in the winter, and I don't know how to be a dragon.'

'You would soon learn,' said Dragonfly.

'As I have learned Wizardry?' Jessamine, shaking her head, picked up her buckets. 'I'm afraid I would be poor at it.'

'How do you know, if you haven't tried?'

This question, being unanswerable, went unanswered. Jessamine left the Mixery, taking the Toading Draught with her, but leaving Dragonfly behind.

*   *   *

'Have you been cleaning again?'

Wizard Garstang, having rung for his third-favourite spell-book to be brought into his study at once, regarded Jessamine with a frown as she came trotting in.

Jessamine, startled, looked down at herself. Had she splattered her gown with Purging Draught and soapsuds, and failed to notice? Or perhaps that mischievous Wishful had got onto her as well as onto Dragonfly.

She saw nothing but mustard-coloured cloth, only slightly wrinkled, and her own unlovely body beneath.

'The Mixery was very dirty,' she said defensively, and set the third-favourite spell-book—less weighty than the first and second, and relatively sober in appearance, a mere dark clothbound tome with silver etchings—onto the low table at his elbow. He was in his best-of-all-chairs again, the thing installed in its regular place before the stone hearth, and somehow contriving to emit a steady reading-light.

'I have other people for that,' he said, making no move to pick up the third-favourite. 'Will you not *use* the Mixery?'

'I thought you liked me to clean, being as you're quick enough to send me for the scrubbing-brushes.'

'Only when I am trying to annoy you, Jess-o'-mine. I can see I shall have to try a different approach.' He picked up the third-favourite at last, and made some show of leafing through it, but Jessamine did not think his mind was on the spells.

'It amuses you to annoy me?'

He subjected her idle question to more depth of thought than she had expected, and after some moments of rumination announced: 'It does not precisely amuse me, but I hope some-day it will benefit me.'

'Benefit you?' Jessamine eyed him with sour disgust. 'I can't see how it could.'

His grin appeared, and a gleam of exactly the amusement she had accused him of. 'No, but I'm persuaded you will. What happened in the Potionery this afternoon?'

'I don't know. The Potions took it into their heads to hold a riot.'

'Again?' His brows went up—*both* of them, this time. 'Why, they haven't done that since Year's Turn.'

'I can't think what set them off.' Jessamine made a move to retreat, navigating carefully between an enormous jarful of twinkling butterflies and a precarious stack of cloth-and-leather-bound tomes towering up from the floor.

'I imagine it was Dragonfly, for some motive of his own. He's restless just at present.'

Jessamine frowned. Her mouth wanted to speak, to tell him about Dragonfly's odd request, and find out his opinion of it. It half-opened, all ready to pour forth the words, but some other instinct shut it again.

'Yes?' said Wizard Garstang, observing this aborted attempt.

'Why is he restless?' she said.

'Dragonfly? Oh, he has a fit of discontent about once a year, and sleeps much of the rest of the time. They say he was an excellent Familiar to one of my predecessors, but that must have been a long time ago.' He bent his head over the third-favourite, and began to read.

A Familiar! Jessamine had always heard that Wizards had Familiars, but *her* Wizard had not seemed to; she'd thought herself mistaken. Was Dragonfly his Familiar?

'Why, he is as bad at it as I am!' she blurted, not making much sense; she'd meant he made as poor a Familiar to the Wizard as she made an Apprentice, and what a pity.

'That being so,' said the Wizard, without looking up, 'I fear our arrangement is to come to an end, for I have taken a new Apprentice. He begins in the morning. I am sure you will show him around the Mixery and the Potionery and so on, before you leave?'

Jessamine stood, transfixed with shock. 'L-leave?'

'Tambul will need your room.'

'B-but—' stuttered Jessamine. 'Where will I go?'

He looked up at last, and directed at her a dark, keen look, as though deeply interested, all of a sudden, in the subject of his erstwhile apprentice. 'Where would you like to go, Jess-o'-mine?'

'I wouldn't like to go anywhere at all!'

'No? Surely there is somewhere that interests you?'

She was silent. To be sure, there might be some other post in Castle Chansany she could take; even were it the scullery, it would be better than nothing.

But he had asked about her *interests*. The world beyond the Castle was large enough. Surely something of it might fascinate her?

'I like it here,' she said. 'With you.'

His eyes were smiling, she was sure of it, though his face remained grave. 'A solution will no doubt present itself by morning,' he declared. 'Do go away now. I simply must finish this cantrip.'

Jessamine, heart-stricken, turned in silence to leave.

'Do not even *think* of cleaning the Potionery,' he called after her.

Jessamine slipped silently out into the passage, and didn't answer.

The potion seared her throat a little as it went down. In its wake it left a burning sensation, more pleasant than otherwise, like the time Jessamine had finished the dregs of one of the Wizard's discarded goblets.

'I could have been the best-of-all-familiars,' she said sadly, 'If only he'd asked.' She dissolved as she spoke, her limbs turning to mist and then smoke and then flame. She waited to disappear, as the boggle had done; down into the innards of Dragonfly, never to be seen again. But she didn't.

'Wizards are no good at asking,' said Dragonfly. 'Not in any of the right words.' His name now made sense to her; he had the wings for it, once stripped of his Dragonskin. He was handsome, too, even if he was hundreds of years old. Perhaps he wouldn't get any older, now.

'I'd stay away from Treganda, if I were you,' she told him with a sniff, wreathing her smokish form around his lithe limbs.

Dragonfly shuddered. 'You do burn, you know,' he said, extricating himself. 'You'll have to watch that.'

'Sorry,' said Jessamine, too busy for remorse; it had struck her that she would never be cold again. Neither cold, nor frail, and the next time Wizard Garstang raised his left brow at her, and said something about the Mixery sink, she'd have exactly the means to annoy him.

No. She would have no opportunity to annoy him, for was she not to leave? She'd decided that herself, just before the potion had gone sliding down her throat. A Dragon need not remain anywhere she did not choose, and she'd have her house with her.

'How does it feel?' said Dragonfly, having stretched out his fairy-limbs ten times over, and turned a somersault that sent him right up to the ceiling. 'Shall you be all right?'

'I shall be the best-of-all-Jessamines,' she told him firmly. 'I can feel it already.'

He grinned, reminding her, for a moment, of the Wizard. 'We thought you'd be perfect,' he said. 'Take care of the Dragonskin. It's the first-favourite, you know.'

'Wait!' said Jessamine. 'Who's *we*?' But he was already gone, vanished out of the meagre window of her little Apprentice's room like a wisp of smoke his own self.

Grumbling, grousing and spitting flame, Jessamine made her way down to the Wizard's study, and slithered her way very carefully between the books. *You do burn, you know.* She had better watch for that.

He was still there, in his chair, with the third-favourite spell-book open on his lap.

'You could not have just asked, I suppose?' she said, taking care not to bathe him in flame. Or not too much, anyway.

He waved her fires away with a flick of his fingers, and set aside the book. 'I did ask,' he said.

'You didn't. I am sure I'd have recalled it.'

'I asked when I gave you the Dragonfly.'

'You did no such thing. I took it out of the Potionery myself.'

'And why did you do that?' The left brow went up.

'Because you wanted him for a customer.'

'In a manner of speaking. I thought a snack might appease the dragon, and that boggle always was an unpleasant fellow.' Garstang blinked. 'Whatever was his name.'

Jessamine, having never known it, could not assist him. 'Dragonfly was the customer?' she spat.

'One might rather consider the boggle as payment for services rendered.'

Jessamine's flames roiled in tune with her dismay.

'I shouldn't waste your sympathies upon him, if I were you,' said the Wizard. 'He was perfectly aware of the risk.'

'But what if there'd been enough of him? You would have got him for a Familiar! I can't think he would have been better than Dragonfly.'

'I thought it of all things most unlikely,' said the Wizard, unruffled.

'What if there hadn't been enough of me? I'd have been dragon-lunch.'

Wizard Garstang looked straight into Jessamine's fiery eyes, and the lurking smile was back in his own. 'You've always been enough, Jess-o'-mine. There wasn't the smallest danger.'

She sniffed, though the tip of her shimmering tail found its way to his wrist, and coiled loosely about it. 'I *am* magnificent, am I not?'

'Beyond anything.'

'Did you complete your cantrip?'

'I can make no sense of it at all. Will you take a look?'

Jessamine draped herself over the back of the best-of-all-chairs, and rested her snout upon her Wizard's shoulder. 'Open it up, then,' she ordered, and the Wizard retrieved the third-favourite, and offered it for his Familiar's perusal.

'I shan't be fed any boggles,' she said, suddenly suspicious.

The Wizard smiled. 'You shall have anything you wish, Jess-o'-mine. You're a dragon now.'

'A ribbon, please,' she said promptly. 'Sky-blue.'

But the Wizard made no move to produce one. He only turned his head, and looked up at her, waiting.

'Oh,' said Jessamine.

It was not a Wizard's power, the magic that stirred in her fiery depths. It was older, deeper, and stranger than that, and Jessamine needed only a thread of it.

'Delightful,' said the Wizard Garstang, with his glinting smile.

Jessamine, decked in ribbons and flame, purred her satisfaction. 'Well, Wizard,' she said, tapping the open pages of the third-favourite spell-book with the tip of her tail. 'About the cantrip.'

THE BEST-OF-ALL-CHAIRS

When the dragon Jessamine slithered into the Wizard Garstang's study in the dark of the night, and undulated her way towards the best-of-all-chairs that skulked in a corner, a voice from the shadows took her by surprise.

'I would not sit there, if I were you,' said the voice.

While disembodied and confusing as to source, it could not be termed alarming; not even though the hour was late, and the night dark and silent. The words emerged too sleepily for that, as though the speaker were at least half asleep.

Jessamine paused. She had not known the sylphs to frequent the study very often, for the Wizard's caprice irritated them, and theirs had the same effect on him. But they were wise in the ways of Castle Chansany, and when they spoke, Jessamine listened.

From a distance of a safe three or four feet, Jessamine inspected the chair.

Nothing so personal to the Wizard Garstang could be modest, either in proportion or design, and so the best-of-all-chairs elevated the concept of *splendid* to new and dazzling dimensions. The tall, engraved back rose to a height of six feet; the seat was wide enough across to fit at least two people side-by-side; and the arms were of proportions eminently suited to the king's own throne. Moreover, while the greater part of an old oak tree had already gone into its construction, in the creation of its spectacular frame, the Wizard had desired that the thing should be soft as well. Hence the profusion of cushions, in hues of emerald and sapphire and gold; above all, the best-of-all-chairs advertised itself as *expensive*.

'Perhaps you think I will damage it, and displease the Wizard,' said Jessamine. 'And were it likely that I should, you would be right to prevent me. But my fires are my own, and shan't do anything unseemly to the chair.'

'The Wizard would never harm his Familiar,' said the shadowed voice. 'However clumsy she had been. But no, that was not my concern.'

Jessamine thought again. 'Perhaps what stands before me is not the best-of-all-chairs at all, but something else in a clever disguise.' She let her tongue unspool, and tasted a leg. The flavour, woodsy and old and dry, did not encourage a second taste.

'Like as not to be, with the Wizard around,' agreed the voice. 'But no, that was not my concern either.'

'Well then, what is it?' said Jessamine, abandoning so un-satisfactory a pursuit. 'I am tired, and I want to sit down. On something *soft.*'

'The Chair is in no mood for company,' came the answer, sleepily, and then nothing.

'No mood?' muttered Jessamine. 'What else does a Chair desire but to be sat upon, I should like to know?'

Nobody answered her, or not right away. A swishing sound came instead, and then into the pool of light cast by Jessamine's own wreathing fires there appeared: a carpet.

It was the thickest one, nicely rounded about the edges, and coloured like forest-moss.

'Aren't you supposed to be in front of the hearth?' said Jessamine, recognising it.

'I went for a perambulation,' said the carpet, settling itself in its accustomed place with a silky *sigh.*

'Refreshing.'

'Occasionally.' The carpet, to all appearances, went to sleep.

Jessamine nudged it with her snout, and when it did not rouse, she delicately bit the corner.

'You are rude,' said the carpet.

'I am,' said Jessamine. 'And since that is the case, I shall not hesitate to make use of the best-of-all-chairs, whatever its mood.' So saying, she flowed fierily up onto the broad, cushioned seat of Wizard Garstang's own chair, and curled up.

Nothing untoward happened. But, just as she was dropping into a comfortable doze, someone said lugubriously: 'I like that.'

Jessamine stirred. 'What's that?'

'Personal Chair to the Court Wizard,' the mournful voice continued. 'Every expense lavished upon me. And then I am made over to an *Apprentice.*'

'But I am not an Apprentice,' said Jessamine. 'Not *now.* I'm the Familiar.'

'You aren't the Wizard,' said the best-of-all-chairs. 'It amounts to the same thing.'

'I should suppose the Wizard to be asleep,' said Jessamine. 'Or perhaps carousing.' She closed her eyes again.

'His fancy's caught,' said the chair. 'His eyes turned another way, and what is to become of *me*, I ask you?'

Jessamine pondered this. 'I think not,' she said. 'He was always more scornful than otherwise, when it comes to the Court ladies.'

The carpet intervened. 'Child, the chair talks of furniture.'

Jessamine sat up. 'The Wizard's got another chair?'

'A gift,' mourned the best-of-all-chairs (or, as Jessamine now supposed, the second-best-of-all-chairs). 'From the Queen.'

'Why would Queen Mellany give the Wizard a chair?'

'It...' The second-best-of-all-chairs paused, struggling in the grip of some deep emotion. 'It *flies*,' it managed at last, and fell into a brooding silence.

'Cannot you fly?' Jessamine enquired. 'I have seen you taking up the best of spots all over the Castle.'

'Not as such,' mourned the chair. 'Not like *that*.'

'Right.' Jessamine slithered off the chair. 'I've got to see this.'

Jessamine would have felt no surprise if the whole tale were to prove itself nothing but hocus-pocus. What the Queen would want with the Wizard such that she would give him a flying chair, well, Jessamine could not imagine. Surely the Queen was too busy ruling the kingdom with the King; what time had she to waste on frivolities such as unusually airborne furniture?

But when at last she discovered the Wizard (he having proved absent from his bedchamber), she found that the second-best-of-all-chairs was right.

The Wizard *did* have a new chair. What's more, the gossamer fairy-wings sprouting from its four graceful legs, and the top of its tall and elegant back, suggested that the tales of its powers had not been exaggerated.

And that the Wizard was enchanted with it could not admit of a doubt, for he was sleeping in it.

He made no attractive picture, sprawled all over the seat, with his legs thrown carelessly over one spindly arm (this chair not having the robust stoutness of the other), and his head gracelessly lolling. Jessamine supposed him to have been engaged in study of this new marvel, with his customary carelessness of time and tiredness, until he fell asleep where he sat.

His sapphire velvet mantle was sadly wrinkled.

Jessamine woke him with a waft of cinder-scented air.

He stirred, grunted something unflattering, and fell back into slumber.

'Wizard,' Jessamine hissed. '*Wizard*.'

His dark eyes opened, and fixed, unseeing, upon Jessamine.

'You make a spectacle of yourself,' she hissed.

Being Wizard Garstang, he had not fallen asleep in one of the many dusty corners of the Castle, a quiet, out-of-the-way place where no curious eyes could fix upon him. Being Wizard Garstang, it would not have occurred to him to take his prize into some such unobjectionable spot, and conduct his investigations *there*. No, not even though he *had* an excellent chamber of his own invitingly titled "Study".

The Queen had presented him with his new, splendid chair in the midst of Their Majesties' Feasting Chamber, Jessamine knew, for that was where the Wizard had remained. And having fallen asleep, had acquired (or perhaps retained) an audience of: two fascinated Court ladies in moon-coloured silks; a Bard's apprentice, the callow youth trailing a lute and a green mantle much too big for him; a rival Wizard from a neighbouring kingdom, judging from the spangled garments he wore; and a pot-boy crept out of the kitchens to see the spectacle, not entirely hidden behind the golden brocade skirts of a banqueting-table laden with sumptuous delights.

Wizard Garstang took in all this in bemused silence.

'He wakes!' cried one of the Court ladies, following this en-lightening comment with a peal of silvery mirth.

'We hope your repose has refreshed you, Wizard,' said her companion, more gravely.

'Yes,' said Wizard Garstang, and sprang out of his seat with one of his abrupt, effervescent bursts of energy. A pair of dancers, failing to foresee this possibility, almost collided with him; the Wizard's satirical brow rose as he watched them whirl away again, scowling. He did not offer the ladies so much as an-other syllable, but bent over his new chair, and became absorbed again in its various contours.

'He will be looking for evil enchantments,' said the rival Wizard, loftily, to the same ladies. 'It is what any Wizard does, upon receiving a new Wonder into his care.'

Jessamine's Wizard did not favour this with any response at all; deeming it beneath his notice, no doubt.

'No such thing,' said Jessamine firmly, and set the rival Wiz-ard's toe on fire with a lick of her tongue. 'The Queen would not give him anything evil.'

The rival Wizard was not long inconvenienced by his flaming footwear, for he smothered Jessamine's promising little blaze with an irritable gesture of his long fingers. The contemplation of the black burn now marring the beauty of his satin slippers distracted him, however, and he did not reply.

'What *are* you doing?' said Jessamine, turning back to *her* Wizard (for he might be every bit as self-satisfied, know-it-all and tyrannical as this other one, but at least he was *hers*).

Wizard Garstang, absorbed, did not reply.

'You have broken your best chair's heart,' Jessamine persevered. 'And it's my belief the furniture will be plotting a mutiny.'

'No, no,' he murmured, running a gentle hand along the edge of one silken, fluttering chair-wing. 'The carpet will keep them in order.'

'The carpet's asleep.'

'Well, and what else would you expect a carpet to do at this hour?'

Jessamine sighed, and slithered under the table, from which sulking-spot she emitted a fine flow of rose-scented smoke.

'I say,' came the Wizard's voice, 'You aren't too attached to these, are you?'

Jessamine peeked under the hem of the brocade table-clothes. The Wizard was chatting with the new best-of-all-chairs, and he had his fingers around the gossamer wings.

'Flying's awfully dangerous,' he continued. 'A high wind and ill-luck and you'll be dashed to pieces against some turret, or fallen into the lake. Care to trade?'

Whatever the chair said in reply, Jessamine could not hear. A soft-spoken thing, by appearances; nothing like the deep rumble of the best— no, the *second*-best-of-all-chairs.

Jessamine hoped its response was favourable, however, for in another moment, the Wizard said: 'Excellent!' and, with alacrity, plucked the glorious wings from the chair's high back. He bent, and a few swift gestures secured those adorning its four legs as well. He piled them all onto the seat, picked up the chair (severed wings and all), and made off with it.

Jessamine scuttled out from under the table, and ran in hasty pursuit.

Wizard Garstang pushed his way through the throng of the Queen's Feasting-Chamber, and once out into the passageways kept up a long, rapid stride all the way back to his study. A word, once fairly through the door, set all the sconces aglow, and the furniture woke up with a start.

The Wizard was no sluggard, when properly inspired. 'There,' he said, a moment later, stepping back to admire his handiwork. 'No ill effect, I think?'

The gossamer wings, taken from the Queen's gift, now fluttered gaily from the back of his erstwhile favourite chair—its back now extra tall and straight with pride, Jessamine judged. The four smaller wings sprouted jauntily from its thick, heavy legs.

The best-of-all-chairs, now restored to all the glory of the position, gambolled.

'Not yet, not yet,' said the Wizard. 'Not till we get outside.'

The best-of-all-chairs subsided.

'They do not match,' sniffed Jessamine.

The Wizard surveyed his chair. 'You are right,' he decided. 'What do you think? Ruby?'

'No! Horrible!'

'You're right,' said the Wizard again. 'Silver.'

'Nothing will do for *you* but gold,' said Jessamine.

She expected the Satirical Brow, in response to this sally. Instead, she received the Glinting Smile. 'Perfect,' he decided, and the wings turned a shimmering and stately gold.

Jessamine slunk up the legs of the Queen's chair (divested of its wings, and waiting hopefully nearby). 'This is my chair,' she announced.

Wizard Garstang's head came up. 'Ah. Yes. Just a moment.' Quite what he did, Jessamine could not tell; she knew only that a surge of magic swept over the chair (smelling, unpleasantly, of wet mud), and as it passed it left behind it an article of furniture much altered.

'Oh,' spake the carpet, softly. 'That's nice, that.'

Jessamine dug her claws into the blanket of soft (and really, scarcely damp) moss that now grew upon the seat of her chair, and stuck her nose into the nearest of the canopy of rose-blooms that hung from the back. The wood itself was no longer a pale deadness of hard edges and turned corners; now it grew in knots and whorls, like a tree again, only chair-shaped. 'Charming,' said she, with rare sincerity. 'Just needs one more thing.'

'The sylphs will see to the watering,' said Wizard Garstang, with a careless wave of his hand.

But Jessamine mustered her own blazing magics (a little musty with disuse, but functional enough), and manifested a spray of ribbons winding jauntily up each leg.

'Those don't match,' said Wizard Garstang, which was true enough, for a living tree-chair had no use for a set of woven fabric adornments.

'Yes, yes they do,' said Jessamine, and went to sleep in her chair.

THE FAR-BELOW

The Object—whatever it was—rapidly disappeared into the impenetrable, milk-white mists surrounding the walls of Castle Chansany. Jessamine listened in vain for the sound of its eventual impact, far below. *Far* below.

An awful silence followed this event, lasting some time.

Jessamine broke it at last.

'Something's fallen over the side.'

Saying it aloud made the terrible truth feel all the more real, and Jessamine's sinuous tail began an uncontrollable twitching. Weren't there supposed to be wards, and such? Invisible but infallible enchantments swaddling the sky-high castle in a comforting shroud of safety? Winds of magic! Currents of gramarye! Nothing was *ever* supposed to go over the side.

And Jessamine had not even the first idea what it had been. She'd strolled out to the balcony to take the air, puffing an amusing stream of perfumed smoke from her delicate nostrils; paused to enjoy the aesthetic delights of the rainbow-coloured forest flowers, rambling from pot to pot, and sprawling languorously along the silver fences; and then—and *then*—it had happened. An Object, small and fast-moving, had gone hurtling down.

She might have sworn, in fact, that the thing had hurled itself off the balcony, and into thin air.

Nobody spoke. She was alone out here, then, not even a sylph wafting about upon the dulcet breezes; hmph. No one to talk the matter over with.

Also, no witnesses.

Jessamine curled up at the base of one ornate, glinting fence and shut her eyes a moment, pondering. If no one had perceived the event save for herself, was it necessary to make anything of it?

Perhaps she hadn't even seen it. Perhaps it hadn't happened at all.

Her draconic lips stretched in a blissful smile, and for some three or four minutes she dozed in the golden sun, comforted by these charming ideas.

But, no. It wouldn't do. Something *had* gone over—something that glittered oddly in the sunlight—and if one didn't put a stop to such behaviour, well, who knew what might go over next? It might be one of the flower-pots, so pretty with their cerulean glaze. It might be somebody's hair comb all over jewels, and the Royal Court wouldn't stand for *that*.

It might be... it might be the first-favourite spell book, and *then* she'd be for it.

Jessamine's eyes snapped open in horror, all thought of slumber gone. Something had to be done. Not a doubt of it.

'I suppose,' she gulped, 'I'll have to fetch the Wizard.'

Her ensuing trek through the castle was of the lengthy character guaranteed to leave her out of breath and patience both; but finally, *eventually*, she ran across the Wizard Garstang—near enough literally. He sat cross-legged upon the floor, his velvet-clad behind parked upon a curlicued rug, and tucked behind an ornate screen in a corner of somebody's bedchamber. Jessamine hadn't the faintest notion *whose*. He sat alone, but the profusion of silver coffee-pots scattered about him, together with far too many cups, saucers and silver spoons, strongly implied he had recently enjoyed company. Rather a lot of it.

'*Wizard,*' puffed Jessamine, her lashing tail toppling a hapless coffee-pot or two. 'You're needed at the Edge.'

'The Edge,' repeated the Wizard. Being face-down in a near-empty pot at that moment, deeply inhaling the dregs of whatever had once occupied it, he took no note of Jessamine's state whatsoever. 'Which Edge, my dear dragon, and why?'

'The Hindmost South-Western Balcony,' she snapped. '*That* Edge, and you're wanted because something's Gone Over.'

That brought him out of the depths of his pot; he raised his head, and blinked his dark eyes several times. Full of steam, she thought, or some such. Perfume. One never knew, with the Wizard. 'Gone Over? Gone Over where?'

'Gone Over *down*.'

'What was it?'

'How should I know? 'Twas a blur of something glitterish, and then gone.'

'You didn't throw it, did you?'

Jessamine began to swell with indignation, but before she had more than half doubled in size, the Wizard grinned, and said, 'I had to ask, Jess-o-mine, did I not? Admit it, you're in just the mood to engage in a spot of target practice.'

'Were your head the goal, mayhap,' she conceded.

'Quite,' said the Wizard, accepting this with admirable grace. 'But it wasn't you.'

''Twas not me. I was sunning myself, peaceful as you like, and there it was gone.'

At last, something like disquiet entered the Wizard's expression. He sat for a moment in thought, tapping a coffee-stained finger against one lip. 'Well,' he said, rising abruptly to his feet, and towering over Jessamine. 'Then something ought to be done, oughtn't it?'

The balcony was just as Jessamine had left it—flourishing with verdure, and empty of company. The Wizard spent some little time with his folded arms resting atop the balcony fence and gazing into the far-below.

Jessamine peeked, too, balanced atop the fence with her long tail wrapped tightly around the bars to steady her. There was not much to be seen for all the white clouds in the way, but perhaps the Wizard's eyes saw more than Jessamine could.

'There appears to be a hole,' he said after a while.

Jessamine looked, but saw nothing of the sort, and said so.

'A hole in the veil,' he clarified, with a trace of impatience. 'The veil, which is *there*, I might add, precisely to catch such things as would otherwise tumble down.'

'Or people,' put in Jessamine.

'Those as well.'

'And how did it get there?'

'The hole? Someone must be tinkering with my arrangements.'

He uttered this in tones of grave displeasure, which one couldn't wonder at.

'What then do we do?' said Jessamine. 'I suppose we must find this person.'

'I suppose we'll have to go down,' said the Wizard instead. 'After all, until we know what the object *was* it is useless to try to guess who wanted it.'

'You think it was a stolen thing?'

'I don't see what other use there would be in making holes in my lovely veil.'

Someone at Castle Chansany was a thief. The notion shocked Jessamine a fair bit, for the Castle did not receive newcomers often, nor did very many people leave; most of those as were in residence were *always* in residence, and how could any of them be so disobliging as to steal from someone else? Her tail began a staccato twitching at its tip, a fair sign of her anger, and since the result was a wobbling and a near-toppling from the balcony fence, she hastily got down. After all, there was a hole in the veil.

'You'll mend the hole?' she said, for the Wizard had put out a hand to steady her, and why would he have done that if he wasn't afraid for her possible demise? He was the forgetful sort, likely to hare off in search of the culprit and leave the problem unremedied.

'In due time,' he said.

'Ah,' said Jessamine. Well, that was that, then. 'So it's down for you.'

'For us, Jess-o-mine. I'll want my Familiar with me. Our culprit and our object both might be down there, after all.'

'Me to go down,' said the dragon with a smoky sigh. 'But it's far-below.'

'You've wings.'

'And little practice at using them.' Jessamine had not been a dragon for long; only scant weeks ago she'd been a half-fae, with two legs only, and not a wing to her name.

'Here, then, is an excellent opportunity.'

Jessamine muttered something, stretched the fiery wings in question, and beat them back and forth. Air moved, but nothing much else. Certainly not Jessamine. 'They're too weak,' she announced. 'They'll never hold me.'

The Wizard's only answer to this was a gust of air—*cold* air—which swirled about Jessamine's clawed feet and wafted her into the sky. He himself had already summoned his favourite chair—the best-of-all-chairs. The thing came swooping in on its gossamer wings, and caught the Wizard up in its velvet-cushioned seat. The pair hovered, and so did Jessamine.

'Tarry a moment,' said she, flailing. 'I tell you, I cannot fly.'

'You must imagine better, my dragon,' said the Wizard gaily, and soared away. Some last few words came drifting back with the winds of his passage. 'The feat is only a thought away!'

Only a thought, and the thoughts passing through Jessamine's mind were not, at that moment, of the sort suited to a public airing. She growled, and spat a little flame over the edge.

It winked out of life in mid-air, smothered to death by all that nothing.

'Well, and so shall I be,' said Jessamine with resignation, and chucked herself over the side.

She had a fair view of the Castle from this inverted posture, and ample time, as she plummeted down, to admire all the beauties rapidly dwindling in size. Those turrets really were *lovely*, all the glass twinkling in the sun so— a frantic flurry of her smoky wings failed altogether to slow her descent— pity she'd not had another of Chef's butter cakes for breakfast, she *could* have, but she'd thought of her girth and refrained, *fool*, for what use had a dragon for a svelte frame if her wings didn't work and she was to be squashed flat in the far-below anyway?

An impact came, sooner than expected; it *hurt*, knocked all the breath out of her in a *whoosh*, but it wasn't the squashing kind of an experience; another breath came.

She'd shut her fiery eyes when she thought of Chef's butter-cakes. She opened them, and saw the Wizard.

'Tsk, dragon,' said he, smiling at her. He'd caught her as she fell, doubtless with a fancy flourish of his Wizarded chair, and she was saved.

'Not so much for flying, these,' she croaked, wafting smoke.

'Since that's so, you might stop flapping them about,' said the Wizard with a cough. 'I'd sooner breathe air than smoke.'

Jessamine, frightened into unwonted obedience, stopped. By the time she'd caught her own breath, and calmed the shaking in her limbs, the Wizard had brought the-best-of-all-chairs to a swooping halt upon some blessedly firm ground, and Jessamine was able to alight from her seat.

The far-below turned out to be leafy in character, and not much else.

'There's a forest here,' said she in surprise.

'Well, of course there is,' said the Wizard, striding off. The-best-of-all-chairs gambolled along after him, far more delighted than either of its passengers at this unscheduled outing. 'What else should there be in the far-below, pray?'

Jessamine had often peeped over the side, but had never glimpsed aught but wafts of clouds and mist; she'd dreamed up many a fanciful thing that may lie beneath, but the Wizard— he'd had the misfortune of *knowing*.

Now Jessamine knew, too, and a few airy dreams slipped away in consequence.

She sighed.

Still, it was more forest than she'd ever seen before, and interest revived. She had no names to put to the trees she saw, but they were vanishingly tall, and broad about their sleek brown trunks. Boughs reached out a long, long way, decked in all that extravagant greenery, and there was emerald-coloured moss up and down them, and all over the floor. She saw ferns, too—these she did know, for some of the Court Ladies liked to keep them in pots, and there were some upon the balconies.

'I'd like a fern,' she announced.

The Wizard was Questing. She knew it from the purposeful stride, and the set to the jaw, not to mention the rapt look in his eyes. But he answered her from some disengaged part of his great Wizard's brain: 'Then you'll have the best of all ferns, Jess-o-mine, but first help me find the Object.'

Yes. The Object. Distracted by all this far-below splendour, Jessamine had forgotten the purpose of the Quest altogether. The Object! Whatever it was had fallen right through the clouds and must have ended up amongst the ferns and the moss, but how were they to find it? Twas a small Object, and a large far-below.

She said this.

'Am I not a Wizard?' answered he. 'And do I not have a Familiar at my elbow?'

Jessamine, being farther away than that, scurried to catch up. He and the Chair were fairly off, trampling ferns aplenty in their haste; Jessamine flitted along behind, unsure what, as Familiar, she was to do.

'There's a cantrip,' said the Wizard. 'Scribed upon the eighteenth page in the volume of thirteen seasons past—' (He meant the second favourite spell book, Jessamine knew that one). 'It is for finding a lost *thing*, and now that I think of it, I ought perhaps to have brought the book with me.'

Jessamine gave a smoky sigh, curling the delicate leaves of a few passing ferns. 'Besides, how are we to use a cantrip on a thing when we've no notion of its identity?' She was looking all around as she scuttled along, her bright eyes on the watch for anything that looked out of place; anything that was patently *not* part of this verdant and squelchy far-below; but she could spend a year at the task and catch not a whiff of it, she knew.

'We must find assistance,' declared the Wizard, after a moment's thought.

'From the second-favourite book?' Jessamine had a vision of the thing, called from far away, and hastening to obey its master's summons; hurling itself over the side, as she had done, and plummeting down.

'No, I have not the book with me. Did I not say that?'

'Then where's this assistance to come from?' said Jessamine. 'For we're all alone, if you haven't noticed.' Not so much as a rustle of leaves had she heard, save those she and the Wizard made themselves. Not even any brisk, scurrying creatures among the undergrowth were there, for with the clamour they were making they'd frightened the lot away.

But the Wizard looked Up.

'Ah,' said Jessamine, espying something feathered, and with a long tail. It wafted along the winds, far above, glimmering blue and red in the dulcet sunlight. She thought it would come down, convinced, in her befuddled way, that all about must obey the Wizard's summons as she did.

But the bird did not come down.

'There,' said the Wizard presently, not deigning to point.

Jessamine glimpsed it, perhaps. A flicker of green, but then there was so *much* green; how was she to tell one sort from the other? 'Something moss-coloured,' she hazarded. 'But up far too high.'

'Here it comes.' The Wizard waited, holding himself unusually still. Rare for the man to adjust his *own* behaviour to suit another's needs; he was trying not to scare the scrap of a creature, decked in wing, that came wafting slowly down.

'Twas a dragon, gathered Jessamine, and couldn't speak for shock.

At least, not for a moment or two. '*Well*,' she spat, curiously affronted. 'If 'twas a dragon you wanted, had you not dragons in sufficient number?' It wasn't even an impressive specimen, being far smaller than Jessamine herself, and all skin and bone. A youngling, barely out of the egg.

'But this one flies,' said the Wizard Garstang, with a smirk at his Familiar.

Jessamine might have sulked, save that the Wizard's expressions were becoming known to her. She detected, beneath the smirk, a conspiratorial smile. Something of fellowship, in this invitation to share a joke, though it came at her expense, and she settled down. Perhaps he was not fixing to replace her with this delicate thing, at that.

The newcomer frisked in delight, under the Wizard's gaze. She would soon be cured of *that*, thought Jessamine sourly, and condescended to sniff the creature, politely enough. It smelled of loam and sap and a whiff of petrichor, not unpleasant.

The Wizard spoke gently to it. It was only a baby, Jessamine reminded herself. It warranted gentleness, even if she didn't. 'Tell me, my tiny fellow. Have you seen an Object lately fall from the heavens?' And he pointed upwards, quite as though the dragon might comprehend.

It didn't. Jessamine read this in its behaviour, perfectly unchanged, say the Wizard what he would. It gambolled, it coquetted for attention—shameless thing—and it made a curious sound, *mrrrr*, and chirped. Someday it might grow larger, and develop, with all its new bulk, an intellect, and perhaps even an identity. Until then, it could hardly be worth talking to—

'Perfect,' said the Wizard, beaming. 'What a fine fellow you are.' He fed it something, Jessamine could not determine *what*, though it smelled sharp, and savoury.

'What,' said she. 'And have you derived meaning from this nonsense?'

'Haven't you? I must say I'm surprised.' The Wizard attempted, with a wave of his bejewelled fingers, to dismiss the dragon. The little creature proved impervious to suggestion.

'You fed it,' observed Jessamine. 'A mistake, that.'

'Well, then you shall have a companion,' decided the Wizard. 'He'll be a fine creature once grown, though perhaps too big for the Castle—'

'Tell me what it said,' interrupted Jessamine, impatient with this vision.

'Something fell,' answered he, in tones of surprise, as though this ought to have been obvious. 'We knew that, of course. But now we have some idea as to *where*.' As if these words had themselves proved a spur, he was off, swooping away in his Wizarded chair.

Jessamine scuttled along in his wake. If she fluttered her wings hard enough, they proved effective to boost her speed, even if not to lift her aloft; she made full use of them, and barely kept up.

The interloper, scarcely inconvenienced by the Wizard's pace, fluttered along too.

'Where are we going?' she called after her master.

'What I truly asked,' carolled he, 'is whether anything fell *that did not belong*, and our little friend has seen only one Object that he could not recognise. It glittered sharply, and caught the sun, and it fell somewhere in this direction.'

Jessamine, growing short of breath, paused, and took in the extent of the damp forest before her. Reams and reams of it, with no end in sight, and all frondy besides. 'Absurd, absurd,' cried she. 'Do you seek to stumble over it, in all this fernery? It'll never happen. We shall be here until Year's End.'

'I don't, at all,' said the Wizard agreeably, slowing. 'But *you*, perhaps—'

'Oh,' said Jessamine, for there it was, lying quietly at her feet. Such an innocent thing, inert among the moss, for all the world as though it had *not* led her and the Wizard a merry dance all the way from the Castle.

'There,' said the Wizard, with vast satisfaction. 'You always had a lucky way about you, Jess-o-mine.'

This being too patently absurd for words, Jessamine ignored it.

'Well, then, and what is it?' The Wizard came swooping back, the wings of his chair stirring the drooping ferns.

'It is a spoon.'

Wizard Garstang halted before this felled treasure, and regarded it in silence.

In point of fact, the spoon was bright silver, recently polished. A fine, wrought thing, fit for nobles to use at table, though in size it seemed more suited to the tea-tray.

Or possibly, the coffee-pot.

Jessamine's mind wandered back a ways, to where she'd found the Wizard. Reposed upon the floor, surrounded by a decimated collection of beverages—and a quantity of spoons.

'It is *your* spoon,' she accused.

The Wizard did not answer.

'It is just like all the others you had about you,' she persisted.

'Nonsense,' said the Wizard, briskly. 'The Castle must be full of such articles.'

'Doubtless,' Jessamine agreed. 'But how would one of *those* come to fall down into the far-below?'

'Well, and how do you imagine a spoon of *mine* should have done so?' He was growing testy, the scowl building upon his brow.

Jessamine, recognising the signs, persevered. 'Because you threw it.'

He scoffed, and spluttered something incomprehensible.

'Perhaps you were in a temper,' said she, serene. 'Or perhaps you were showing off, for I doubt me not that there were ladies present. Was it not so?'

The Wizard, unusually, was silent.

'If anybody *else* were to throw a thing with sufficient force to hurl it over the side, its descent should, in all likelihood, be prevented by your Wizardly veil.' Jessamine, becoming smug, permitted herself a snicker. 'But if *you* were to throw it, Wizard-mine, how different a story. There's a fine hole burned in your veil, I'll be bound, and a long afternoon's work ahead to mend it.'

The Wizard bent, and collected the spoon. He examined it briefly, and then tucked it away into a pocket in his velvet coat. 'Tell no one of this, Jess-o-mine.'

'I might, perhaps, be encouraged to hold my peace,' she conceded. 'If I were to be suitably recompensed.'

The Wizard Garstang sighed. 'Shall it be comfits again? I'll speak to the kitchen.'

'Comfits aplenty,' said Jessamine sternly. 'And two or three butter-cakes.'

The Wizard eyed her. 'You could ask more.'

'But I shan't, for I'm a reasonable dragon.'

'And are you to assist me in mending this hole I've burned in the veil?'

Jessamine gave the matter due consideration. 'No, I shouldn't think so,' she decided. 'For the sun is not yet gone, and I've a nap to finish.'

THE QUEEN'S PHILTRE

Have you ever been to Castle Chansany?

Perhaps you go there as a pedlar, selling ribbons and cosmetics and jewels to the inhabitants of the Royal Court.

Perhaps you are a cook, or an ostler, or an apothecary, tending to the residents' many and varied needs in exchange for a few silvers for your own.

You may be a Wizard or a Wizard's Apprentice, oft to be found in the Libraries in the small hours of the morning, weary-eyed in pursuit of an elusive cantrip.

Or perhaps, just perhaps, you are a noble yourself, attending the Court in your satins and silks and making your bow to Their Majesties.

Have you, then, met the Queen?

Queen Mellany, they say, is a lady of surpassing handsomeness (if not, precisely, beauty). Doubtless her velvets and her jewels would grant handsomeness enough, even were she insufficient in feature. An air of majesty and power would supply the rest, would it not? And a queen must have a surfeit of both.

She is a little younger than His Majesty the King, but not much, with honey-coloured hair not at all given to grey (so they say). Her eyes are the colour of amethysts, proclaim the fanciful (or the fawning). Others speak of her voice, low and mellow, melodious as a lady's voice should be.

Perhaps these observers have seen her from afar, in Their Majesties' Feasting Chamber, or at a Royal Ball. They cannot have seen her in person, not up close. Not in the intimate fashion of a friend or an associate.

For if they *had*, they would sing a different tune.

If *you* have ever chanced to glimpse Queen Mellany in private—as she sits, almost unattended, in her glass-house, say, or before she retires to her bed—you might not speak of handsomeness or velvets, or of jewel-coloured eyes.

You might be more disposed to say: Her Majesty is *tired*.

'Fetch me the Wizard Garstang,' said this lady one eventide. She spoke in the dusty, whispering tones of profound exhaustion, so faint the syllables that one must strain to catch them at all.

But her lady-in-waiting (Aramanta, today) had sharp ears. 'Yes, your majesty,' answered she, and left the glass-house at once in a flurry of emerald silks.

The queen was left alone, which seemed to suit her, for she sat motionless, her eyes half-closed. There is at least one advantage to weariness: there is a peace in it, for if one has not the vitality to go rushing about the world, one must by necessity place oneself somewhere comfortable, and stay.

A deep serenity enveloped the glass-house once Aramanta was gone, for everything else in it was passing into slumber. The sun's blinding rays were gone, dipped below the horizon, leaving a tranquil blue haze in their wake. The queen's flowers had furled their petals and stood dreaming in the dusk. Even the winged things that occupied the upper reaches of the rambling vines were silent in their nests.

A luna moth drifted slowly by, its silvered wings glinting in the moon-coloured light of the queen's crystalline lamps.

The night wore on and turned into morning, and the Wizard Garstang did not appear.

There came, though, another voice. A dry, smoky cough stirred the air near the queen's knees, and then somebody spoke. 'Majesty?'

Queen Mellany's eyes opened. They appeared a faded blue, barely any colour left to them at all, but perhaps it was a mere trick of the light.

A dragon crouched by her feet, the proud, ruby-shimmering head dipped in a show of respect (or possibly uncertainty).

'Yes?' said the queen, still in those dusty tones, for there was no need to exert herself *here*.

'What manner of service is it you want?' said the dragon, curling a long, fire-tipped tail around clawed feet. Something in the voice told Her Majesty that this creature was of a female persuasion, and she was looking expectant.

The queen achieved a frown. 'I am not acquainted with any red dragons,' she said, slowly. 'And I do not recall that I asked for one.'

'I wasn't either,' said the dragon in answer to this first observation. 'Until recently, when I turned into one. But I am not always red, as it happens. I was blue yesterday, and perhaps I shall be golden tomorrow.'

The frown deepened.

'And you did not summon me,' continued the dragon, helpfully. 'You called for my master Garstang, but being as he's the Wizard, well, he's nowhere to be found. They're rarely anywhere you want them, Wizards, and if they are it's like to be a week late.'

Queen Mellany said nothing, but the befuddlement creeping into her pallid face said enough.

'I'm Jessamine,' said the dragon. 'I was the Wizard's apprentice, once, though I cannot say as I was any good at it. I'm the Wizard's Familiar now, though, and I *am* good at that. Were you wanting anything a Wizard's Familiar might be able to do?' This last question was uttered with a note of anxiety, as though the creature were uncertain of her own relevance to the situation.

Her Majesty, however, had not the first idea. 'I need a new Philtre,' she said. 'The Wizard Garstang enchants them for me, and he must do so again, at once.' It took the poor lady some time to utter so many words together, but Jessamine did not lack for patience. She waited, politely enough, until the queen's words had ceased.

'It'll not be the classic sort of Philtre you're wanting, will it?' Jessamine mused. 'You've the love of his majesty the King already, not to mention a castle full of courtiers and a kingdom full of subjects. That's enough love for anybody, I should think.'

'Indeed,' said the queen.

Jessamine subjected her liege-lady to a long look and a deep scrutiny. 'Something along the restorative lines, then?' she offered.

'Indeed,' said the queen.

'Hm.' Jessamine, perceiving that Queen Mellany lacked either knowledge of the subject or the capacity to express it, asked no further questions.

'If the Wizard's anywhere to be found, he'll be along soon, I make no doubt,' she said. 'But that's as may be. The matter's urgent, I judge.' She performed a fleeting bow, a dip of her rubescent head all wreathed in smoke, and grinned. All her long, pearly teeth showed. 'I will see what I can do,' she promised, and scuttled off.

The queen, bemused, said nothing, but slipped back into her half-slumber.

*   *   *   *   *

Queen Mellany was a merry figure, Jessamine would previously have said; merry and formidable in equal measure, a fair bit of each. A distant being of bright gold hair, a flashing smile, and an air of majesty only a born queen possesses.

But not today, alone in her glass-house, without her pomp and her ceremony. Without her Court. For a moment, Jessamine had felt the larger of the two, and she being but a small heart and a shrinking soul herself.

Which was the true queen?

The Wizard would know, but the Wizard was not to be found.

Jessamine scurried through the winding labyrinth of the Castle, barely aware of the passages she slithered down and the chambers she passed by. Her mind (small it may be, but it was keen, for all that) occupied her with reflections of a new kind: who among her acquaintance was all that they seemed to be? The Wizard, for instance. What might lie behind the vibrant, glittering colours of the man? Was he, too, a poor quailing thing beneath the arrogance and the laughter, like Jessamine?

Or wearied to his very soul, like the queen, and only pretending otherwise?

The thought prompted a snicker. Inconceivable.

The door to the Potionery stood shut fast, with the impregnable demeanour of a locked and bolted barrier. A muffled clattering emanated from within, and a curse or two in Tambul's hoarse voice.

Jessamine made of herself a puff of smoke, and wafted underneath.

'What's amiss?' said she, reshaping her draconic curves upon the other side.

Tambul, the Wizard's new apprentice, turned an aggravated face upon her. His hair, never very well-behaved at the best of times, appeared to be staging a full-scale revolt, for every white wisp of it stood on end. His compact form bristled with indignation; the little man fair radiated rage.

'You look like to fly into pieces in another minute,' said Jessamine. 'Can you not mellow yourself a trifle?'

'It's those *sylphs*,' he spat, staring wildly at the empty air around him. 'They've taken the Wizard's Wishful Elixir, and I have but *just* finished Mixing it. He'll not be pleased, and then who'll be to blame?' He swiped uselessly at the air, coming up with nothing.

Jessamine, seeing nothing resembling a floating phial, judged the thing long concealed. 'Come, now, is this the truth?' she called. 'It is too bad of you.'

A chorus of laughter answered her, and then the phial reappeared. It was one of the larger ones, Jessamine saw, airy glass, and filled to the brim with a parti-coloured liquid. Tambul had made a lot. 'But he is no *fun*,' breathed a voice in her air, even as the phial floated its way (sulkily) into Tambul's reaching hands.

'Aye, but you make him still less so with such treatment,' Jessamine reproved. She could not disagree with their judgement; she hadn't taken to the new apprentice herself, he being of a sour disposition, and not seeming sensible of his immense good fortune in assisting the Wizard Garstang. But he had talents far exceeding her own, this she could not deny, and the Wizard seemed contented with him.

She received only a gusty sigh in response. Tambul snatched up his phial and stuffed it immediately into the velvet potion-bag hanging from his belt. 'This'll not come out again until it goes into the Wizard's own hands,' he informed the air, scowling.

'Tambul,' said Jessamine.

The look he gave her might be irritable, but no more, the return of his Elixir having mollified him a shade. 'Yes?'

'We've an emergency.'

That word, to Jessamine's surprise, operated powerfully upon the Wizard's apprentice. He snapped to attention, forgot his grievances in an instant, and seemed somehow taller for it. 'What's the matter?'

'It's Her Majesty, the Queen, though not as I ever saw her before. She looks like to fade away any minute, Tambul, so tired as she is. I'd swear she was a century old, and never mind the golden hair. She wants a Philtre from the Wizard, but can't say as what's in it, and no one can find him.'

Tambul attended closely to this jumbled recital, and did not plague her with questions. 'The Queen's Philtre,' he mused. 'Seems to me as I've heard mention of it before, but I've no notion how it's made. And we have nothing of *that* sort in the Potionery just now.'

Jessamine's heart sank. 'Then do you know where the Wizard has gone?'

His brows quirked. 'If the Familiar hasn't a notion, how then should I?'

Jessamine, flattened, gave a wispy sigh. When had anybody kept pace with the Wizard Garstang, after all? Not even *he* could keep up with himself, she'd wager. Things fell out of his brain as rapidly as they wandered into it.

'Then what are we to do?' said she. 'Where did you hear of the Philtre, Tambul? Did the Wizard mention it to you?'

'No,' said he, wiping his hands on the colour-stained apron he wore, before tearing it off. 'I've not been set to make any such thing. Twas in a book, methinks—'

'One of the grimoires?' interrupted Jessamine, her heart rising.

'Aye, but I'm forbidden to go into them except in the Wizard's own presence. *You* ought to recall that.'

'I do,' Jessamine agreed. 'So you would be. But *I* am not. I'm the Familiar these days, and he hasn't said as I'm to leave them alone *now*.'

'He hasn't *said* as much,' repeated Tambul. 'But does that mean he hasn't intended it?'

'It hardly matters,' Jessamine decided. 'We've need of those grimoires, and if the Wizard's unhappy with me he may tell me all about it later. For now, we're to the secret library, and quickly.'

The Wizard's study seemed a lively place, when the Wizard was in it. Not so much when it stood empty. It *echoed* in rather chilly fashion—an oddity, given the profusion of carpets and cushions and curtains; and it only did it when Garstang was off someplace, as though his absence had disembowelled it of something.

The-best-of-all-chairs stood in its customary spot in the best corner, towering over the more mundane articles of furniture, and sporting all the best of the soft things. It didn't speak as Jessamine and Tambul came in.

Neither did anything else, in fact, until Jessamine lightly kicked the mossy carpet that lay before the empty hearth.

'*Whissht*,' uttered the carpet, a sound not unlike a sneeze. It quivered. 'Well, what is it?'

'Is the Wizard handy?' said Jessamine, to start.

'I've no notion at all.'

Not, then. 'Well, and is the Library about?' she tried next.

The carpet fluttered, a helpless little gesture. 'You'd have to ask the shelves.'

The Library should not, strictly speaking, be its own entity at all, being as it was a collection of shelves itself—and books, of course, always those. But things about the Wizard had a way of turning *odd*, and in this case, the Library had a will of its own.

Jessamine turned to the shelves, at least those she could perceive. Not part of the Library, these, or not officially; they were the ones that hung about in the open, where just anybody could see them, and housed only the lesser books. But if you wanted to find a Library, a bookshelf was always a good place to begin.

Jessamine redirected her question to these humble creatures, wrought all of polished, dark wood as they were, and burdened with weighty tomes and bejewelled things. They occupied the wall several feet above her head, a lofty position, from which they loomed over everything except the-best-of-all-chairs.

A silence followed, rather a long one.

At length, a dusty voice said: 'And what would you with the Library?'

'I need a grimoire,' said Jessamine, promptly and firmly. If you sounded like you were uncertain of your right to things, people tended to get obstructive ideas. 'The Queen's in trouble, and the Wizard has the answer, and I've to find it. Quickly.'

'Righto,' said the shelf, and the wall behind it shivered. It had no right to perform so delicate a manoeuvre, being, probably, a foot thick and made of solid stone. It did, however, and it creaked as well, and *groaned*, and then—stopped, and fell silent.

Nothing had moved, not even the wall, and Jessamine experienced a profound confusion—until it occurred to her that all was changed. The shelf she'd spoken with was gone, perhaps, or only altered—hard to say, when everything was made from the same deep-brown wood and held a similar array of leather-bound spell books. But these were different books, and that was a different shelf.

'Oh, splendid!' she cried, and swarmed up the Wizard's favourite chair. The back of it rose quite six feet high, a suitable vantage-point from which a dragon (and but a small dragon, at that) might peruse the spoils.

Tambul stood upon the chair's seat. He would be made into gloves, Jessamine reflected, if the Wizard came back and saw him at it, but that was his own look-out.

Besides, they had a queen to save, and heroes were obliged to perform daring manoeuvres, once in a while.

Jessamine seized upon the best spell-book, the chief grimoire, the Wizard's prized collection of cantrips. Being as it was such, the book was of mighty size and sumptuous demeanour, its covers sapphire-blue and gilded and its manner self-satisfied. It harrumphed a little as Jessamine leafed through its pages, but it didn't object.

'The trouble is, I hardly know what I'm looking for,' she commented to Tambul.

'Aye,' said he grimly. 'It's not like to be helpfully labelled. "The Queen's Personal Tonic, in Case my Familiar and my Apprentice Should be Obliged to Mix it in My Unexplained Absence"—that'd be nice.'

'You'll get used to it,' offered Jessamine.

'By *it*, I suppose you mean *him*, and I may at that,' grumbled Tambul. 'But not before I lose my wits altogether.'

Jessamine permitted herself a small, smoky snicker. Really, it was invigorating to have someone to grumble with; someone who understood, as she did, how *maddening* the lofty Wizard Garstang could be. Indeed, the Wizard delighted in being so, the wretch; if he had not been threatened with defenestration by a maddened subordinate, he considered the day wasted.

'Oh, but,' she said, arrested in the midst of these pleasant reflections. 'But, Tambul, it *is*.'

'It is what?' Tambul set aside the emerald-bound tome he had been perusing, and Jessamine passed the grimoire down to him.

His face turned thunderous. 'The Queen's Excellent Philtre,' he read aloud. 'For the Information of my Inferiors, Should I be Unable to Oblige Her Majesty.'

The tip of Jessamine's tail began an irritated, staccato twitching.

Tambul's face only darkened further as he read on. 'This is some manner of joke,' he announced. '*One measure of cochineal, ground up fine, dissolved in aqua pura. And let a simple Cantrip be uttered over it, that it might manifest a Starry Radiance.*'

'That doesn't sound too hard,' said Jessamine hopefully.

Tambul shut the book in disgust. 'You really were the worst apprentice, weren't you?'

'Yes,' said Jessamine placidly, having never felt the slightest interest in the mechanics of potion-making. 'So you had better explain the source of your indignation, hadn't you? What's cochineal?'

'*Cochineal, ground up fine*, is the parts of an insect,' he answered. 'Powdered.'

'Some fine, magical insect,' said Jessamine, smiling. 'With healthful properties, for Her Majesty the Queen.'

'A red insect,' said Tambul.

'A powerful, strong colour.'

'No. An insect that is red *only*, with no mystical qualities, Jessamine, not even of any kind. It is a charming colour, I'm told, often used to stain the lips of Court Ladies, and that is all.'

'The... the Cantrip, then?' Jessamine faltered. 'The Starry Radiance—'

'Looks pretty, I grant you, and impressive, if you're disposed to enjoy such things.' Tambul's sour tone left his own feelings on the subject of *sparkles* very clear indeed. 'But of no use to the Queen's health, or anyone's.'

Jessamine turned this information over. 'So we're to mix up a red liquid that looks pretty,' she concluded.

'Yes.'

'And which does nothing at all.'

'Yes.'

Jessamine enjoyed a brief, fervent desire to set fire to the Wizard Garstang's study, but with a strong effort of will, she refrained. 'It isn't a joke,' she offered.

'It must be.'

'It can't be. How could he have known to arrange it? For all his odd talents, clairvoyance was never among them.'

'The whole Library is probably a jest,' muttered Tambul. 'Put here merely to torment us. The *real* Secret Library is somewhere else.'

But Jessamine knew better. She had *one* advantage over Tambul, ignorant as she may be about the potions, and that was seniority. The Library was the real one, and so was the first-favourite-spell-book.

So the Philtre described there must be the one he gave to the queen.

'Was there nothing else written there?' she asked. 'With the measures for the Philtre.'

Tambul scowled, wrenched open the grimoire again, and leafed through it.

'More nonsense,' he said. '*Let it be administered in Her Majesty's Glass-house, at the Golden Hour of the day.*' He shook his head in disgust. 'What possible difference the *place* should make when a Philtre's taken, I can't imagine. And what's the *Golden Hour*?'

'The Golden Hour changes through the year,' said Jessamine. 'Haven't you ever noticed it? It's late after the noon, when the sun sinks low, and all the world is bathed in gold light.'

Tambul's brows rose. 'No,' he said. 'I haven't noticed.'

Tambul clearly possessing the aesthetic sensibilities of a block of wood, Jessamine abandoned all further attempts to enliven his mind. 'The sun's coming up,' she said, uncurling herself from the top of the Wizard's chair, and creeping down. 'We'd better hurry along, if we're to have the stuff by the afternoon.'

'You cannot mean we're to pursue this absurd plan?' Tambul spluttered. 'We're to feed *Her Majesty the Queen* coloured water with stars in it, and call it a Philtre?'

'Yes.'

'But 'tis trickery.'

'If it's trickery, it's the Wizard's trickery,' said Jessamine firmly. 'And once in a while, you know, he has sound reason for the doing of it. To the Mixery, Tambul. We have work to do.'

The Philtre (such as it was) took no time to prepare, Tambul being handy enough at the art. But before that could be managed, there was the cochineal to unearth (the Wizard not being the organised type, he had left his jar of it, open and half-empty, in the south-facing breakfast parlour). Then a suitable cantrip had to be chosen, for the making of the stars; Wizard Garstang had not seen fit to record his own, preferred charm in the book, and Tambul said, somewhat aggrieved, 'I have not been much in the habit of making things twinkle.'

Jessamine assisted as she could, scurrying hither and thither, and anxiously watched the sun's progress across the sky. More than one carpet, or set of drapes, began to smoke as she passed, and had to be hastily beaten.

At last, though, the mixing was complete, and Tambul declared himself satisfied. He handed a clear bottle filled with carmine liquid to Jessamine, who curled the tip of her tail around the neck of it, and carried it high.

She'd reached the Mixery's stout oak door before she realised he was not following.

'Come along,' said she, giving off sparks.

'My task is to Mix,' he said, rather loftily, gazing down at her from beneath dark brows. ''Tis the Wizard's to administer, or in this case, yours.'

'You think it won't work,' said Jessamine. 'And you'd rather it were my fault, when it fails, and not yours.'

'Of course it will not work. It is coloured water.'

'Will you have a *little* faith in the Wizard, if not in me?'

Tambul's scowl deepened.

'*Something's* bound to happen when the queen drinks your *coloured water*. Do you want to see what it is, or not?'

Tambul heaved a great sigh, and took off his colour-stained apron again. 'Very well.'

'And if it doesn't turn out well, we can always blame the Wizard,' added Jessamine cheerily. 'After all, it's *his* spell-book.'

'That being so—' Tambul agreed, and he swept up the grimoire in question—as proof, no doubt, for when he needed to explain himself to the queen.

The afternoon was speeding by, and the sun was sinking; Jessamine wasted no more time on words, and sped along herself, trusting to the Wizard's apprentice to keep up as he could. The route from the Mixery to the Queen's Glass-house was a winding one, and couldn't be got through quickly.

At length, however, Jessamine burst through the gilded doors and found herself once again embedded in green verdure. The enchanted windows shimmered in the golden light of the dying day, and the place seemed, indeed, different. Warm and mellow and sweet, like bathing in honey.

Queen Mellany sat where Jessamine had left her, in her handsome chair, framed by long-leafed ferns and dreaming lilies. A songbird, feathered in purple and blue, sat on her shoulder, singing.

The queen sat still and slumped, her eyes half closed. But when Jessamine approached, those eyes opened, and fixed upon her. Did they seem a trifle less faded than before, or did the dragon's hopes mislead her?

'Majesty,' panted Jessamine, prostrating herself before royalty—or every part of herself save her tail, which she carried higher than ever. 'We've the Wizard's Philtre for you.'

'But not the Wizard himself.'

'No, Majesty,' Jessamine admitted. 'I haven't seen him.'

'Nor I,' added Tambul, bowing again.

The queen frowned.

'He'll turn up,' Jessamine assured her. 'He always comes back, you know. Like bad weather, or a headache.'

'The Philtre?' answered the queen.

Jessamine swarmed up the arm of the royal throne, and permitted Her Majesty to take the bottle from her. She had to concentrate to keep her sparks and her smokes to herself, and not waft them about; she was a trifle unsettled.

The queen wasted no time, but removed the bottle's stopper at once, and quaffed the starry contents. A smile crossed her weary face immediately—not so *very* dazzling a smile, only a little one, but it was a start.

Then she gave a slow sigh, and settled deeper into her chair.

Jessamine felt a pang of disappointment, having hoped the lady might, with new energy, surge out of her chair, and dance a jig about the glass-house. Or if not quite that, then something equally rewarding.

Tambul's knowing look seemed gloating.

But the queen's posture was losing its *slump*, rather. The smile had not gone away, and her eyes were brighter. She opened them wider, and looked at Jessamine with more interest, and attention, than she had exhibited before.

She scrutinised Tambul, too.

'The Wizard's Minions, is it?' she mused. 'Almost as a good as a whole Wizard, between you.'

'Better,' said Jessamine stoutly. 'For we've not mislaid ourselves.'

'Nor left a whole jar of cochineal out in the open, where anything might have got into it,' said Tambul, less relevantly.

The queen gave a tiny, decorous belch, and out came a star, and floated off. 'He usually stays to talk,' she observed. 'Once I've drunk the Philtre.'

'We could do that,' offered Jessamine. Tambul looked ready to object; she frowned him down. 'What would Your Majesty wish to talk about?'

Queen Mellany considered this, shifting in her chair. It was the first real movement she'd exhibited since the previous eventide. 'Tell me of your day,' she commanded. 'And the making of this Philtre. And the Wizard. Is he good to you? Is he a stern master? I feel that he would be, *quite* stern, but you've such a charming degree of disloyalty towards him I feel I must be wrong.'

'Quite wrong, Your Majesty,' agreed Jessamine, and launched into an account of all that had come to pass; aided, here and there, by Tambul, whose reflections tended towards the sour, but the queen only laughed.

And as the afternoon wore away, and the Golden Hour slowly faded, Jessamine realised that what the Queen needed was less the Philtre and more the friend who brought it.

'You'll come again, will you?' said Her Majesty at last, rising from her chair as the light faded from the skies.

'But of course,' said Jessamine, smiling, and showing all her teeth. 'You'll need another Philtre, won't you? Shall we say tomorrow?'

'The day after,' decided the queen, stretching, and drifting towards the door. 'I shall be quite well until then.'

KNIGHT ERRANTRY

A Wizard in all their glory is a fine sight, as any Court Lady will tell you. They're a peacocking bunch as a rule, fond of their silks and velvets, and like to be lavishly bedecked in jewels. And, after all, why not? To be the *wonder-workers* of the world, the *wielders of cantrip and myth*, the *masters of magic and mystery*, and, above all, the *fixers and mixers of myriad problems (and quaffable solutions)*; this is no insignificant role. Their grateful petitioners are minded to shower them in gratitude; the moveable sort, by preference, composed of *worldly goods* and all that glitters, and why should not they revel in it? The Wizardly arts are not for the faint of heart.

For those of us unused to the splendours of silken mantles and perfumed locks; of rings set with rubies and diamond-studded combs; of embroidered shoes with curling toes, of cloth-of-silver surcoats and tunics gilded in gold, a Wizard in his, or her, natural state, may make an intimidating prospect. Theirs are personalities to match: you'll always know when a Wizard enters the room. Those smiles are like to be felt on the other side of the Castle, let alone the dining-chamber; they draw attention the way a candle draws moths, and rightly so. A Wizard is *never* ignored.

Formidable, then, a Wizard in public; but what of a Wizard in private?

What, moreover, of a Wizard in *disguise*?

Those flashing colours and shimmering silks serve a sobering purpose, after all. The jungle-cat's patterned hide serves as warning to its prey, so it's sometimes said. A tree-frog's jewel-coloured skin warns away its predators. If you *know* you're in the presence of a Wizard, you know to be on your best behaviour, or at the very least, on your guard.

How much more formidable, then, is a Wizard who's pretending to be somebody else?

And what could he *possibly* mean by it?

To skulk about in disguise is not among the Wizard Garstang's regular habits, to do him justice. His self-satisfaction is of an order that suffers diminishments only begrudgingly. To shed his own, glittering persona; to affect the semblance of some other (and, by definition, lesser) being; this pursuit, be it ever so entertaining, can only grate upon so magnificent a mind.

It could only be undertaken in the case of important business, then. No mere *whim* could separate the Wizard Garstang from his magnificent tunics, or from his enchanted chair. It must be an errand so sacred, so profoundly important, that no one but the Wizard himself could be trusted to undertake it. And yet, an errand that would *not*, in this rare instance, benefit from the open display of all his elegance; not a common occurrence, you might think? Indeed not.

Yet, it happens.

It is known, at the present time, that the Wizard Garstang is not at Castle Chansany (or at least, he does not appear to be). This was discovered by the usual method: when called for, the Wizard did not come, and he kept this up for rather a long time. Long enough to suggest that absent-mindedness, distraction or self-indulgence (the usual culprits) were not the cause of his tardiness, on this occasion. In fact, the Wizard was gone.

Yet nobody saw where he went, not even his faithful Familiar, Jessamine. Subtlety not being a strong suit with the Wizard, this can only have been by design.

He left the Castle by moonlight, as it happens, and alone. By the time his absence was both noted and accepted at Castle Chansany, he was already some miles distant; clad in attire one could only term nondescript and shrouded in a cloak of a plain, unremarkable blue, with the kind of hood whose express purpose is the hiding of the face.

Where was he going?

'To be perfectly honest, madam, I haven't the faintest idea,' said the Wizard Garstang. This question had been put to him by a brisk, sensible sort of woman, not much given to smiling *or* nonsense. He had got as far as the River Ballam by then, and proposed to proceed by boat. The lady and her good husband were ferry-folk, with a small boat between them, and an eye to the Wizard's custom. She had, not unreasonably, asked him where he intended to go.

'We can take you to High Oaks or the Greywater,' said she, unfazed.

'Neither is suggestive of much adventure,' answered the Wizard.

'There's a larger town. Tiven-by-the-Water. But it will take all day to reach it, and it'll cost you dearly.'

The Wizard applied his magnificent mind to the prospect of Tiven Bywater, and was not transported. 'I don't believe that is my destination, either,' he said.

The ferry-woman shrugged, a little disappointed. The Wizard might not have been wearing his jewels, but he had the speech and the bearing of a man of means, and might have made her morning. 'There's naught else within reach of a boat,' said she. 'You've to follow the road down to Balla'dale, then, and try the crossing there. Two days' walk, if you're on foot.' Her glance suggested she had no notion *why* the Wizard was on foot, for he hadn't the look of a man without the means to ride.

She was turning away when the Wizard said: 'No, no. I must go on the water, and it must be here. Your boat seems a splendid craft.' He spoke truly, for these ferry-folk cared for their vessel well. Its hull was clean and sound, its small sail looked in good order, and at the prow rose the carved semblance of a dragon's head. The creature reminded him, passingly, of Jessamine.

'Then choose a destination,' said the woman, patient still, though with an edge to her tone. If the gentleman didn't want her services, there'd be others who would.

'I will know it when we get there. Can you not permit me to board, and simply—go?' He flapped a hand in a down-river direction. 'It's that way.'

He received a narrow look by way of reply, and a long silence.

The Wizard's patience expired. 'I'll pay you five times your usual rate. In fact, here.' He rummaged inside his enveloping cloak, and produced a small pouch. The thing *clinked* as it settled into her outstretched hand.

Not only did it bulge enticingly with coin, but the pouch itself was wrought from a fine-woven fabric most would feel privileged to acquire in a shirt, or perhaps a gown. The ferry-woman's frown vanished in a trice. 'Come aboard,' said she, affable now, and the Wizard settled himself near the dragon-headed prow.

They were not long in departing, for the lady and her husband were true river-folk, happiest afloat. The Wizard turned his face to the wide, silver-lit water, glittering in the rising sun of the morning, and waited.

'Is it that you're looking for something?' asked the ferry-woman's husband, once the business of casting off and setting the sail was completed. He'd taken up an oar and settled into an easy rhythm, slow and steady, for the wind was doing most of the work.

'I am,' answered the Wizard.

'What might that be?'

'I'm uncertain.'

This obscure response befuddled the ferry-man. He fell silent, and remained so, as did his wife. If he'd known he was talking to a Wizard, he wouldn't have given the matter a second thought; Wizards were odd folk, as everyone knew.

An hour passed, and another. The ferry-folk spoke to one an-other, on occasion—an observation on the wind or the water, a murmured instruction or request. The Wizard didn't speak at all. He sat with his back to those plying the oars, wrapped up to his ears in his heavy blue mantle, and watched the rolling green shores slip by.

What he saw, or sensed, with his Wizard's eyes, no one could have said. He seemed half asleep, dozing the morning away, save that some small sign of tension in his hunched shoulders suggested otherwise, and his eyes were not more than partly closed. He watched for something, and waited, but the morning was gone before it came.

'Hm,' said he, all of a sudden, and sat up straighter. Those keen eyes opened wide at last, and searched the shore intent-ly. They had come to a wooded space by then, grown thickly with fine old trees; possibly the town of High Oaks was near. The ferry-folk looked, and saw nothing of note, not a hint of movement among the green-dappled boughs. But the Wizard's attention was chained.

'Stop!' cried he, some minutes later. 'Stop at once, stop *here*, if you please, I must go ashore.'

This was easier said than done, for the far shore was a distance away, and across a strong current. The ferry-man was heard to utter an oath; his wife maintained a tight-lipped silence.

To do them justice, they tried; pulled hard upon the oars, made what adjustments to the single sail they could. But the river-water carried them far and fast, and the Wizard gave a strangled cry of protest. 'Did I not say *stop?* We are gone too far! Go back! Go back!'

'We cannot go *back*,' growled the ferry-man. 'I haven't the strength to out-master this current, and neither's my wife. We will set you down when we can.'

The Wizard, impatient, shook his head. He cried out something incomprehensible to the ferry-folk, a few words in a strange tongue none but Wizards understand. And then the true nature of their passenger stood revealed, for what should come soaring over the tumbling river-waters but a *chair*, a very grand chair, with gossamer wings fluttering at all four of its legs. This chair swooped upon the boat, scooped up the Wizard, and sailed away, and that was the last these good ferry-folk ever saw of the Wizard Garstang.

He might, perhaps, have done better to fly from the beginning, save that this errand was to be performed *incognito*, and a flying chair does rather give one's Wizardly nature away. Besides, some stray sense had told him the river was important, and so it had been. He sent the chair upstream a ways, following some direction only he could determine, and when (for some reason) he was satisfied with his location he called, 'Here! Yes, thank you, set me down. Charming. Delightful. Excellent, excellent.' Muttering these various praises, and patting the high back of his favourite chair, he alighted. His boots landed right on the river-bank, the high oaks marching away before him, and he set off without a moment's hesitation, striding away with the water at his back, and his chair bumbling along cheerily behind him.

He seemed to become aware of this well-meaning company only after a few minutes, and turned with some impatience. 'No, that won't do. Cannot you see that I am in disguise? Off with you, my *good* chair, and come back when I call.'

After that he was alone, and seemed at pains to make himself appear harmless. He took down the hood of his mantle, and ruf-fled up his dark hair (usually so scrupulously ordered, but needs must, after all). He even adopted a pleasant, amiable expression; no easy matter, but he performed the role with admirable ded-ication until, at last, he came to a halt, and looked about.

He'd stopped beneath an oak-tree much like all the others; high-grown and gnarled, abundant with curled-edged leaves in the freshest green, and sprouting grass-coloured acorns in preparation for the autumn. Below its branches, the forest-floor was earthy and littered with twigs, and had little to recommend it to anyone's particular notice, save for one thing: there lay upon it a bowl.

Earth crusted the bowl so liberally that its precise nature lay hidden. The Wizard noted only that it was large enough to hold a great many of Jessamine's favourite butter-cakes, if she chose to store them there, and it was rather cracked. Shallow, too; more of a basin, perhaps, and so it shall be termed henceforth.

He paused to consider this spectacle, his eyes alight. Two, then three turns around the basin did he take with slow steps, scrutinising the thing from every angle. The basin, as one might expect, did not react—until he bent down, hand outstretched to touch, or perhaps to collect it.

Then it moved. It emitted a thin sound, in fact, like a smothered shriek, and jumped a full four inches away from the Wizard's reaching grasp.

'Oh, come now,' said the Wizard Garstang, crossly. 'I shan't hurt you. In point of fact, I may be able to mend you. Wouldn't you like that? Just look at these cracks! And all this dirt. My Jessamine would be scandalised, and rightly so. She'd have you in the sink and washed-up in a trice, and then you'd gleam like the moon. Hm? Who wouldn't want that?'

The basin seemed unconvinced. When the Wizard tried, again, to sweep it up into his possession, it fluttered and scuttled away, crying pitcously. Garstang was obliged to chase it, and he did so, stumbling after, a clumsy gait most unsuited to a Wizard's dignity. This did not improve his temper.

Nonetheless, when he succeeded in laying hands on the fleeing crockery, he did so gently enough. The basin bore its defeat with equanimity, for though it shivered and sobbed, it made no further attempts to escape.

The Wizard applied his sleeve to the encrusted dirt, and wiped some of it away. Underneath, something shimmered golden.

'There, and I thought so,' said the Wizard, incomprehensibly.

When the chair came soaring back, not long after, it took up the Wizard and his new friend both. The basin rode upon the Wizard's lap all the way back to Castle Chansany (there being no further need for subterfuge, now). Garstang clutched it close, his long, agile fingers slowly stroking the basin's rim. His air of amiability was now quite gone; in its place was the light of some anticipation brightening his eyes, and an atmosphere of suppressed excitement.

'A basin,' said Jessamine, upon the following day, when the Wizard was at last to be discovered again where he was supposed to be: in his study. 'You spent days wandering the world—quite without leave or warning, recall—in pursuit of a basin?'

'I did,' said the Wizard gaily, fair frisking about his library. 'A most successful venture.'

'In what fashion, pray?' said the dragon tartly, for she'd had a busy time of it in the Wizard's absence, and was not best pleased.

'Why, *look* at it,' answered her master, and swept an arm (dramatically, flamboyantly, as was his wont) in the direction of the beleaguered basin.

'I am,' said Jessamine, unimpressed. 'A grubby specimen, and broken. Haven't we crockery enough, somewhere about? Could you not have asked the kitchen, if you wanted one?'

'I could have,' agreed the Wizard.

He did not elaborate. Jessamine was not, ordinarily, a slow-witted dragon. It was annoyance that fuddled her wits; but once, with a smoky sigh and a strong effort, she recovered her equanimity, she perceived at once that something must be unusual about this particular basin.

A cursory inspection revealed nothing of the kind, if one discounted the faint glimmer of gold where someone (the Wizard, she concluded from the state of his sleeves) had attempted to polish it. A golden basin, what of that? The Castle was full of such things.

Something else set it apart, then, but perhaps its true nature was beyond the perception of a Familiar. 'It had better be cleaned,' she decided.

'It had indeed. Shall you supervise, Jess-o-mine?'

'If you will.' The sylphs, summoned by some silent request of the Wizards, were already in motion; the basin was swept up by an invisible wind, and borne away to the door. Had it *squeaked* as it rose?

Perhaps it had. Being on excellent terms with the moss-coloured rug, not to mention the best-of-all-chairs and the bookshelves, Jessamine accepted the probability without a qualm.

Even *that* didn't make a basin special, around here.

The basin did not submit quietly to a thorough scrubbing. Jessamine did not so much supervise as stand guard, for the unhappy crockery made several attempts to leap out of the deep stone sink of the Mixery, and make a bid for the door.

The sylphs were brutal, however, and determined, and at last the procedure was complete. The basin stood revealed as glimmering gold from lip to base, and a fine specimen, though no amount of washing could heal the cracks that ran quite through it.

Gold was not prone to developing cracks, thought Jessamine; an oddity, of sorts. And what was so large and valuable a piece of tableware doing out in the depths of the woods at High Oaks, skulking around all by itself?

'There is something fishy about you,' Jessamine informed it.

Once released from the torments of soap and water, and briskly dried, the basin no longer seemed unhappy. In fact, its transformation pleased it, for it stood taller than before, and radiated a smug pride. Its answer to Jessamine's observation was a twinkle she might have been inclined to term roguish, if a basin could be said to possess a capacity for mischief.

'Well, it's better than all that sobbing,' she decided. 'I've to take you back to the Wizard, now. You'll come along peacefully, if you please. I haven't the energy to go chasing through the halls at this hour.'

The basin submitted quietly to being scooped up and swooped away, without so much as a single sob of protest. Jessamine approved of this more cheerful state. Why, at this rate she might even come to *like* the thing.

It was destined for some pride-of-place spot in the Wizard's own lair, she judged, among his many curiosities and rare paraphernalia. That yet another valuable oddity could be worth his sudden departure from the Castle, and a three days' quest to procure it, she still couldn't explain. But Wizards, they had the feathers of peacocks and the hearts of magpies, and one didn't question them if one was wise.

Jessamine wasn't often wise.

'So,' she said, flowing on a wave of smoke back into the Wizard's study. He'd collapsed into the arms of his favourite chair by then, divested of his drab blue mantle, and sat admiring the ruby-red glow of his rings. 'It's a pretty thing, that I'll grant you. But what's so special about it?'

The Wizard beheld the basin's transformation with a vast approval. 'Does the answer yet elude you, my Jess? I am disappointed.'

'And I am growing irascible.' Jessamine breathed a tongue of flame at the Wizard's toes—not quite enough for his velvet slippers to catch on fire, but near.

He laughed. 'Very well, behold. I'll answer this mystery in a moment.'

Jessamine heard these words with a profound scepticism, for the Wizard could be amused by torment. She curled up near the hearth and half-shut her eyes, prepared for a long wait.

She was to be satisfied far sooner than she expected, however, for he sprang out of his chair almost at once, and paced around the basin. It sat in the centre of the moss-coloured carpet, glimmering to itself, and smiling. Perhaps it quavered a little when the Wizard loomed over it, but Jessamine did not think poorly of its courage, for all that. Most people *did* quiver a bit, when the Wizard took it into his head to Loom.

'Well, well,' uttered the Wizard softly, subjecting the basin to a hard stare. Abruptly he sat down on the carpet, cross-legged, and set his chin upon his hand, fingers drumming a rhythm on his own cheek as he thought. 'I *think* I'm correct in my surmise,' he decided after a time. 'But we shall see, shan't we?' He gestured, and a flurry of sparks went up; he cried out a sharp, harsh word in one of his befuddling *other tongues*, and in a waft of blue smoke the basin disappeared.

Jessamine heard a man's voice shouting something, but it was not the Wizard.

When the smoke dissipated, and the study gradually returned into focus, the basin was gone. A man lay sprawled where it had been, inelegantly, as though he had forgotten how his limbs worked. He was dressed head-to-toe in cloth-of-gold; he wore rings and bracelets enough to rival even the Wizard's excesses; and his shoulder-length, reddish hair had been arranged, by someone's careful hand, into a profusion of perfect curls.

In the grip of profound surprise, Jessamine forgot herself so far as to cough embers onto the carpet. 'Forgive me,' she said vaguely, as the carpet writhed and spat to put itself out. She skulked forward on her belly, her tongue unfurled to taste the air near the gold-glittering man.

Royalty.

'You're the prince,' she gasped.

Prince Armael bestowed upon her a dazzling smile. He wasn't handsome, poor soul, as a prince *ought* to be, but with that smile and those clothes he came very near it. 'A dragon!' he announced, in a rich, deep voice. 'I don't recall that we had a dragon before. I'm quite charmed.'

'I'm Jessamine,' she informed him. 'Familiar to the Wizard Garstang.'

'A noble position. I believe I owe my present, immaculate state to your tender ministrations and I thank you.' He spoke cheerfully enough, and he smiled, but his eyes were too wide, and there lay somewhere in the depths of them a wild, hunted look.

'I was his Apprentice before, but I wasn't very good at it,' she observed, babbling. 'Er, your highness? How came you to be a basin?'

A positively enormous question, when it came to it, for the prince had been missing for nigh upon a year. He'd gone out hunting one glorious, autumn morning, and never come home. He had simply gone adventuring, many believed—among them, His Majesty the King. It could have been true.

It *was* true, in fact, for the prince said: 'Do you know, I haven't the faintest idea? I was more than halfway to the sea, last that I recall, and after that—' He shrugged, and embarked upon a lengthy and confused tale, involving a separation from the rest of his party; a thief who'd tried to steal his bow; a chase all the way to High Oaks and beyond; a trading caravan he'd fallen in with thereafter, and kept up with for some time, for no reason he cared to explain; and then an abrupt end came to his recollections, for he'd become a basin, and couldn't recall how it had come about.

'You ran into a Wizard, I shouldn't wonder,' surmised Garstang. 'And made him wroth with you, in some fashion. Or *her*, perhaps. Was there a lady in the case?'

The prince grinned rather sheepishly. 'Perhaps there was,' he allowed. 'Ah well. If so, then she's had her revenge.' He accepted the hand the Wizard offered, and got to his feet. He swayed where he stood for a moment or two, then seemed to gather himself, and turned about.

'I'd better go to Their Majesties,' he decided. 'They'd like to hear what's become of me, I suppose.'

'I imagine they might, at that,' agreed the Wizard. 'Her Majesty in particular, perhaps. She's missed you sorely.'

Prince Armael appeared affected by this news, which raised him in Jessamine's estimation, just a little. 'I'll go at once,' he agreed, and went.

Jessamine considered the Wizard, standing tall, and so pleased with himself. He watched the prince go with a grin of pure self-satisfaction, and then fell into the arms of his favourite chair with a happy sigh. 'Excellent,' he beamed.

'Aye, you'll be peacocking all over the Castle for many a day,' said Jessamine, drifting back to her spot by the hearth. 'Did you know, when you set out, that it was the prince you'd find?'

'Not in the least,' answered Garstang, retrieving a curly glass pipe from some hidden pocket, and lighting it with a flick of his finger.

'Then why did you go? And how did you know *where*?'

'A Wizard learns to pay attention to his Instincts,' said Garstang, with due emphasis on the word.

'I daresay.' Jessamine, disgusted, closed her eyes.

'As does a Familiar,' added Garstang, unexpectedly.

Jessamine's eyes snapped open again. 'Instincts? I'm fair sure I don't possess any.'

'Then you haven't learnt to pay attention.' Garstang puffed a puff of lavender-drifting smoke in her direction, and smiled. 'Take note, Jess-o-mine. Some other day, it could be you hauling an errant prince home to his mother.'

Jessamine favoured the Wizard with an unflattering reflection on the possible nature of his parents. Then, to the sound of the Wizard Garstang's cackle of laughter, she curled her tail over her nose, and went to sleep.

STRANGENESS ALOFT

The clattering and rattling, scuffling and banging (not to mention an occasional *thud*) had been going on all day.

Not consistently, or Jessamine could not have borne it. No, there were intervals of peace and silence, just long enough for an irascible and increasingly aggravated dragon to tuck her nose beneath her tail and drift halfway back into slumber...

...and then there it came again, with, if anything, extra slithering and dithering and general to-do, and it sounded horribly as though *something had got into the walls,* and was making itself at home there. And that could only be bad news, for today of all days, *today*, Jessamine had other things to occupy her.

Prince Armael had returned to Castle Chansany. Everyone knew it, for there had already been considerable pomp and celebration. Everybody knew the Wizard Garstang's part in it, too, of which Jessamine disapproved, for it made him — somehow — smugger than ever.

Despite all this, soon there was to be a ball, a grand ball, in honour of the wayward Prince's return (and, indeed, his rescue from the ignominious state in which he had been discovered and rescued: that of being, embarrassingly, obliged to take up state as a household object). Their Majesties would preside over the festivities, naturally, and the Wizard Garstang would be feted as befit his service to the Crown (wearing the best of his most salubrious attire, naturally, and lording it insufferably over all and sundry).

Someone had even managed to rustle up some foreign dignitaries. Such persons did not often attend Court at Castle Chansany, the kingdom being but a small one, and the Castle somewhat out of reach. That being so, the presence of *a fair few* extra nobles and royals, ministers and wizards, was no small thing.

They were all coming to gawp, of course, at this handsome (or nearly handsome) prince, the man who had, through riotous adventure, developed an unusually close sympathy with the daily plight of household crockery. There wasn't another person alive, probably, who could tell you, with such exactitude, how a plate might feel when it was heaped with edibles and then swept into the sink; how a tankard or a knife experienced the raising and draining of beverages by hungry mouths, or the slicing and dicing of slippery comestibles. Nor, indeed, how it felt to become a man again, and take up walking about on two legs, and talking, and such practicalities, when he had, for some time, been obliged to occupy himself with neither.

There was curiosity.

And there was, therefore, so much for a Jessamine to *do*, that she had no time whatsoever for unnameable things making a racket behind the walls.

'Got no right to be living in the walls,' she declared, spitting a cinder or two, when another such clamour woke her from her pleasant doze, and brought her scaly head up in rank disgust. 'Stars! Do they think that's what we put them there for, to be bustled about in, and bashed to pieces?'

The chair, her own chair, answered her. 'Who?' it said, in its high, fluttery way (matching, rather, the fluttery and tendrily plants, and other such bits, that clambered up the legs, and twined about the arms).

'If I knew that, I'd have turfed them out again, wouldn't I?' said Jessamine. She gave a great sigh, for half her words disappeared under the tumult of another great *messing-about* happening. She'd have to get down, and investigate, just as her own, dear chair had made itself so comfortable!

'What a bother,' spat she, and got down.

The chair had parked itself in the Wizard Garstang's study, where it often liked to sit. The Wizard's own best-of-all-chairs often lurked there, too, together with a quantity of other, congenial furniture; Jessamine liked for her chair to go where it had friends.

But that meant that the scuffling sorts behind the panels were likely of a magical nature, and *that* meant that the problem couldn't possibly be the simple sort, over and done with in half-an-hour, and straight back to sleep.

No. It would be difficult, and delicate, and obstreperous, and befuddling, and *awkward*, and what with all things considered, Jessamine felt that life had delivered more than enough of those things, for the time being.

'I prefer the sapphire,' said she shortly afterwards, having tracked the Wizard Garstang down in his dressing-chamber. He was decent at the time, being bedecked in silks and velvets, with a tunic all covered in embroidery, and prancing before a long mirror. 'The crimson's very fine, I grant you,' she added, 'but it makes your nose look bigger.'

The Wizard had vanity enough to catch at the thought; he studied his dark-visaged face in the mirror, frowning. 'No it doesn't,' he said, rather curt. 'You jest, Jess-o-mine.'

She did, but would not own it. Instead she sniffed, and slithered over the stone-flagged floor to join him before the looking-glass. 'Much bigger,' she insisted. 'Her Majesty would never approve.'

'Her Majesty does not concern herself with the proportions of my nose,' answered Garstang, and with spirit. But he removed the crimson mantle and cast it over a nearby chair.

Jessamine waited.

'The sapphire, you said?' said he next, and shortly thereafter presented himself, properly attired, for her inspection. He cut rather a dash, as a general rule, even Jessamine could not deny. Today, he looked handsome indeed, for someone had done something intriguing with the thick waves of his dark hair, and he shone with an energy and a vigour which could not help but attract.

'You'll do,' said she.

The Wizard smiled. 'Did you come here to criticise, dragon, or was there some other purpose?'

'We've a problem,' she answered.

'Oh, no. No problems today, I forbid it.'

'I tried that my own self,' she said. 'It didn't work.'

He sighed, and pinched the bridge of his nose. Probably his head was hurting him. 'Very well then, let me hear it. Quickly, quickly.'

Jessamine told him.

'The *walls*?' he repeated, frowning. 'What walls?'

'In your study.'

'Oh,' he said, and was silent for a moment. 'Oh, dear.'

'You've some notion as to who it is,' she observed, misliking the look of things.

'You intrigue me, dragon,' he said, which was not at all an answer. 'Not a *what*, but a *who*, you ask.'

'I've learned a thing or two, keeping company with you,' she retorted. 'Even a basin may have opinions, it seems.'

His glittering smile flashed; he gave a crack of laughter. 'Well,' was all the answer he made. He was gone in the next moment, out the door and striding away down the passage. 'Come along, Jess-o-mine!' he called back, and she hastened to scurry after him.

Typically, they arrived at the Wizard's study to find the chamber shrouded in apparent peace and slumber. The silver candelabras had dimmed their flickering flames and sat dreaming upon the tables; the rug lay, quiet and silent, before the cooling hearth; the best-of-all-chairs gave a slight snore, its wings sleepily stirring.

'Not much amiss, at present,' observed the Wizard, in a hopeful tone.

'Give it time,' answered Jessamine, swarming up the legs of her chair to repose herself, once more, upon the seat.

Wizard Garstang did not excel at waiting, as a rule. He hadn't the patience for it. He displayed little now, pacing about back-and-forth before the hearth, and fidgeting with the cuffs of his tunic, quite as though he had never had to wait upon anyone else's convenience in the whole course of his life.

Jessamine ignored him, and ignored the walls, too. Her weary mind gladly returned to its half-doze, and she lay, occasionally snoring, until the tumult resumed — with an ominous *crash*.

The Wizard froze mid-step.

'Well, and they *are* getting rowdy,' Jessamine remarked. 'Because you're here, no doubt. Perhaps they've got a message for you.'

Wizard Garstang did not immediately reply. His attention seemed all focused elsewhere; he did not even glance at his familiar, instead gazing into the indeterminate distance with his ears manifestly pricked, listening through every renewed *scrabbling* and *rabbling* and (eventually) another great *crash*.

Then he heaved a vasty sigh, did terrible things to the ordered waves of his hair with impatient fingers, and uttered an oath.

'There's nobody in the walls, dragon,' he informed her. 'What an absurd idea.'

Jessamine, mildly affronted, did not reply. *Absurd idea*, said he, scornfully, as though absurd things were not a daily occurrence in Castle Chansany!

When the Wizard offered nothing more, at last Jessamine said: 'Well, what strikes you as a more *reasonable* explanation, then?'

'It's perfectly obvious what it is,' he retorted. 'And could hardly be more ill-timed. When we have the Princess of Fayence here! Not to mention the Count of Darstven-Deep, *two* royal dukes, and gawkers beyond counting. *Ill-timed*, dragon.'

'It wasn't my doing,' snapped Jessamine, her own patience wearing thin.

'Wasn't it?' He eyed her, narrowly, his dark eyes oddly gleaming. 'You were not sleeping there in that chair of yours, dreaming up impossible wishes and peculiar ideas?'

'I don't see why the walls should attend to my wishes, even if I was.'

'Nor do I. But the chairs do, and the carpets, and all the rest of the furniture. You've a way about you, Jess-o-mine.'

She sniffed, and flicked the flaming tip of her tail. 'I am sure I don't know what you're talking about.'

His surprising grin flashed. 'I believe you don't, at that. Well.' He cast another look around at the walls in question, finding them as stony and unremarkable in appearance as ever. With a shrug, he seemed to abandon the problem; he said, lightly, 'Oh, well. Nothing to be done about it now. Shall we away to the festivities?'

'You don't mean to do anything?' Jessamine repeated, awed.

'There is nothing I *can* do, dragon. And when a disaster proves beyond one's capacity to alter, the only thing left to do is enjoy it.'

He strode away upon these words, leaving Jessamine to reflect, with some disgust, that she might have known the Wizard would have some odd, bottle-brained attitude that would be of no help to man or beast.

But if he were resolved upon enjoying himself, then so too would she be.

'Be careful,' said the carpet, surprisingly, as she scuttled across it.

'I'll do my best,' said she. 'Only I've no notion what it is I've to be careful of.'

Awe-inspiring though its size might be, the ballroom at Castle Chansany still proved insufficient to contain the sprawling extent of the party. The revelry spilled far beyond the borders of the marble-floored, balconied, handsomely-gilded chamber, spreading into the salons adjacent, and a large hall, rather windy (the cause of this mysterious), whose purpose had long since been forgotten, and which was rarely put to any particular use. Indeed, as Jessamine scuttled from the Wizard's study, down long and winding corridors and through many a flung-open doorway, she began to encounter revellers as far away as the music rooms.

There would be no peace at Castle Chansany until the morrow, most like. Or possibly the day after.

Truth be told, it had been a long time indeed since last there had been real, *high* revelry at the castle. There were banquets aplenty, of course, with dancing after; a Royal Court could do no less. But a proper, solid, overdone extravaganza, such as was called for by the prince's return... well, nothing of its like had been undertaken since before his highness had disappeared.

Small wonder, then, if the castle, so long stoppered-up, should uncork itself with a *bang*.

The music, jaunty and festive and *loud*, as though a thousand pipes had leapt from slumber all in a tussle and burst into frenzy — Jessamine couldn't hear herself think. Which, all things considered, was no great drawback, for her thoughts were not much worth listening to, today. She kept a weather eye out for shenanigans, as she scurried from door to door; if the walls hereabouts were as minded to misbehave as the Wizard's, well, she would hear nothing of that either.

And good riddance to it.

She had hoped to slither into the party unnoticed. Considering her diminutive size, this was no unreasonable expectation; but, either ill-luck or Prince Armael's unlooked-for alertness were against her, for no sooner had she set one delicately scaled foot over the threshold than a shout went up, containing, somewhere in its muddled depths, her name.

'The Wizard's Familiar!' someone cried, a hanger-on of his highness's, she supposed. He had a gaggle of them about him, all richly dressed and all (in Jessamine's private opinion) fatuous. 'And what role did the little dragon play in your rescue, Highness?' continued the voice, and here came a fatuous face bending down to inspect her, grinning, and smelling of the festive beverages concocted in the cavernous kitchens.

Prince Armael smiled, an expression a shade less foolish than his friend's. 'Why, she took charge of the scrubbing!' he cried.

'And a proper job of it she did, too, for I emerged without a speck on me.'

'I've washed a pot or two in my time,' said Jessamine shortly.

The prince made her a low, sweeping bow. 'And I am a grateful recipient of your expertise, madam.'

Jessamine, in spite of herself, softened a bit. He did have excellent manners. 'And where is the Wizard?' she asked. 'He's as like as not to get himself into trouble, if someone doesn't keep an eye on him.'

'If you can keep him out of trouble, madam, it is more than anybody else has ever been able to do.' The prince pointed. There was her wizard, surrounded (inevitably) by Court Ladies, and in a mood of high good humour. He stood right in the path of a flurry of dancers, with typical obstructiveness, and barely noticed as waves of them broke around him, and reformed on the other side.

Something was wrong with his smile, Jessamine thought. It was plentiful, today, which was not so unusual a happenstance; but there was a glitter to it, and a bit of a twist, as though it were prompted by more (or less) than mere merriment. He glanced, once or twice, at the walls about him, and occasionally at the ceiling.

He was waiting for something to happen, Jessamine thought, and moreover, he knew exactly what it was like to be.

'Master Wizard, do you call yourself?' she told him, once she got nearer. 'Master Mischief, more like. What horrid surprise do you mean to spring upon the company?'

'*I* mean nothing of the sort,' he retorted. 'But the Castle does not bow to my whims, you know.'

'How curious of it to be so stubborn, when everybody else does.'

'Ah! Except you, Jess-o-mine, and so I am kept honest.'

She eyed him sourly. 'The pleasure is all mine, I'm sure.'

He grinned. 'I would tell you, dragon, truly, only I should not like to cause a ruckus before time.'

'It's to be bad, then.'

'For a little while.'

'And then?'

'And then all shall be well, I daresay. Does not everything turn out well, eventually?'

Jessamine, gifted with no such sanguine expectation, only sniffed. Though, to be sure, they *were* celebrating the end of the prince's absence, an occurrence which had, against all apparent odds, turned out extremely well.

Perhaps all was not to be entirely lost, after all.

'Ah,' said the Wizard then, his head coming up, his eyes scanning the walls with a keen, eager look. 'Do you feel that, Jess-o-mine?'

She did; indeed, everyone did, for the floor, enlivened, perhaps, by the music and the dancing, had taken it upon itself to join in. It began to shake, and shiver, and the walls rattled with a deepening, deafening, ominous *rumble*, as though the stones might fly to pieces.

'Your horrid surprise, I perceive, is to bury the lot of us under rubble,' she gasped, attempting, with little luck, to dig her claws into the marble floor. Clinging was no good; she ought rather to run, but where to? The whole castle was a-shake.

'Oh, I don't believe it will come to that,' answered the Wizard merrily. He was grinning again, a wild expression, which struck Jessamine as sinister.

'Oughtn't you to *do* something?' she cried, as a quantity of glasses shattered all together, eliciting a chorus of shrieks from the guests. The floor was tossing now, lurching and groaning, *tortured*, Jessamine might have said — and then there came a swift, rushing sensation that left her light-headed.

'I could swear we just went — up,' she said, more softly, for with the surge of motion came relative peace. The rattling and groaning had stopped.

'And why should we not go up?' asked the Wizard, not un-reasonably.

'Were we not high enough in the air before?'

The ruckus had felled Prince Armael's entourage like a bun-dle of dropped sticks. They lay every which way, uttering oaths and curses unfit for a young dragon's ears; Jessamine ignored them.

The prince, though, lay comfortably on his back, his head cushioned on his folded arms, and grinned up at the Wizard. 'Oh, it *has* been a while, hasn't it? I don't believe we've gone wander-about since I was a child.'

'We were due a year past, if not before,' answered the Wizard. 'It's waited for you.'

The prince unfolded his limbs, and patted the pale marble floor, rather affectionately. 'Dear old castle.'

'Wander-about?' Jessamine spat. 'Do you mean to say we've flown off?'

'And why shouldn't we?' said the Wizard. 'It would be tiresome, always to remain in the same spot. Now, would not it?'

'Most buildings manage it,' muttered Jessamine.

'And a dreary lot they all are.' Having, with these few, sweeping words, confined every structure in existence to the midden of conversational interest, Garstang forgot them altogether. 'Come with me,' he said to Jessamine. 'We will investigate.'

Now that the castle had ceased tearing itself to pieces, Jessamine would prefer to remain where she was, enjoying the suddenly blissful sensation of a still floor and a quiet set of walls. But, investigating with the Wizard was not without its appeal; and so she went, scurrying to keep pace with his long strides. They wove in and out of the scattered guests, gathered together in chattering knots; wended their way out of the ballroom and the salons and through the windy hall; dashed up several staircases; and fetched up at last at the top of the tallest tower, where there hung a balcony over the far-below.

The queen was already there. She smiled gaily upon the Wizard as he entered, and upon Jessamine also. 'Is not this nice?' she declared. 'I began to think we were stuck fast.'

They were flying indeed, Jessamine perceived, for silvery wafts of cloud sailed past, not so very far overhead. Even the stars seemed to dip and whirl in the black bowl of the heavens, a dizzying effect; Jessamine shut her eyes.

'But where are we going?' cried she.

'To the next kingdom, of course,' said the Wizard. He leaned far over the railing, courting disaster; if there were any justice in the world, he ought to fall over it. 'You did not imagine Her Majesty to reign over a single, paltry little land, now did you?'

'I was brought up in the scullery,' Jessamine reminded him. 'Cannot say as I ever heard anything about it.'

This fetched the Wizard's attention; he turned to stare at her, narrowly, as though something offended him.

But when he spoke, he merely said: 'You must take some improving lessons, Jess-o-mine. With Tambul, perhaps.'

In all her hurry and alarm, Jessamine had forgotten her courtesies to the queen. She hastened to repair this omission, prostrating herself suitably. 'Forgive me, your majesty. I was distracted.'

'Come up here, where you can see,' came the queen's answer, and Jessamine found herself hoisted — an event injurious to her dignity — and deposited atop the balcony wall. Where, if you please, she could fall to her death at a moment's notice.

Her claws found tiny cracks in the stone, and gripped.

The view, she had to admit, made up for the danger. Below her spread some few, stray wisps of cloud, like puffs of steam streaming by — and farther below, a dark, endless expanse of deep water, glimmering silver under the moon.

'We're going a long way,' she observed.

'We will be there by morning,' said the Wizard, comfortably.

'And where is "there"?' she demanded.

The Wizard smiled. 'Wherever we're supposed to be.'

KNAVERY

You may not be wholly surprised to learn that a castle, once aloft, is not swift-moving.

Jessamine, hanging with her snout over the edge of the topmost balcony of Castle Chansany, was in no way enlightened as to the direction the Castle had taken it into its head to go in. The pearly clouds swirled so thickly around the craggy stones of the soaring building as to obscure everything that might be passing below.

This also made it difficult to determine the velocity of travel. After an impressive surge at the beginning, and motion swift enough to set the flags whipping in the wind, the castle had slowed down; this was as much as Jessamine could determine.

She rather thought that it had slowed down a lot.

'I could get there faster if I walked,' she muttered, though this was something of a lie; presumably the castle knew where it was off to, but since Jessamine didn't, she would have to wait, and be carted along at the castle's own pace.

'Like a sack of potatoes,' she spat, slithering down from the balcony.

There being little so serviceable to treat a poor mood as confectionery, Jessamine deemed it time to pay the kitchens a visit, and see if Chef had any butter cakes lying about.

She often visited the kitchens in pursuit of a treat, or possibly two, and had never done so without finding them bustling with activity. Today proved no exception. Chef reigned over a small battalion of staff, among them two pastry-chefs, a saucier and assistants uncountable, employed to chop and peel and blanche and mix and roll and shape all day — and half the night, too, if Chef should require it. He frequently did.

The hour was far advanced, and the moon had been wafting silverish through the thick, dark blanket of the sky for some hours already. A few of the choppers and mixers had retired to their beds, but plenty remained. Jessamine entered the main kitchen only to dodge, swift on her scaled toes, as a behatted assistant came charging across the flagstone floor with a boiling pot in his hands. The tumult of knives hitting wooden boards, copper pots bubbling, pans hissing, men and women shouting and rolling pins thudding into thick dough assailed her ears.

The aromas, however, made up for the assault. Jessamine breathed in a pungent melange of frying onions, roasting meat, fresh-baked bread, and spices, a smile curving her lipless snout.

She scuttled in, weaving her way past several pairs of legs, and skulked around the side of the huge, oaken-planked table in the centre of the floor. Chef Paglar, discernible by the height of his black hat, occupied a station in the corner farthest from the door. He proved to be making marchpane.

'Chef,' panted Jessamine, the long journey down and down, from the balconies to the cellars, leaving her out of breath. 'I am in sore need of comestibles. It's *urgent*.'

'Isn't it always,' answered the chef, unimpressed. 'What's the matter now?'

'We're on the move.'

'What of it?'

'I haven't travelled by flying castle before. It's turning my stomach.'

'Then you ought not to be eating, methinks.'

Jessamine paused. 'Perhaps if you've got something with ginger,' she suggested. 'Good for an unsettled belly, that.'

'Pepper cakes over there.' Paglar's elbow flapped, vaguely indicating a dish piled high with golden-brown *somethings*. Jessamine pointed her nose thither, and received a lungful of spicy fragrances: ginger for certain, and other things besides.

'Don't take too many,' Paglar warned, as Jessamine slithered over to the dish. 'They're for Their Majesties, and the Court gentlefolk.'

Jessamine claimed two. Then, on second thought, a third. They were still steaming hot, but she was proof against such trifles as heat, in her dragon-scaled suit.

She retired to a corner under the table, a droplet of drool leaking from her jaws.

'Chef,' she said, paused on the point of devouring her spoils. 'Something's different.'

'Same recipe as ever.'

'Not the cakes. Something's different about *you*.'

So intent had she been upon the rumblings of her stomach, not to mention the challenge of traversing the kitchen without being trampled or tripped over, that she had scarce paused to observe Chef Paglar with any particular attention. Only belatedly had it penetrated her befuddled thoughts that his voice had altered. Not as deep as it used to be, she thought; higher in pitch, smoother in timbre.

And there was more. Jessamine clutched her pepper-cakes to her scaly breast, and peered out from under the table. Was he wearing a dress? He was. Black, of course; everyone wore black in the kitchen, but unmistakeably a gown.

Jessamine sidled around, planting herself as near to the chef as she dared. There, she hadn't imagined it. His beard, formerly black and luxurious, was gone. Not shaved away. His cheeks were smooth and plump, as though they'd never grown hair at all.

'You're a woman,' she discovered.

'Saw the Wizard,' Paglar said, nodding.

'Ahh,' said Jessamine knowledgeably. 'A transformative draught.' She'd assisted in mixing one or two of those, when she had been the Wizard's apprentice, and not his Familiar. They couldn't turn you into just anything, whatever the name implied. They made of you whatever you most wished to be; or, perhaps, whatever you *ought* to be.

They weren't cheap. But neither were Paglar's skills.

'Ought I to be calling you something else, then?' she enquired.

Paglar took her eyes off her marchpane comfits, long enough to shoot Jessamine a glance. Jessamine gulped, but the chef wasn't displeased. There were crinkles at the edges of her eyes.

'It's still Paglar,' said the chef. 'But I'm a *she*, if you please.'

'Right you are, milady.' Jessamine made the chef a little bow, and took the opportunity to cram a pepper-cake into her mouth.

Bliss. Ginger, strong and uncompromising. The zing of black pepper. Fragrant cardamom and nutmeg and mace. The sweetness of honey...

...smoked eel? And *pastry*, the thick, dense kind that went into raised pies. Meat-jelly. And cherries.

Gagging, Jessamine spat. A half-chewed glob of food fell onto the flagstones, and lay there, glistening. It *looked* like pepper-cake, as far as she could tell. Smelled like it, too.

'Chef,' said Jessamine.

'I *am* busy,' Paglar replied. 'Her Majesty's marchpane won't finish itself.'

'I daresay, but there's something funny about this pepper-cake.'

Chef Paglar's chin came up at that, and she darted a narrow-eyed look at the towering dish of cakes. 'What is it? Are they underbaked? Too much pepper? Not enough ginger?'

Jessamine watched queasily as the masticated lump of pepper-cake turned pale and slimy. There was the eel.

'Try one,' she suggested.

She held up one of her two remaining pepper-cakes, offering one to Paglar.

Steeling herself, she shoved the other into her maw.

Her eyes locked with Paglar's as she chewed. As such, she witnessed the confusion in the chef's face as she received a mouthful of perfectly spiced pepper cake...

...and then the dawning horror.

Jessamine spat out the second cake, shuddering. '*Garlic,*' she gagged. 'And stewed apple, and port-wine, and not a little betony.'

Lion-hearted Paglar swallowed her mouthful of cake, though not without a grimace. 'Lavender,' she reported. 'And ginger, which might be well enough, were it not for the pork crackling and the quince jelly.' she shuddered, and added, 'And then the *strawberries.*'

'We've confectionery that thinks it's an entrée,' Jessamine said. 'Or the fish course.'

Chef Paglar set her hands upon her ample hips, and surveyed the bustling kitchen grim-faced. 'It's a problem, right enough,' she agreed. 'There's nothing for it. We'll have to fetch the Wizard.'

* * ✳ * *

As a rule, Jessamine's was not the sort of nature to take pleasure in other people's misery.

Unless it was the Wizard Garstang, in which case, she thought, fair was fair.

As such, she secured the biggest, best-looking of the pepper cakes for the wizard's delectation, and carried it off to his study on a silvery tray she'd swiped from the pantry.

'Chef's made pepper cakes,' she announced without preamble, scuttling over the threshold of the wizard's begloomed lair with her tail coiled tightly around the tray.

His favourite chair proved empty. Instead, Jessamine spotted her erratic master seated tailor-style upon a table that had not been there in the morning, staring at a bare patch of wall.

He did not respond to her announcement; did not even twitch. It was as though she wasn't there at all.

'What are you doing?' she said, pausing at the foot of the table. It was a tall article, made from a dark, heavy wood, with legs as long as the wizard's. Jessamine had to stretch herself a long way to bring her tray within her master's reach.

'Thinking,' he said. He hadn't blinked.

'*Cake,*' she insisted, proffering the tray.

Wizard Garstang's eyes flickered. He took a second look at the contents of the tray, then said, with supreme indifference, 'That is not a pepper cake.'

'Why not?' retorted Jessamine. 'It looks like one, doesn't it?'

'Perhaps.' The wizard went back to the contemplation of his wall.

Deprived of her prank, Jessamine shook her silvery tray, making the spurned cake jump. 'Try it,' she hissed. 'It's delicious.'

She regretted the lie, a little, as soon as it was uttered. A jest was one thing; a deliberate falsehood another.

The wizard subjected her to a narrow-eyed look, but took the cake, and crammed it, whole, into his mouth.

He chewed, chewed, chewed, swallowed, and thought.

'Has Paglar changed the recipe?' he mused.

'Something's changed, but it isn't the recipe,' Jessamine grumbled, discarding her silvery tray, and hurling herself upon the dark boards of thc floor. She slithered under the table, and skulked there, fuming.

A tendril of smoke wafted upward.

'Needs some adjustments,' the wizard decided. 'I wouldn't have used bilberries, myself. Not with the herring.'

This wisdom dispensed, he returned to his wall, and his wizardly thoughts.

'Is that it?' Jessamine demanded. 'A crisis in the kitchen, and you're babbling about bilberries!'

'A crisis? What crisis?'

'The *cakes*,' Jessamine spat. 'They're not supposed to taste of herring.'

'That's what I said.'

'They are pepper cakes, made with no herring, or bilberries either, but you try telling that to the cakes. They're all confused.'

'Oh!' Garstang sat up; the table creaked ominously. 'They've gone change-about.'

'Change-a-what?'

'Change-about.' He didn't elaborate, but sat tapping his fingertips upon the table-top. 'Dragon. Is the whole kitchen topsy-turvy?'

'I don't know. I left Paglar to investigate.'

'She won't be happy.' He chuckled, to Jessamine's disgust, then leapt off the table and strode to the door. 'It might be because we're on the move,' he mused aloud, as Jessamine scuttled after. 'But I'd think not. Nothing else is going change-about, after all.'

'No? That table you were sitting on didn't used to be, for example, a chair?'

'A chair? Don't be absurd. It couldn't more plainly be a table.'

'Then what were you doing sitting on it?'

'I told you. Thinking. No, Jess-o-mine, it isn't the altitude or the speed. This is a clear case of Knavery.'

Returning to the kitchens in the wizard's wake, Jessamine plunged into uproar. Paglar and her staff had abandoned cooking in favour of a furious debate, laced with panic; Paglar broke off as the wizard swept in, and said, wild-eyed, and with a sweep of her arm which indicated the entirety of the kitchens, 'Garstang. It's all of them. Everything. What am I to do?'

The Wizard Garstang took immediate command, which consisted of advancing into the centre of the room and adopting an imposing posture. 'Every dish you've made is changeant?' he said to Paglar.

'Every single one. I've to serve Their Majesties shortly, they've guests, there's a feast in full swing. It's a disaster.'

'Peace, Paglar. I shall advise Their Majesties to proceed with the dancing early, and we shall have plenty of time to resolve this little difficulty.'

'Little? *Little*?' Paglar advanced upon Garstang, rage darkening her face with every step. 'You know what they'll say, out in the castle? "That Paglar's gone change-about her own self. It must have got into the food." Everything I touch will be seen as tainted.'

Garstang, for once, appeared abashed. Slightly. He made a placating gesture, and offered, 'I won't let that happen, Paglar.'

'It may already be too late. I can't answer for the beef ragout, it's already gone out. Not to mention the soup.'

'Then we must work quickly. I believe you may have hit upon the explanation, at least in part. Is there anyone at the castle who bears you some manner of ill-will?'

'For certain,' said Paglar bitterly. 'Especially since…' She gestured at her plump, and now womanly, curves clad in a neatly buttoned-up dress.

'Anyone in particular?'

Paglar's rage and panic dissipated all at once, leaving her more weary than afeared. She sank down onto a three-legged stool by the wall, and gazed helplessly at Garstang. 'I don't know. No one's made any threats, not directly.'

Garstang turned. 'Dragon. Go to the Potionery, and ask the sylphs what's become of the last batch of Transformative Draught.'

'You think it's got into the food,' said Jessamine.

'It may have. Talk to Tambul, too. Be quick.'

'And what will you be doing?' she demanded.

'Conducting an inquisition,' he said grimly. 'The door's to be locked behind you, Jess-o-mine, and no one's to leave until this little matter is resolved.'

He thought one of the kitchen staff might have done it, she surmised. A glance about the kitchen revealed a sea of tense, unhappy faces; doubtless they were all worried for their jobs, same as Paglar. Nobody looked shifty, or guilty, but that meant nothing. Some people hid their feelings all too well.

'Right you are,' said Jessamine, and dashed for the door. 'I'll roar when I want to come back in.'

Jessamine barrelled through the door of the Potionery fast enough almost to collide with the shelves on the other side. This process was aided by the curious fact that the door was already open when she arrived.

'Hello?' she called, coming to an abrupt halt. She lifted her snout and sniffed the air. A strange aroma lingered, but she couldn't say of what.

Nobody answered her, but she heard a low muttering, and followed it around a heavy set of oaken shelves laden with potions. 'Tambul? What are you doing here at this hour?'

The Wizard's Apprentice cast her a look over his shoulder, his face creased with the annoyance he usually displayed around Jessamine. And something else. Something *shifty*. 'I'm taking an inventory,' he snapped.

It could have been true, stationed as he was atop a tall stool perusing another set of shelves, and with a large ledger spread open upon a table nearby. But that shifty look... he hadn't told her everything.

'And why would you be taking an inventory at midnight when there's a feast afoot and we're on the way to who-knows-where besides?' she demanded.

'Feasts have nothing to do with me,' he said curtly, turning his back on her. He selected a jade-coloured potion from the shelf, gave it an experimental shake, and noted something in his ledger. The display, Jessamine thought, was for her benefit.

'That doesn't answer my question,' she pointed out.

Tambul growled something inaudible.

'Tambul,' Jessamine snapped. 'We've a crisis in the kitchens. Everything's gone change-about and the Wizard's fit to be tied. Did you have something to do with it?'

'Change-about?' Tambul stared at her in horror, his face draining of colour.

'The food. Topsy-turvy and entirely without sense, and there's no reasoning with it. The Wizard's holding the staff hostage until answers are found, so if you know anything about this I charge you: out with it.'

Tambul blindly restored the jade-shaded potion to the shelves, and stepped down from his stool. Then he sank down upon it, and put his face in his hands. 'Oh no,' he said indistinctly.

'Here, none of that. Paglar's already in convulsions and we don't need the both of you stewing.'

'You don't understand.' Tambul didn't emerge from behind his hands. 'It's my fault.'

'How?'

'The Transformative Draught. I took it down for Paglar, and I forgot to put the rest away. And now it's gone. I don't know where.'

'Right.' Jessamine, more shaken than she would own, found the sight of the irascible and seemingly untouchable Tambul reduced to jelly a shade unsettling. 'The Wizard will want to know. Where was it left? And do you have any idea who took it?'

'You can't tell the Wizard! He'll dismiss me. I'll never work as a Potioner again. They'll throw me out of the castle.'

'They will do no such thing, and nor will the Wizard. Come, Tambul, you've got to help. What do you know?'

Tambul lowered his hands, and took a steadying breath. 'Right. I left the bottle in the Dispensary. I locked the door behind me, or so I thought, but it was open when I went in and — the bottle was gone.'

'Might you have forgotten to lock the door?'

'I don't know, do I?' snapped Tambul, his old irascibility coming back. 'Does it matter?'

'Yes. Because if you locked it, someone's either got hold of a key or done something to the lock. Not everyone could do either.'

'I don't think I forgot, but I can't be sure.'

'Very well. And do you have any ideas as to who got in and took the draught?'

'No. I didn't see anyone.'

Jessamine paused for a moment, her brain alight with ideas. Hmm. 'Where do you leave your keys?'

'Leave them? I never leave them.' Tambul lifted his tunic to reveal a belt wrapped around his waist, and shook the brass keyring hanging from it. A quantity of keys jangled. 'I don't even take them off when I sleep.'

'But the Wizard also has keys, doesn't he?'

'Of course.' Tambul's face brightened with hope. 'Do you suppose *he* lost his keys?'

'He might have. He's careless. I'll ask him. One more thing, Tambul. Did anybody know you'd left the Transformative Draught in the Dispensary?'

'You mean, did I wander about telling everyone I met that a priceless potion was lying about on the bench, for just anybody to take? Of course I didn't.'

'Then somebody must have seen you take it in there, and come out again without it.'

'I didn't see anyone.'

Jessamine heaved an inward sigh. Tambul was inobservant to the point of obstructiveness, wandering about with his head in Potion Land and noticing nothing.

'I'm going to the Dispensary,' she announced. 'I want a look at that lock.'

The lock on the Dispensary door was as stout as the Wizard's arts could make it. Not merely a contraption of metal tumblers and levers and whatnot; Garstang had also enchanted it. Jessamine could smell the stink of magic on it.

'If you tried to pick this, I'd wager you'd get a nasty shock,' she observed to Tambul, who'd trailed woefully after her, out of the Potionery and down the hall to the Dispensary.

Tambul sniffed. 'Naturally. There are valuables in here.'

'But the key,' she went on. 'If you've got a proper key, enchanted with a counter-spell, you'd be all right. Is that how it works?'

Reluctantly, Tambul nodded. She surmised he was still worried about being blamed. After all, only he and the Wizard held the enchanted keys.

'Well,' she said, with one last, grimacing sniff at the lock. 'Since the enchantment appears to be intact, the intruder must have had a proper key. And if it wasn't yours, then it can only have been the Wizard's.'

Tambul let out a breath. 'Do you think so?'

'Assuming you haven't been lying to me.' Jessamine fixed him with a severe stare.

'I haven't! I swear!'

'Right, then. We've only to consult the sylphs, and I believe we'll have our answer.'

'And where are they?' Tambul lifted his face and searched the empty air with a keen gaze, as though he might discern their airy, invisible shapes if he only *looked* hard enough.

'Search me.' Jessamine stepped away from the Dispensary door and scurried back down the hall. 'But they're often to be found in the Potionery. Ladies?' she called as she darted back through the door. 'Sylphies? I'd like a word?'

'We do have the answer you seek,' answered an ethereal voice, like a clear, chiming bell. 'But we've promised not to tell.'

Jessamine sneezed in disgust. 'Promised! Promised *who*, I'd like to know? And why would you do a thing like that? If somebody's making off with the Wizard's precious potions, he ought to know about it.'

'It won't happen again,' said the sylph.

'Oh, won't it? You know that for certain, do you?'

'She *promised*.'

She. That was a clue, at least. 'Promises are lovely,' retorted Jessamine. 'Until they become inconvenient, and then they often turn out to mean nothing at all.'

Silence.

'Your precious *thief* is all too likely to try it again, and well you know it.'

The air fluttered. 'We were given surety.'

Jessamine sneezed again. Her nose always itched when people said foolish things. 'You mean you were *bribed.*'

The silence, this time, was palpably shame-faced.

'Right,' said Jessamine with a short sigh. 'Two can play at that game. Shall it be the usual?'

The air brightened, as though filled with smiles. 'Delightful,' whispered the sylph.

Jessamine shook her head. Why the Wizard relied so much on the insubstantial things, she'd never understand. They had the moral fibre of a blade of grass. 'Tambul,' she said to the little apprentice. 'Get me a cauldron of lemonade, a jar of every-flavour comfits, and a basket of ribbons in seven colours.'

Tambul blinked at her in blank incomprehension. 'What?'

'Quickly!' she barked. 'There's no time to be lost if the banquet's to be saved. And if you want my help to shield you from the Wizard's ire, you'd best make yourself useful.'

Tambul, pale as the underbelly of a fish, swallowed any further objections and rushed away.

An hour later, Jessamine was on her way back to the kitchens, her tail high and waving in victory. She was moving as fast as her short legs could carry her, for though she'd carried her point with the sylphs, it had taken far too much time.

Not that Tambul could fairly be blamed. He'd come up with the comfits and the ribbons in double-quick time; so fast, she had to suspect him of some complicity with the Court Ladies.

Never mind that, though. The lemonade. There was the delay, for every drop of the beverage had been sent to the Queen's table, and there wasn't so much as a thimbleful to be had from the buttery.

Persuading the sylphs to accept ginger beer instead proved no easy task, but Jessamine could be wily, when she had to.

'It's every bit as good as lemonade,' she'd insisted. 'Zingy. Tart. Refreshing.'

'We do not like beer,' the sylphs had said.

'It isn't beer.'

'Ginger not-beer?'

'By all means, let's call it ginger not-beer.'

This confusion had taken some further time to resolve, and still more to coax the elusive sylphs into trying a drop or two.

But now they were suitably bought off, and Jessamine had the all-important information for the Wizard.

Tambul, the coward, had left her to face Garstang's probable wrath alone, a decision Jessamine had greeted with another, hearty sneeze and a derisive flick of her expressive tail.

No matter. She was more than a match for the Wizard.

'Ho, the Wizard!' she boomed, upon reaching the kitchen portal (still firmly locked). She added a violent roar for good measure.

The door swung open, revealing a harried-looking Garstang on the other side. 'At last. You've been ages.'

Jessamine did not grace this observation with a reply. 'Is there a maid in here called Maggot?' she barked, bypassing the Wizard, and dashing into the kitchen.

'Maggot?' repeated Garstang, slamming the door behind her. 'That can't be right.'

'It's what the sylphs said,' Jessamine insisted.

'Moggat,' said Chef Paglar. 'That's her.' She pointed, indicating a maid of plump aspect, with carrot-coloured hair and a face wan with dread.

'Well, there's your culprit,' said Jessamine, without sympathy. She sat down upon the cool tiles of the floor, feeling rather weary. All the dashing about, and at this hour of the night! The knave had led her a merry dance, and received a flinty glare for her trouble. 'Tambul left the Transformative Draught in the Dispensary,' she explained. 'And before you propose to fly off the handle over it, Wizard, it was likely *your* keys she filched in order to unlock the door.'

Wizard Garstang's dark brows rose into his hair. '*My*—'

'She likes to chat with the sylphs, from time to time,' Jessamine went on. 'They told her about the Draught in the Dispensary, and were bribed to keep quiet about her having taken it. And I suppose she's spent this evening adding a bit to every dish in the kitchens.'

The maid, Moggat, stared at the floor, twisting her hands in her begrimed apron.

'What I haven't discovered is: why,' Jessamine concluded. 'Perhaps she has some kind of grudge against the chef.'

'You won't work in my kitchens again, that I can tell you,' said Paglar, grimly.

Moggat's head came up at that. 'I don't want to work in your kitchens! I don't want to work in any kitchen! I want to be a Potioner.'

Garstang had been, thus far, silent, regarding the disgraced maid with a gimlet stare. 'I remember you,' he said abruptly. 'You petitioned me for Tambul's role, didn't you? After Jessamine resigned it.'

Jessamine snorted. *Resigned.* In a manner of speaking.

'I did,' said Moggat, lifting her chin. 'I've always wanted to be a wizard. But nobody would look twice at a lowly servant, would they? Including you.'

Garstang contrived to look stern and a little shame-faced at the same time. 'Well, and so you hatched this scheme?' he pursued. 'Why?'

She sighed. 'I thought, if Tambul's carelessness was exposed, you'd want a replacement. And maybe you would reconsider me.'

Jessamine frowned at that. Tambul wasn't usually careless, though it could happen, on occasion. The scheme seemed cruel;

but she had to admit, Tambul didn't endear himself around the castle. He was habitually rude. 'But why put the Draught in all the food?' she asked. 'Surely taking it would have been enough.'

Moggat, curiously, blushed. 'That wasn't my original plan,' she confessed. 'I thought of that part later.'

'To what end?' uttered the wizard, in awful tones.

'I was curious about what it would do,' said Moggat, her voice ringing with enthusiasm. 'So I put a bit in a batch of the pepper-cakes, and it was so interesting that I put some in the soup, too. I wanted to see if the effects differed depending on the recipe, see? And they do!'

'You've ruined the feast,' Jessamine growled. 'Did that not occur to you?'

'I suppose I thought, maybe, it would be… fun,' said Moggat.

'Fun? Fun! I still haven't got the taste of smoked eel and cherries out of my jaws!'

'Mine was ginger and pepper and raspberry,' said Moggat, reflectively. 'Quite good, I thought.'

Wizard Garstang folded his arms, and narrowed his eyes at the maid. 'An underhanded scheme, irresponsible, and unworthy of a person of any honour,' he pronounced.

Moggat's face fell, and she nodded. 'I know, sir. I suppose I got carried away.'

'Also a bold scheme, and clever, and betraying a bright, in-quiring mind,' he continued.

Moggat blinked.

'I'm not sure what's best to be done with you, but I'll think of something.'

Moggat's eyes grew very wide. 'You mean...'

'I'm not sure what I mean, yet. I'll have to think about it.'

'Out of my kitchen, Moggat,' insisted Paglar. 'I could well have been blamed, not Tambul. And what then?'

Moggat turned red again, and removed her apron in subdued silence. 'I *am* sorry,' she said, without looking at Paglar. 'I didn't think of that.'

Jessamine sighed, and sagged into a weary heap upon the floor. 'Oh well. No harm done there, I suppose.'

'But the feast!' said Paglar. 'It's too late to make any more food.'

Wizard Garstang appeared to be manifesting a smile. It took him some few moments, but once it had fairly worked its way onto his features it quickly became fiendish. 'Ah! But perhaps Miss Moggat has the right of it,' he declared. 'You know best of all, Paglar. A recipe's success or failure has much to do with how it's presented.'

'I don't think making it look *pretty* is going to work,' answered Paglar sourly.

'Oh, it will,' said Garstang confidently. 'But we're going to do something different. Make up platters with a bit of everything on each one. We want an intriguing mix. And this will be no ordinary feast. We're going to call it "The Feast of Surprises", and I'm much mistaken if it won't prove a hit among the Court.'

Jessamine sneezed, twice in a row. 'Stars above. Surprises! I'll say.'

She thought the Court would prove the Wizard a fool, but she was mistaken, for they enjoyed the feast immensely.

The Wizard's smug smile lingered for many days afterward.

AMONG HIS MAJESTY'S ROSES

I t is time to speak of His Majesty, the King.

A quiet man (an uncommon quality in a monarch), he appears at banquets and feasts, because he must. He holds Court once every turn of the moon, because it is his duty. But left to himself (which occurs more often than one might think), he is most often to be found in one of three places about the castle: the library (where he studies languages, philosophy and history); the solar (where he watches the clouds by day, and the stars by night); or, best of all, the rose garden.

It might be more rightly called *his* rose garden, for few would disturb him there. Not out of fear of retribution or rebuke; King Griffin, besides being of a quiet disposition, tends towards mildness of manner, too (though one would not wish to find oneself on the wrong side of one of his long, silent stares, on the rare occasions upon which some fool has displeased him). He is left to his peace and his perfumes out of respect, for as the Courtiers of Castle Chansany understand, to deprive the king of either would be to deprive him of sense and sanity as well.

There comes a strained look about His Majesty's eyes when a banquet runs on too long, or when a Court-holding day proves over-filled with petitioners and pleas. He grows straighter and taller in his seat, the better to counteract the slumping of his shoulders, the shrinking-in upon himself, as though these di-minishments in posture might hide him from the world. If he is not soon released from bustle and hurly-burly, one might detect the presence of a growing ache in the royal head by the unfocused look in his grey-washed eyes; and soon after *that*, he is like to turn abrupt, acid in his manner; what might be termed *irritable*, in a less august person than himself.

The King, then, needs silence and safety, and he finds both among the green, sleeping sanctuary of his roses.

On Castle Chansany's strange journey to Somewhere, His Majesty has been spending more time than ever wandering the winding, cobbled paths between the ivory stone walls, greeting blossom after bloom, and thinking. The Castle not only aloft, but sailing; sailing to *somewhere*, a place unknowable; King Griffin does not, perhaps, bear so well with motion, or perhaps with suspense. Powerlessness does not belong to a king; it is not his province.

Being more in need of solace than ever, then, it is unfortunate that, some few days into the Castle's sudden wanderings, the King was to be interrupted after all.

His visitor entered like a gust of wind, awhirl with noise and purpose, and already talking. 'Griffin! I have waited since three o'clock yesterday afternoon and not a sign of you has there been.' This, we must suppose, was the closest to the courtesy of an apology this visitor was likely to offer, being none other than the Wizard Garstang, and not accustomed to finding himself quietly wished elsewhere. 'I've need of speech with you,' he continued, tracking the King down to the south-west corner of the rose garden, where he had been in silent communion with a flower he called the White Heart of Midnight.

'Oh?' said the King, without looking up. A pity he did not, for he missed the sight of the tall and imposing figure of his Court Wizard engaged in a brief tussle with a clambering beauty of a rose, its thorns hitching possessively into the trailing length of Garstang's deep emerald cape.

Still, the Heart of Midnight, with its dark, velvet core, more than deserved a king's attention.

'More rightly, it's Baldringa I want to speak to,' said Garstang, admonishing the grasping rose with a narrow-eyed stare.

King Griffin did not appear enlightened by this news, or not immediately. He roused himself from his contemplation of his rose one slow blink at a time, and was obliged to say, 'Baldringa. I do not recollect—' before recollection blessed him after all. 'Ah! My mother's Wizard.'

'The Court Wizard before me,' agreed Garstang, with a trace of impatience. 'Long gone now, of course.'

The King nodded, befuddlement fading, but realisation not quite dawning, yet. He looked about at his prized blooms: a tall and verdant tree at his elbow, profuse with flowers the colour of raspberries; determined climbers mapping the walls with silken green foliage, velvet petals in lilac and saffron and black; sturdy shrubs raising thorned branches to the clouds, turning their honey-coloured faces to the sun. This wandering survey complete, he asked: 'But where is she?'

Garstang appeared taken aback. 'Somewhere hereabout, surely?' he answered, performing a circling turn where he stood, his dark gaze sweeping over forty or fifty roses in moments, and taking in none. Whether he meant the roses or the walls or the rest of the castle beyond, he didn't say.

King Griffin smiled, a little. 'I'm afraid I am unacquainted with the Wizard Baldringa. We have not spoken since I was a boy.'

'Well, that won't do,' came Garstang's reply, together with a frown. 'I have questions for her.'

The King's attention drifted, inevitably, towards White Heart of Midnight once again. 'I shall be glad to help you,' he said, mildly enough. 'Once I know how.'

Garstang, knowing himself dismissed, made a small sound illustrative of impatience. 'Thank you,' he said, only a little curt, and belatedly bethought himself to bow.

This done, he marched away again, taking his noise and his vitality with him.

The King took a slow breath, inhaling serenity with a smile, and returned to the comforting depths of his own, silent thoughts.

*   *   *

Any Court worth mentioning possesses not only a monarch and a Wizard, but a Court Dragon, too.

In the private opinion of Wizard Garstang, the dragon of Castle Chansany ranked among the very best of the latter. But the Wizard being loath to praise rather than provoke, his Familiar remained oblivious to his good opinion, and a trifle irascible because of it.

Thus it was that when her own repose was interrupted, like the King's – hers being conducted in the full sunshine to be found atop the highest walls at that hour of the afternoon – she obeyed the peremptory summons with a feeling of resentment.

It was the sylphs who brought notice. 'You're wanted,' said one of them, suddenly, close to her left ear.

Jessamine twitched. 'No I'm not,' she snapped, without opening so much as a single eye (for though denial of inconvenient truths has never been known to accomplish much, who amongst us can resist just one more ill-starred attempt at it?).

'You are,' persisted the sylph, and Jessamine felt an insistent breeze whirl about her shivering ears. 'It's the Wizard.'

'Can he not manage his own affairs?'

'Never,' said the sylph, with an airy laugh.

Jessamine did not consider this point worth debating, it being too patently true. 'I'm comfortable,' she informed the pestersome sylph. 'I'll be down later.'

'He says to bring you at once,' sighed the sylph. 'Immediately, and right away.'

Jessamine's eyelids lost their delicious heaviness, and snapped open. Her irritated gaze took in the stupendous sight of a prismatic blue sky, clouds drawn across it in lazy drifts of sunlit white and grey; the great, glittering expanse of a nameless ocean somewhere below, above which they were presently sailing, at ponderous speed; and the soft, golden, gently crumbling mass of the castle's walls, sun-baked and glinting, atop one of which she was presently draped.

She took all of this in with a single blink of her fiery eyes, and dismissed it with a growl. 'Wizards,' she grumbled, and slithered down off the wall. 'What manner of mess has he got himself into?'

'He did not say,' whispered the sylph, dreamily. 'Only that *she* proves elusive, and someone must go after her.'

Jessamine flexed her brains as she toddled down the many stairs from the towers, thinking. If the Wizard hadn't meant Jessamine herself – and it seemed he had not – who then did he refer to when he spoke of a *she*?

'Might be Her Majesty the Queen,' she muttered, scuttling down a long, cool corridor. 'Or one of the Court Ladies. Though I'd think as not, the latter. He hasn't the patience for them.'

The Queen, then. But why would Her Majesty be hiding from the Wizard? And what did he need Jessamine for, to find her? Any passing errand-runner would do, for so slender a task. It wasn't a queen's business to be hard to find, as a rule.

If it weren't the Queen, then she had no further ideas. Garstang had many acquaintances but few confidantes; herself excepted (and the Queen), she was aware of no other lady he might urgently be in want of, on a balmy afternoon somewhere over the sea.

She had not long to wait for an answer to this burning question, for the moment the *click-click* of her curling talons was heard crossing the threshold of the Wizard's study, he spoke.

'Baldringa,' he announced in a mighty voice. 'Fetch her for me, Jess-o-mine.'

Unlike the King, Jessamine required neither time nor prompting to remember the name. 'The Old Wizard? She's dead,' she informed him shortly. 'Must be.'

'She is nothing of the kind,' Garstang said testily. 'A Wizard is never dead, dragon, until they mean to be. Baldringa was ever fond of a nap. I am merely unable to determine which nook or cranny she has squashed herself into this time.'

Jessamine's draconic brain reeled. Somewhere about the Castle, an ancient Wizard (who ought, by rights, to be worm food) had been lying about sleeping these many years, without anybody being any the wiser.

'You are sure, I suppose?' she said, sceptical.

'Perfectly.'

'Then it's a pity you gave me to Dragonfly. *He* could probably tell you, were he still corked up in his bottle in the Potionery.' Dragonfly, former Familiar to the Wizard Baldringa; once housed as a potion upon a high shelf among the Wishful Elixirs and the Changeful Draughts, and now – who knew where? He had given his dragonskin to Jessamine, and gone.

'And what do you want with Baldringa?' she demanded tartly. 'Cannot some other, less elusive Wizard satisfy you?'

'Certainly not. I have questions only she can answer.'

'Questions of burning urgency, I perceive. Not one could wait until we come to stop flying, for example.'

'No, dragon, for it is precisely the *flying* I want to enquire about. Shall you be lending me your assistance, or must I ask Tambul?'

Jessamine drew back, horrified. 'Tambul! Lawks, no. Only I don't see as how I can help.'

'The sylphs,' said Garstang distinctly. 'The pesky, wispy, omnipresent-until-you-need-one sylph-ladies of the Castle, with whom, I have previously had occasion to note, you seem to have a *way*.'

Jessamine thought a moment, and had to give the Wizard due credit for brains. Those sylphs went everywhere, and few could catch them at it – not even she. If anybody might know where (or how) Baldringa had hidden herself, perhaps they would.

'I don't see why you couldn't ask them yourself,' she muttered as she slunk back toward the door.

'We have quarrelled,' he said shortly.

He did not explain when or why, but Jessamine scarcely required details. The Wizard came to quarrel with people, from time to time. It was one of his Qualities. Sometimes, Jessamine suspected he considered it a sport.

She trailed out of the Study and went into the Potionery. A few of the sylphs lingered there rather often, for no reason Jessamine understood, save perhaps for the entertainment of causing mischief — the Potionery being full of breakables and shakeables, after all.

'Ladies?' she piped up as she puttered in. 'If you'll excuse me interposing on your leisure time? The Wizard's having a crisis, and has sent me to appeal to your better natures.'

'The Wizard,' answered a fluting voice, 'has been rude, and has not apologised.'

'It's his way,' Jessamine sighed. 'To be rude, that is, and not to apologise. At least, not in apology-words. He'll sometimes find roundabout ways of making amends. Like ribbons. Or beverages.' He had done both for Jessamine, at different times: a saffron-coloured ribbon once, when he had cursed at her in a fit of high irritation, and sent her scuttling out of the Study in fright. And another time a bowl of drinking chocolate, *with* cream, when he had stamped upon her tail (she was fairly sure it had been accidental, for it was not the Wizard's habit to cause deliberate harm; but he had been very careless).

'I see no ribbons,' answered the sylph. 'Or beverages either.'

'I could bring some of either, or both, if it would help.'

There came a wisp of a cool breeze floating past Jessamine's nostrils: a sylph-sigh. 'What is it that he's wanting?'

'Why, it's an entire mystery! There is another Wizard somewhere about, I'm supposed to believe, and he wants to talk to her. Only she must be well hidden indeed, for I hadn't a notion, and even Garstang cannot find her.'

'Baldringa,' said a different voice, surprising Jessamine.

'That's the name. Why, do you know her?'

'Not I. But 'twas a name commonly spoken about the Castle, once.'

'So it was. Well, we've to find her, and I beg your aid most humbly, or I'll be at this errand until next Year's Turn.'

A third voice spoke, very softly, near Jessamine's ear. 'She was a jug, once.'

Had the sylph spoken so softly as to evade comprehension? 'A jug?' Jessamine repeated. 'A *jug*?'

'Another time, a tapestry. It hung on the wall behind the King's throne for three years together.'

Jessamine heaved a long and smoke-wreathed sigh. She was not altogether unfamiliar with people turning into peculiar things; had not Wizard Garstang himself rescued the Prince from ignominious status as a golden basin, not long since? A curse of sorts, that time; not a state chosen by Armael himself.

But Wizards, as everyone knew, were strange.

'So she might be a carpet, today,' Jessamine concluded gloomily. 'Or a saucepan. Or a book, stuffed into the library shelves amid a thousand others.'

'Or a ribbon,' said one of the sylphs, happily. 'A chocolate pot. A silver fork, a golden spoon.'

'A chamber pot,' suggested another, improbably, giggling.

'An ornament in Her Majesty's hair, all over jewels! A garter about the King's hose, with diamonds in!'

'A grand chair, upon which royal arses repose,' said the second again, the one who'd mentioned the chamber pot.

'A throne, then,' said the third sylph, tartly.

'That is what I said,' came the reply, with a chortle.

Jessamine threw up her claws, emitting an irritated puff of sulphurous, stinking smoke. 'Ladies. Please. Will you help me find out *which* of these many ordinary articles the Wizard Baldringa might be hiding in?'

'Hiding *as*, I should think,' said one of the sylphs, pertly.

'That's as may be,' said Jessamine firmly. 'Will you help me? There's ribbons and lemonade in it.'

'Not-beer,' countered a sylph immediately. 'Please.'

'Ginger not-beer. Very well. Is that a yes?'

'Yes, yes,' said the sylphs together, and streamed away, for she heard not a peep out of them after that.

This left Jessamine alone in the Potionery with no notion where to look her own self, though a glimpse of the bright-sparkling glass bottles with which she was surrounded gave her an idea.

Donning her thickest dragonskin, at least in her own mind, she went, next, in search of the irascible Tambul.

*   *   *

'Tambul!' roared she shortly afterwards, upon finding the erratic apprentice Potioner nose-deep in something blue and sweet-smelling. He was in the Mixery, concocting Something.

'Look sharpish! And I'll have none of your nonsense today, for we've urgent business afoot.'

'There's always urgent business afoot,' snapped he, not inaccurately. 'It's the Wizard again, isn't it?'

'Of course.' She scuttled over to the stool upon which he (somewhat precariously) balanced, arms blue up to the elbows, hands deep in a sink full of ooze. 'The errand's mine and you aren't to worrit yourself over it, but I've need of a Potion.'

'We have those,' he said, stirring the ooze until it wafted up a pungent scent of lilies.

'I need to See better.'

That caused him to turn his head; he squinted down at her eyeballs, frowning. 'Nothing amiss with your sight.'

'Not in an ordinary way, but this is Wizard's business, and far from sensible. I need to See through Wizardly curses and cantrips.'

Tambul's bushy eyebrows both rose together, signalling incomprehension.

Jessamine huffed a testy sigh. 'Prince Armael,' she began. 'When he was a basin, *I* had no idea. Neither did you. But the Wizard knew. How? He Saw through the curse, that's how, by some mysterious Wizardly means, and I've need of it.'

'You'd have to be a Wizard,' said Tambul, dismissively, and went back to stirring his perfumed sludge.

'I only need it for a little while,' Jessamine retorted. 'Temporary-like. I've not the smallest desire to bother myself with curses and cantrips *always*.'

Tambul stopped stirring again, and stared off into the distance. Jessamine waited with as much patience as she could muster. She was growing accustomed to Tambul's odd ways, and this was one of them. Thinking.

'I might have something,' he decided at last, and hopped down off his stool, spraying blue slime all over the floor. Jessamine, too slow to dodge, received a trail of it over the long, scaled curve of her snout, and sneezed.

'Mind you,' said Tambul, pausing again. 'If it's Wizard-sight that's wanted, why cannot the Wizard chase about the Castle himself? He's got it already.'

'You have met the Wizard,' sighed Jessamine. 'Brain like a box full of butterflies. He'd get as far as the Library, or the Queen's breakfast-parlour, or the south-west tower topiary garden; catch sight of a fascinating book, or a curious tea-spoon, or a rare songbird; and that would be that. All else forgotten, until to-morrow morning after breakfast, by which time it would be far too late.'

Tambul knew the truth of this far too well to contest it. He merely sighed, and stalked off to the Potionery, trailing blue ooze, Jessamine, and a quantity of irritable dragon-smoke.

Jessamine waited quietly enough while he fetched a ladder – he was not a tall fellow, Tambul – and set about clambering up and down the shelves. It took him some time to identify whatever it was he sought, but at length he clattered down to the floor again, arms coated in dust now as well as slime, and handed a jar to Jessamine.

The thing was elderly, by the look of it: thick with dust (and slime, now, thanks to Tambul), the lid so tightly shut Jessamine had to sneeze on it to open it.

Inside, something murky lurked.

'I've to imbibe this?' she said, doubtfully, and sniffed.

'Only a little,' Tambul cautioned. 'Or you'll be seeing far too much, most likely forever.'

Daunted, Jessamine mastered a brief impulse to shut the lid again, and hurl the jar from the Castle walls, for good measure.

Instead, she sighed (inwardly cursing the Wizard's good name), and took a pinch of the stuff in shrinking claws. It wobbled, nastily, tasted worse; but it went down easily enough, only a brief grimace, a momentary retch – and gone.

'Oh,' she said, after a moment, for the empty air was suddenly full of airy shapes, like begowned clouds. They had twinkling eyes and wafting hair and impish smiles and they were all, every one of them, clustered about Jessamine.

'Ladies,' she said, thinking it prudent to make them a courtly bow. It was one thing to *know* they were there, and capable of any mischief at a moment's notice; quite another to be faced with them all, all at once, and abruptly grasp just how many of them there were.

They were never still, either, the sylphs, any more than the wind was. Jessamine was like to grow dizzy with the watching of them, and for a moment she shut her eyes.

They were giggling.

'You see us,' whispered one. 'How *enchanting*.'

'Not for long, mind,' Jessamine warned. She took a gumption-boosting breath, opened her eyes again, and drew herself up. She could be almost as tall as Tambul, if she tried, and in terms of guts and gumption, much taller. 'Now, then,' she said decisively, and set down the stinking jar. 'If you'll permit me, ladies, I've a Wizard to find.'

Baldringa was not in the Potionery, or the Mixery either. Jessamine did discover sundry other oddities: a stirring-spoon that had once been a cat, by the look of it, and still wore its striped tail; a book with a lady's maid folded into it, squashed flat, like a pressed rose; a matched set of game-pieces, severed from their attendant board, which sang soft laments in discordant harmony.

If this was the sort of thing that Garstang saw when he wandered about the Castle, Jessamine wondered less at his propensity toward distraction. She began rather to wonder how he ever got *anything* done.

'I can't stop,' she apologised to a drinking goblet – heavy silver, and all over engraved – which tried to ask her questions.

'But there is a potato pie in the buttery!' protested the goblet. 'And what has become of the strawberry comfits, with the marzipan in them?'

'That's all very well,' Jessamine said, stopping after all, 'but I'm on a quest. Have you happened to encounter a Wizard recently?'

'No,' answered the goblet, sadly. 'Not since Queen Harindra danced a pavanne with the Prince of Jorland.' It quivered, and added, in a lower tone, 'I carried wine, that day. Honey wine, for the Queen.'

'Baldringa danced a pavanne?' Jessamine was, briefly, arrested by the thought. Baldringa had been young and lively, once – like Garstang, perhaps.

'She wore jonquil ribbons,' mused the goblet.

Jessamine shook herself out of this dream of ages past, before it could quite carry her away. 'That's all very charming,' she said, 'But I need to find Baldringa now, not years in the past. Haven't you seen her more recently? Think.'

Was a drinking-goblet capable of thought? It was not in possession of brains, of course, but it seemed to be trying; it shivered a little, and rocked back and forth. 'I saw the jonquil ribbons,' it offered.

Jessamine frowned. 'Many another person wears jonquil, I've no doubt.'

'But these were *ribbons*,' insisted the goblet. 'And just the shade.'

'And who, or more likely *what*, was wearing these lovelies?'

'Twas a rose,' whispered the goblet dreamily, as it began a swooping sort of dance. 'Petals of silk and velvet, coloured like wine, and the ribbons twined about it, like a wreath.'

Jessamine blinked. 'Roses do not commonly wear ornaments,' she observed. 'Being ornaments themselves. You may be onto something, Goblet.'

'My name is *Petua*,' hissed the silver vessel, affronted, and ran away, bristling, like a cat.

Jessamine paid it no mind, arrested in reverie. Roses. One did not see a great many roses about the Castle, as a rule; flowers aplenty, of course, but the roses were special. The roses were delicate, and loved, and prized, and they needed particular care.

The roses dwelt in His Majesty's own garden, where few others presumed to go.

Jessamine, for a moment, quailed. To barge in upon the King's solitude, like a boor! To trespass on His Majesty's most sacred of spaces, like a heedless peasant! Was she not a dragon of *manners*?

Still, there was the Wizard to answer to, if she didn't. She could tell *him* to do it, perhaps, but small chance that he would. He would only say, testily, 'Then bring me this rose, dragon, and quickly,' and she'd have to go into the rose-garden after all.

Jessamine sighed, and straightened her spine. Perhaps kings were not so *very* alarming; Her Majesty the Queen had been rather charming, after all.

King Griffin did not immediately perceive the fiery little crea-ture whose stealthy presence invaded his peace. Jessamine was green today, by accident or design, and her emerald-scaled hide blended, well enough, with the satiny foliage beneath which she skulked.

The king was in conversation, with a rose.

'How beautiful the ocean looks, from above,' he was saying, in his soft, low burr of a voice. 'Few have ever beheld such a sight, I suppose, which is a great shame. Beauty lifts the spirit, does it not, and enlarges the soul.'

'Then you might permit more besides your royal self to wan-der the rose-gardens,' came Jessamine's voice, tartly, before she could stop herself.

The king turned his head, mildly surprised, and still did not discern Jessamine until she moved, and the leaves rustled. 'A visitor,' he said, smiling. 'Hello.'

Jessamine crawled out, and sat up on her haunches, shaking verdure and cobwebs from her ears. Belatedly, she thought to bow. 'Majesty.'

'You are right, of course,' he murmured, taking in the un-common sight of a tiny and irritated dragon without visible surprise. 'Perhaps it is selfish of me to reserve this space for my own use. Though, you know, I have never made any such decree, nor am I displeased to receive a visitor, once in a while. The people of the Castle seldom come here, regardless.'

'Perhaps they're afraid of you,' Jessamine suggested, boldly, though she doubted as she spoke. King he may be, but Griffin's quietness was not the menacing sort indicative of a sleeping ragefulness, nor the deceptive, soft-spoken mildness of malice and spite. His was the gentle sort, the subdued manners of a man without bluster or bombast, and despite her trepidation Jessamine had already begun to relax.

'That may be,' agreed the king, without rancour.

Jessamine sighed, and deflated a little. 'More likely it's because they like you,' she admitted. 'And they respect that you need the roses more than they do.' She thought a moment, and corrected herself. 'The roses, and the peace, for there'd be roses still even were half the Court squashed between the walls.'

King Griffin smiled. He looked a little weary, Jessamine thought, like the Queen. Perhaps ruling was not all that it was cracked up to be. 'What brings you to the roses today?' he asked her. 'Or was it the peace that drew you?'

Jessamine had, for a moment, forgotten her errand. Now she remembered it, all at once, and cast a sharp look at the rose the king had been chatting with, when she'd come in. Yellow petals, and no ribbons. Not Baldringa. 'I'm on a quest,' she said importantly, and drew herself up. 'On the Wizard's authority.'

'Ah,' said the king.

'I've to find another Wizard,' she continued. 'A different one. A lady, this one, or she was that, before she was a tapestry. Or a jug. Or a rose.'

The king glanced at the yellow rose, rueful. 'Well, my dear?'

Jessamine narrowed her eyes, looked again. "Coloured like wine", the goblet had said, and this one was nothing of the kind.

But then, it *had* mentioned honey-wine, for the queen, and would that not rather be yellow than red?

And now the rose was nodding its pretty head, and there were the jonquil ribbons flowing out like smoke, and then it spoke. 'I've had a long rest,' said the rose, in the flat tones of a quite ordinary person (like Jessamine). 'I am up to a little conversation, provided it don't take all night.'

King Griffin smiled, and stepped back, gesturing for Jessamine to take his place before the Wizard Baldringa.

'Oh, no,' said Jessamine, shrinking back. 'I was told only to *find* the Wizard, not talk to her. Besides, I don't know what his Wizardliness wanted with her. "Questions", that's all he said. Typical.' She sniffed.

The rose snorted with laughter. 'No matter. I know what Garstang would ask me.' She sniffed, too, just as Jessamine had, and said: 'He tires me.'

Jessamine could not suppress a giggle, at that. 'Truth to tell, he tires everybody,' she confided. 'Especially himself, I think.'

The rose that was Baldringa nodded its beautiful head. 'I've told him to slow down, again and again. He'll wear himself to flinders.'

'I don't think he can,' said Jessamine.

'Perhaps you're right. At any rate, little dragon, I chose not to answer, when Garstang stormed in here earlier today. I'd rather not call him back now. I'll talk to you.'

'But I don't know what he wanted to ask you,' Jessamine protested.

'That's all right,' said Baldringa. 'I do.'

The King glanced up at the sky, prismatic blue as it was, and awash with daubed clouds, like streaked paint. 'The Castle flies,' he noted. 'It didn't always.'

Jessamine gave a draconic snort of surprise. 'You mean it was once just a *castle*? Plunked on the ground and stationary, like any other?'

'Certainly,' said Baldringa. 'And so it might always have remained, but for me.'

'You're the reason we're airborne.' Jessamine said it flatly, half a question, half a condemnation (for she had by no means resigned herself to this absurd flitting-about, quite as though the gigantic building were a pigeon, or a bat).

'I am,' said Baldringa. She was silent a moment, and added, 'Not that I meant to be. And that's what Garstang wants to question me about, I'll be bound. He wants to know where we're going *to*.'

'Do you know?' Jessamine asked.

The Baldringa-rose rattled with mirth. 'Not the foggiest, dear.'

'Oh,' said Jessamine, faintly.

'I'll tell you how it all came about, if you want to hear it.'

Jessamine scuttled closer, and hunched there, snout up-turned, her pointed tail wrapped around her toes. 'A story,' she breathed, with shining eyes. 'Yes please.'

'Well,' said Baldringa, as the King drew up some favourite chair, and reposed his royal behind in it. 'It all began many years ago, when I was dancing a pavanne with the Prince of Jorland...'

BALDRINGA'S BLUNDER

'I think,' said the Wizard Baldringa, 'I may have made a mistake.'

She spoke for the benefit of her familiar, Dragonfly, who lay curled in a tight spiral upon her lap. His forked tongue flickered, tasting the pungent roseleaf smoke unfurling from the bowl of the wizard's clear-glass pipe.

Drifting as he was between slumber and leaf-induced bliss, Dragonfly made no immediate reply. Several moments passed, pregnant with meaning, before the spine-chilling words penetrated the rosy fog wreathing his smiling brain, and wiped his contentment away.

'A mistake?' he echoed, his emerald eyes opening upon a world gone mad. A *mistake?* The Court Wizard did not make mistakes. *If,* by some unlucky happenstance, she did, then the last thing she would ever do was own it (that duty being among the eclectic mix that fell to Dragonfly's unenvied lot).

Perhaps he had misheard. His burnished silver talons tightened upon the wizard's knee, and he waited, breath suspended, for her to tell him that the roseleaf had addled his wits. Or hers.

'Mm,' said the Wizard Baldringa, meditatively.

Another cloud of rosy smoke wafted over his head, thick and fragrant. He coughed.

A sense of inescapable dread settled over him like a miasma.

'You'd better make a clean breast of it,' he said, gathering what passed for his courage. 'What is it you've done?'

'I've broken the Castle,' said Baldringa.

As if in answer, the walls shuddered.

'Yes,' decisively said now, no lingering note of doubt to soothe a dragon's fears. The Court Wizard lurched suddenly out of her chair, her comfortable bulk moving at a hitherto unknown speed, and spilled the curled and recumbent form of Dragonfly onto the cold flagstone floor.

He lay there a moment, dazed and blinking. Baldringa sat, by habit, in a corner of the cavernous kitchens, a nook tucked out of the way of the bustle and scurry of the harried cooks (mostly). They were used to her down there, scarcely noticed her large, dreaming form as she rocked her creaking chair back and forth, eyes fixed and intent upon unknowable things unfathomably distant.

They noticed *now*, though. If it were not the indignant sneezing of Dragonfly as he picked himself up off the floor, then the sight of the large and (typically) slumbrous Wizard hurling her ample form at the soot-scarred wall by the fireplace, and vanishing into it – well, that would get anyone's attention, even were you a hassled and hurried scullery maid passing by with a teetering tower of besmeared pots.

Or Chef, intent upon a barrow's worth of marchpane and pastry, weaving up fragrant confections for Their Majesties' table. 'What's got into the Wizard?' said he, staring in awe or perhaps horror at where Baldringa had been, marchpane all forgotten.

Dragonfly snarled something too smoky to be intelligible.

Chef nodded, and returned to his confectionery.

I've broken the Castle. No one had heard that save Dragonfly, it seemed, and a good thing, too. The last thing anybody wanted was a panic, not while the Wizard was being so *odd*.

'Perhaps she exaggerates,' mused Dragonfly to himself, without much heart. Disappearing into walls – that was a something he hadn't seen before, let alone that the operation had been conducted with such haste. Baldringa was not a Wizard of haste. Baldringa was a Wizard of sloth and sluggishness, of long afternoons dreamed away by the fire, her begrimed fingernails stroking trails of contentment down Dragonfly's spine as he lay inert in the nest of her robes.

She wasn't even being quiet in there. Somewhere under the clattering of pots and utensils, the hissing of hot oil and boiling water, the chatter and (occasional) cursing of the kitchen folk, Dragonfly heard – *felt*, perhaps, in his bones – a deep, resonant thumping, as though someone inside the stout stone walls were striking great, ringing blows upon them with a hammer. Or a staff.

Dragonfly began to pace, his silver talons wearing scratches into the stones. His feet would not stand still, not with that racket going on.

He ought to have sat down. *Ought*, if he'd had any sense, to have crammed himself into some safe, dark spot, and come out only later, when the thumping and the shuddering had stopped.

If he had, he might have fared better.

As the *thumping* gained in volume, amplified by magic and foreboding alike, and the walls shook harder than ever, even the kitchen folk took note; gradually, all activity ceased, all sounds faded away save that deep, thunderous drumming.

Then came a lurch, and a *rushing* of air. Dragonfly slipped, tumbled, fell; crashed hard into the far wall – how had his head come to be in the vicinity of *that* wall, he had been pacing near the hearth, where it was warmer, like any dragon of sense – the impact upon his fragile skull left him dizzied, so befuddled he thought the Castle had *tipped itself sideways* – he squeezed shut his eyes, talons scrabbling uselessly, clutching at nothing—

'There we are,' came Baldringa's voice. He opened an eye, and there she was: the roseleaf scent of her, the reassuring bulk of her, the white-whiskered, wild-haired, smiling *oddness* of her. She spoke briskly, as though a tricky task of some importance were just completed.

Dragonfly risked the opening of a second eye. The kitchen swam in his befogged vision, but the wreck of it needed no clearer focus: pots and pans and knives and spoons lay scattered across the floor, gathered in jumbled clusters in corners; and all of Chef's sauces and salads, fragrant meats, pastry pies and marchpane comfits had erupted from their containments and landed, streaked and smeared, over every polished wooden surface, every worn stone tile. Dragonfly himself had landed in a cushion of plaited loaves, golden and steaming and crushed (dragon and bread, the both).

A groan emerged from Chef. He lay with his limbs all akimbo, like the rest of his staff. His black coat bore a glistening adornment of sugared almond paste, and honey.

Crinkles appeared at the corners of Baldringa's eyes, and curse her, they were merrily a-twinkle. 'Is there any butter cake left?' said she, with an enquiring look at Chef.

He croaked something, coughed, and said, more clearly: 'Wizard. What have you *done*?'

'Oh, we shall do very well now,' she answered, incomprehensibly.

Dragonfly said nothing, yet. The rushing of air had not yet ceased, and if he could rely on the sensations of his stomach (and usually, he could) then there was some manner of *swooping* going on.

'Wizard,' he finally ventured. 'We are airborne.'

Her smile broadened.

'*Why* are we airborne?'

She gave the question some little thought, but without much effect, for at last she only said: 'Well, and after all: why not?'

*   *   *

The roots of this disaster lay some days before – or perhaps months, for the first sylph had arrived at Castle Chansany at the previous Year's Turn.

Before that, the Castle had been, if not quieter, then more restful, despite the clamour of courtiers and craftsmen, of traders and servants, of hounds and horses and – yes – of Wizards and dragons, too. A single sylph, invisible to the eyes of all but Baldringa; so insignificant a creature, a mere wisp of wind, a cool breeze ruffling the hair, a whisper at the edge of comprehension – one might imagine only *one* such could scarce throw the life of the Castle into chaos.

Yet, she had. She could not be persuaded to stop bathing herself in the bubbling vats of lemonade prepared in the kitchens, and served up in silver pitchers above-stairs; no marchpane comfit was safe, unless she were given a handsome share; she filched ribbons from the coiffed locks of the Queen's Ladies, turned courtiers' hats inside-out and whisked them away, set the hounds to chasing rabbits made of naught but smoke and wizardry.

At first, these antics enlivened the castle's inhabitants, the sylph's airy laughter bringing joy to the ears of those privileged enough to hear it. Only at length did the tide of approval turn, and some few among the Court began to feel wearied of it, and to look to Baldringa in mingled accusation and plea.

For it was Baldringa who had invited the little sylph – or conjured her up, perhaps, out of air and nothingness, in a great cauldron made of copper and magic. No one knew why, the ways of Wizards being, generally, inscrutable.

When at last she upset a tureen of turtle soup all over Their Majesties' brocade table-cloth, ruining the sumptuous garb of more than one lord and lady in the process, and burning an unlucky footman rather badly about the hand, Their Royal Majesties, as one, beseeched – indeed, commanded – the great Baldringa to do something about it. Please.

The distant moon had waxed to plumpness and waned again since, an insignificant span of days. Yet; at the end of them, a regretful Wizard and a broken Castle.

What happened was: this.

'I suppose she is lonely,' mused Baldringa, beholding the solitary sylph with dispassionate eyes as the wispy thing disported herself with an array of golden cutlery. 'The only one of her kind within a day's ride of the castle, I shouldn't wonder. Perhaps the distance is greater still. How should we all feel, were we so alone among strangers, and of another kind to ourselves?'

A line of thinking by no means so bad, for a Wizard. It displayed a transitory compassion, at the very least, even if it was misdirected. Baldringa summoned up another sylph, from wherever it was she had procured the first, and it was with a great sense of personal satisfaction that she released the second whirling gale of mischief to join her fellow.

The mischief, approximately, doubled.

The Queen's favourite lady-in-waiting lost a prized pair of hair-combs, and a quantity of hair with them, snatched as they were out of her braided black locks by careless, covetous little hands.

Chef lost seven bowls of freshly whipped cream one after another, each one whisked out of his grasp no sooner than he had finished the mixing of it. The bowls were later discovered scattered about the castle's corridors, one of which caused His Majesty's Chief Herald to trip upon it on his way to his bed-chamber, and measure his considerable length upon the crimson carpet, nose-first.

Even Dragonfly raised his smoky voice in complaint, setting fire to the hem of Baldringa's ancient velvet robe as he enumerated the sylphs' depredations upon his personal collection of butter-knives and soup-spoons. The fire was put out, as was Dragonfly, for several days afterwards. (The knives and spoons were never recovered).

'I seem to have blundered,' decided Baldringa at last, surveying the remains of a collection of plant pots, wrought in good pottery, and once very fine. A pair of gardeners rescued what could be preserved of their contents, an array of peonies and roses in sad condition.

'I'd say so,' agreed Dragonfly, sitting sourly at his master's heels and spitting smoke.

Baldringa spent some time in silent consideration.

'They must be bored,' she concluded. 'They are like unoccupied children: bound to poke their fingers into every possible amusement.'

'That might be it,' answered Dragonfly, doubtfully.

'What if I were to give them an occupation?'

'You would not like to simply – get rid of them?'

'By what means?'

Dragonfly stared at a smear of earth upon the balcony floor, silenced. 'Just – send them away,' said he, vaguely.

'I could ask them to stop breaking pottery, with much the same success.'

Dragonfly made airy, magical gestures with his talons. 'Send them into the aether. Merge them with the wind. Tear them to *ribbons*. They like those.'

'Vicious, my Dragonfly,' said Baldringa reprovingly, but she laid one great hand briefly upon his scaly head. 'I shall not make ribbons of them.'

'Just the wind bit, then. They are half of a gale already.'

'I will find something for them to do.'

Dragonfly sighed. 'As you wish.'

She set them to work in the kitchens, much to Chef's disgust. If they could eat whipped cream, then they could make it, too, and for a time the gambit seemed a success: their little hurricanes whisked gouts of cream into airy castles in no time, saving Chef and the kitchen-maids a great deal of labour. They were set to whip mounds of the whites of eggs, too, and to turn fat, pale almonds into powder. Even the sylphs seemed to take to the labour, weaving and diving about the cavernous kitchens with inexhaustible energy and merriment.

For a day, that is, and most of a second. Then, the novelty inherent in turning flowing wet matter into quivering peaks of substance (or the other way around) dissipated, and the sylphs absconded with all of the cream, and the almonds, too.

'Never again,' proclaimed Chef, pointing a sharp knife at Baldringa.

'Very well,' said the Wizard, and turned away.

Next they were dispatched to the forge, a low building crouched at the base of the castle's walls. After all, what need has a smith for bellows, with a pair of sylphs to fan the flames of his furnaces? And fine service they performed for him, too; never had a fire burned so steadily or so hot, and for a scant few days the smith replenished every one of the golden utensils that had mysteriously gone missing (and a few of Dragonfly's butter-knives, too).

But a bored sylph with a fire to play with is a dangerous business. So the smith soon found, and he may think himself fortunate that only half of the timber-framed workshop burned to the ground.

'Never again,' thundered the smith, pointing a sizeable hammer at Baldringa.

'Very well,' said the Wizard, and left.

'How came there to be three of you?' said Baldringa, the next day, upon finding a trio of hurricanes idly stirring her tea of a morning.

They only smiled, their ethereal faces bright with delight, and drifted away. Three of them.

Baldringa shook her head. More urgent than ever, then, that they should be put to some purpose: she tried the conservatory, next, and the Court's music-master. 'May they swell your songs, and carry your melodies high,' she informed the musicians, a noble thought, and unwise. For they did, of course; carried the dulcet music so high, the strains of harp and lute were heard as far away as the village of High Oaks. Nor were they quite the melodies their owners had intended to play. Something stranger, fey and frantic emerged instead from the quivering strings, and it was delightful until it wasn't, and the music-master sent them away.

'They're of no use at all!' cried she to the Wizard. 'Sheer trouble! We don't want them.' And she slammed the door to the conservatory in Baldringa's face (and hopefully the sylphs', too).

The next day, four sylphs danced a pavanne in the courtyard of Castle Chansany, their insubstantial forms discernible to the majority through the quantity of silken ribbons they wore (stolen, every one of them, from the dressing-rooms and coiffures of the Court's Ladies).

The day after that, seven bells jangled a discordant cacophony from seven different quarters of the Castle. The clamour did not stop until noon, when Chef contrived to distract the culprits with comfits and lemonade.

A week later, thirty-two sylphs attached themselves, silently and unnoticed, to the trains of the Ladies' Court finery, wafting the silks and velvets so high as to expose their owners' undergarments. Since this occurred during an important Court function, at which several foreign ambassadors were present, Their Majesties felt an uncommon degree of displeasure (as did the Ladies).

'The matter has got out of hand,' Baldringa mused late that night, having effected the sylphs' removal from the dancing chambers by means she would not discuss, even with Dragonfly. 'Thirty-two of them there are! Soon there will be more sylphs than courtiers.'

She reposed in her chair by the kitchen hearth, politely ignored, as always, by the few sleepy cooks and pot-washers still alert. Roseleaf smoke coiled from the bowl of her pipe: faintly blue, that day, and sweet-smelling.

Dragonfly had taken refuge under the chair, judging it best to go unobserved, should a sylph appear.

'And where are they now?' murmured the dragon toothily.

'Somewhere they can cause no further trouble,' came the stout and sturdy answer.

Dragonfly permitted one eye to drift open. 'Put those sylphs where you will, Wizard, be assured they will find a way to cause trouble.'

'Psh,' said Baldringa, and puffed. 'To every problem there is a solution.'

Dragonfly returned to his doze, finding conversation with so stubborn a Wizard unprofitable.

Both fell into slumber at last, the Wizard in her chair with her pipe fallen upon her knee, the Familiar curled upon the cooling tiles at her feet. Upon the dawning of the following day, as the first of the cooks came in to mix up the dough, Dragonfly stirred first. He crept out from behind Baldringa's battered shoes, and filched a nugget of pastry (uncooked) from a bowl unwisely left unattended.

He paused halfway through this sweet repast, for the floor had seemed to shudder under his talons. Only a momentary sensation, and soon gone, as though it had never been; he'd imagined it.

Ten minutes later, Dragonfly's jaws (still sticky with butter) met the stone-flagged floor with a *smack*. Fallen, and face-first! But a clumsy pot-washer had bumped him on her way into the scullery, that must have been why.

By the time Baldringa roused from her dreams (or nightmares), Dragonfly had all but forgotten these occurrences. Thus he greeted her cheerfully enough, bringing her a pastry (cooked) and a flagon of weak beer for her breakfast.

'Not a hint of sylphly activity today, yet,' he informed her. 'All's well in the Castle.'

'It's as I told you,' said Baldringa, her mouth full of almond paste. She washed it down with a gulp of beer, and wiped her lips with her sleeve. 'They won't be bothering us yet a while.'

Perhaps she was right, after all. Ought not he to have some faith in his Wizard? They were not like other mortals, Wizard-folk. They were a cut above. That was why they were so arrogant.

So when the shuddering came again, and went all up and down the walls, Dragonfly sunk his talons into a stout table-leg, and (preserving himself from a tumble, this time) thought nothing of it.

'What was that?' said Baldringa, sharply.

'I don't know!' answered Ella, Chef's best pastry-crimper. 'It's the third time at least.'

'You mean to say this has been going on all morning?' Baldringa sat up, all the way up, and glared at the nearest white-washed wall as though it had insulted her. 'What's got into the walls?'

Dragonfly peeped up, turned fearful of a sudden. 'Believe we were fixing to ask *you* that, Wizard.'

The shaking subsided, and did not return; not for an hour, at least. Baldringa got out of her chair, and performed a slow turn about the kitchen, tapping at the walls, and peering into a crack in the whitewash. 'Stop that,' she said, once or twice, and sternly.

This admonishment proved effective, so the Wizard concluded, for she ceased remonstrating with the stonework and returned to her chair. But she did not speak again, after that, ignoring all remarks addressed to her person; her thoughts were far away. Her pipe came out again, and the roseleaf; Dragonfly, feeling unsettled, crept into her lap.

'I think,' said the Wizard Baldringa at length, 'I may have made a mistake.'

And thus we return to the beginning of our tale, and our Wizard's most uncharacteristic admission of error. Dragonfly, half-asleep, turfed out of his nest of robes; Baldringa's abrupt vanishment into the walls; the curious sensation, soon thereafter, of the Castle and all its contents sailing up into the distant skies.

And the Wizard's complacent remark: *Oh, we shall do very well now.*

The Castle, airborne. And well, after all, why not? A castle may be a castle just as well in the air as on the ground. Nay, better, for word of the magnificent floating Castle Chansany travelled far and wide, and brought many a prosperous and curious visitor to the gates. The reputation of Chansany's Wizards has ever, since that day, been of a towering nature abroad; a distinction they do not, in all likelihood, deserve, but when has anybody minded having anything that is too good for them?

The reprehensible sylphs have never, since that day, kicked up mischief in any excessive degree, being too much occupied with the maintenance of the flying palace. Why it should so amuse them to hold a vast and weighty structure a full league above the ground is anybody's guess; no Wizard has yet been able to answer the question, at any rate.

Should a sylph's attention wander from this noble occupation, they are like to be found in the Potionery, or the Mixery. It is only fit, after all, that their mischief should be confined to the Wizard's domains, since 'twas a Wizard who saddled the castle with them. Once upon a time, they are even known to be of help.

And so it came to be that Castle Chansany and all its inhabitants took up a bird's eye view over the rest of the world, and stayed there. Odd, isn't it?

Odder still, though, its tendency to wander about while it's up there. It doesn't happen often. When it does... well, Their Majesties and all their Court are at the mercy of thirty-two wayward sylphs. Who knows where they are like to end up?

SYLPHISH AND STRANGE

The Wizard Baldringa (presently represented by a rose, with jonquil ribbons) fell silent, abashed, perhaps, by the rampant foolery of her tale. Sylphs! Everyone knew they were tricky creatures. Had to handle them carefully, you did, or who knew what might happen?

A silence followed, heavy and cumbersome, like a castle improbably afloat. Jessamine broke it at last.

'You mentioned a pavanne.'

The rose stirred. 'I did what?'

'A pavanne,' Jessamine repeated. 'You said it all started with a pavanne. You were dancing it with the Prince of Jorland. Where does that bit come into the story?'

'Oh. Well, it doesn't.' The rose shook her pretty petals, and droplets of dew fell, glittering. 'I thought it made it sound nicer as a beginning, that's all.'

Jessamine, disappointed, said no more. She'd never danced a pavanne herself, with a prince or anybody else either.

His Majesty, King Griffin, heaved a sigh. 'Sylphs,' he uttered, lugubriously.

'Sylphs,' agreed Jessamine, flatly. 'And I've to tell the Wizard, now, and he won't be happy.' She narrowed her eyes at the rose-that-was-the-Old-Wizard, tempted to kick it, but didn't. Wizards were tricky creatures, too.

'It may all turn out for the best,' suggested the rose. 'We might be going somewhere wondrous.'

'That we might,' Jessamine conceded. 'And we might be going somewhere terrible. What was wrong with where we were, that's what I'd like to know.'

'Best to ask the sylphs, dear,' murmured the rose, sleepishly. The dewy petals fluffed, and curled; to all appearances, Baldringa went to sleep.

'Well, I like that,' muttered Jessamine, kicking her feet at an unoffending leaf instead of the Wizard. 'Causes all manner of trouble, and then drops off into slumber, peaceful as you like, leaving the rest of us to fix it!'

The king smiled, faintly. ''Tis the way of Wizards, is it not?'

'It is. And that being so, I wonder why any sensible Court should want one.'

The king, it seemed, had no answer to offer.

Jessamine scuttled off, in search of Garstang — at least, at first. Her little heart quailed at the prospect of the Wizard's wrath, however, and halfway down a twisting staircase she stopped dead, and thought.

Maybe she did not have to tell the Wizard about the sylphs, yet. Maybe she could resolve the problem herself — and *then* tell him, after. He might be pleased, instead of angered, and wouldn't that be pleasant?

The problem being but a small one (the answer to the one-would-think simple question: whither goest the castle), Jessamine had only to track down the strange, sylphish sorts that infested the Potionery (or the Mixery, or the Dispensary) and ask them.

Easy.

The Potionery being the closest, Jessamine turned her steps thither, and hurried. Before she was fairly through the door, her jaws were already shaping the words (at a hearty roar) 'And what manner of mischief have you all got us into now? I warn you, I've been told! The whole story!'

But it was not the sylphs whose dulcet tones rang in her thoughts with pleasing alarm: it was Tambul she found, whirling away from a shelf full of rainbow-coloured concoctions, and staring at her with reddening countenance. 'Mischief? Me? I shall beg you to watch your tongue, dragon!'

Jessamine skidded to an abashed halt, though only briefly. Dragon, was it? Only the Wizard got to call her by so ignominious a name (and grudgingly at that, the simple truth being that she could not stop him). 'It is Jessamine, to thee,' she informed him in tones severe enough to match his. 'And I was not addressing you.'

'Oh.' Tambul settled down, hackles visibly deflating. Were Jessamine less occupied with her own errand, she might have detected signs of guilt in the Apprentice's demeanour and defensiveness. The opportunity passed unnoticed.

'It is the sylphs,' Jessamine said in disgust. ''Tis they who are taking us someplace else, and I am here to give them a piece of my mind about it.'

'You, and not the Wizard?' enquired Tambul, scratching at his wild shock of hair, his eyes narrow as they studied her.

Curse Tambul and his wits: sometimes very lively, especially when one least wanted him to be paying attention. 'I shall be informing the Wizard,' she answered loftily, 'once I have gathered more information with which to enlighten him.'

To her surprise, Tambul made no further objection. 'Right you are,' he said, with — she was almost certain — a look of understanding. He turned back to his ordered rows of rainbow liquids, content, apparently, to ignore her henceforth.

But he offered one last nugget of insight first, that being: 'I believe they are congregating in the Mixery.'

'And are they Mixing something?' she demanded tartly. 'Or merely hobnobbing?'

'The latter, it's to be hoped.' Tambul shrugged, and fetched down something grass-green and pungent.

Jessamine sniffed in disgust, and wandered away along the corridor.

The door to the Mixery proved firmly closed, which inconvenienced her somewhat. She rapped her sharp claws against the heavy oak, producing a hollow (and rather satisfying) boom, and lifted her voice to a bawl. 'Sylphs! If you please, you shall let me in at once.'

A faint, airy chuckle answered her, and nothing else. The door remained closed.

Jessamine raised her reedy voice still further. 'You'll not be pleased if I am left to say my piece out here. I have a veritable graveyard of bones to pick with the lot of you.'

The chuckling ceased. In another moment, the door swung slowly, ponderously, open.

Jessamine scurried in. 'Thank you,' she said, slightly mollified.

She saw nobody in the Mixery, of course: the sylphs rarely chose to make themselves visible, least of all to her. But there were signs of habitation. One of the great, stone sinks, filled to the brim with sudsy water, was bubbling gently, as though idly stirred by small hands, or kicked by mischievous feet. An enormous wooden spoon stirred and stirred the contents of some vast basin, stationed, seemingly innocuously, in a corner: its contents smelled floral, and a little sharp.

There were wet footprints all over the stone floor.

'Well,' said Jessamine, as the door closed behind her. 'I have heard Baldringa's tale.'

She waited, but no gasp of guilty comprehension favoured her twitching ears.

'The one about the castle,' she went on, severely. 'Which did not always float, so I am now informed! That's your doing.'

'So it is,' breathed a sylph in her ear, the words accompanied by a chill little breeze.

'What that means,' continued Jessamine, 'is that the castle's present mobile state is your doing, too.'

She waited in hopes of receiving some confirmation, but nobody answered her.

'Well!' she uttered briskly. 'All that remains is for you to tell me where we are off to, and why, and I shall be able to leave you in peace.'

'But you shan't,' whispered the sylph at her ear. 'You will take these tidings to the Wizard, will not you? And he will by no means keep his distance.'

'If you hoped to take the castle waltzing off across half the kingdom without attracting the Wizard's notice, then I shall have to call you an unflattering name or two,' Jessamine spat. 'Not to mention that Their Majesties are like to be most displeased with you. What can you mean by kidnapping the Royal Court?'

''Tis not kidnapping,' objected another, affronted voice.

'What else would you like to call it?'

''Tis adventure!' answered one.

''Tis a duty,' whispered another.

'A duty?' Jessamine pounced on the word, being the more out of place of the two. 'A duty to what? Or whom?'

'We did promise not to tell.' Two of them spoke at once, united.

'You do not mean to tell me that somebody put you up to this,' said Jessamine in a dangerous tone. 'And made you promise not to tell! As though 'twere a mere trivial bit of folly! And you, all of you, have carried it out without so much as a thought for the consequences—'

'We thought of them,' interrupted a sylph. 'That's why we do not wish you to summon the Wizard.'

''Tis cowardice, that. If you do wrong, you ought to take the results, whatever they may be.'

'But why, if we do not have to?'

'You will have to. Answer my questions, or I shall fetch the Wizard this moment.'

A susurration of soft voices followed: a sylphish consultation.

Then, some appointed spokesperson said: 'We do not mean to let you.'

'I—' began Jessamine, but no more time had she to express her disapprobation of such a threat, for she was whisked up into the air; all tumbled about, like a leaf in a hurricane; and when the world righted itself again (and she felt courage enough to open her tightly-squeezed-shut eyelids) she was not in the Mixery at all. She was in a cupboard, she judged, for the cramped quarters bore just space enough for a quantity of folded linens (and one small, disgruntled dragon).

The door, of course, proved firmly locked.

'Well,' sighed she, with a pungent puff of smoke. 'And that's me fair punished for my own cowardice.' For she ought, of course, to have fetched the Wizard right away, the moment she had left the King's garden. But she had quailed, and tarried, and now look what had come of it.

She briefly contemplated the satisfying efficacy of bathing the locked door in the flames of her wrath, which ought to open it in a trice. But being surrounded by flammable materials, no good could come of that. Why, she might burn down the Mixery entirely, and everything near it, too.

Given sufficient time, she might contrive to dredge up from the depths of her brains an unlocking cantrip; surely she'd witnessed such, on one of her various perusals of the Wizard's Books. But she'd had no especial reason to pay attention to the details, never expecting to find herself stuffed up in a cupboard, with a solid slab of oak between her and duty.

Heaving a disheartened sigh, she made a nest for herself on a low shelf, amidst a pile of lavender-scented potion-bags (only slightly shredding them with her sharp claws), and drifted off into a nap.

*   *   *

The Wizard Garstang, the while, oblivious to these mishaps and doings, was engaged in pacing the circumference of the tallest tower at the castle. Not the smallest suspicion had he that the sylphs were to blame for the building's predicament — being, in his periodic arrogance, assured of their docility. They could kick up a lark on occasion, to be sure, but theirs was not the way of serious mischief (he thought).

Perhaps he, too, ought to have performed his own labours, and not sent his hapless (and quite little) Familiar off to do the dirty work for him. If he had, he would have been present for Baldringa's tale, and would now be in some position to act upon the information it contained.

Instead, he paced, impotent and irritated, watching the clouds sail by far below, and wondering.

He was not entirely without an inkling as to their possible direction, it has to be said. He hadn't owned such to anybody else, least of all Jessamine, but he was not devoid of resources. They had, clearly enough, been drifting chiefly westward; and while he had little means of determining the speed at which they travelled, he knew well enough where they would (eventually) come to if the castle were not stopped.

He did not particularly wish to go there, not at all.

He had tried everything in his Spell Books, every charm or cantrip at all likely to affect such a gigantic and inflexible article as a castle. He had even tried communing with the stones themselves, thinking (rather wildly) that some latent awareness might linger somewhere deep in the bones of the building. There wasn't, of course, but Wizards have seen stranger things than that about the world.

If the sylphs and Jessamine were avoiding the Wizard, well, the Wizard was avoiding Their Majesties with equal vigour. For he had no answers to offer them; not a single one. And a helpless Wizard, ignorant and without resource; a Wizard made a fool of, and by a sprawling pile of stonework! What use might a Royal Court have for so humbled a creature? There were Wizards enough eager to fill his curl-toed shoes. Swarms of them. Younger, more flamboyant, more dazzling.

No, he could not admit to Their Majesties the extent of his failures. He could only dither way up there in the air, awaiting the moment of arrival, and practicing what he might choose to say when the appalling moment came.

He did harbour some faint hope of Jessamine's endeavours. She was a dedicated dragon, she'd proved that, and surprisingly wily. If anybody might weasel up some answers — nay, even a solution — it might, just possibly, be her.

But many hours had passed since he had sent her on her errand — the one he ought, of course, to have performed himself — and she had not returned. Were he in the habit of thinking much beyond the end of his own nose, it might have entered his thoughts to feel some concern; but what could befall a Jessamine in Castle Chansany? No one could possibly mean so beguiling a creature harm. Not here.

Let us leave the lofty Wizard Garstang, then, to his hapless (and helpless) wanderings, and return to his underlings, for in their less illustrious hands rests the power to overcome these not insignificant obstacles.

Jessamine having been out-witted by a sylph or several, the next move belongs to the unlikely Tambul. Perhaps that proves a surprise?

We left him uninterested in Jessamine's errand, intent upon something gooey and bubbling in jars. Doubtless this was important work, for despite all his faults Tambul contrives to be a dedicated Apprentice Wizard. Perhaps it is to his credit that he should be so inflexibly studious, even at so exciting, and uncertain, a time. But it was not much to Jessamine's satisfaction, for it took him nigh upon three hours to effect her rescue.

It came about at last because, finished with his efforts at cataloguing in the Potionery, he wandered into the Mixery, with his head full of a Swiftly Sparkling elixir he wanted to try. Jessamine, having taken a comfortable two-hour nap in the intervening period, was by then intent upon effecting her own rescue; and at the cost of several deepening bruises to her skull, was attempting to beat down the cupboard door behind which she unwillingly reposed.

The dull thudding sound penetrated even Tambul's abstraction, and thither he went, a beetling frown darkening his brow, for the method of mixing his Swiftly Sparkling was leaking out of his thoughts. 'Why, what can have got itself stuck in the cupboard?' he mused, imagining some castle cat or like creature.

'It isn't a cat,' chortled a sylph in his ear.

Tambul stopped several steps from the door, and glared at the insubstantial air. 'Sylphish mischief, is it? I ought to have known. And what is it you've got stopped up in there, pray?'

'Tambul!' roared Jessamine at this juncture, somewhat muffled through the thick planks of the door, but audible enough.

'What!' Tambul dashed forth, but his moment of heroism was instantly foiled, for no key stood in the lock. 'Let her out this instant! What can you be about, to use poor Jessamine so?'

Not that he hadn't been sorely tempted to serve her a mischievous turn himself, a time or two, when his temper got the better of him. But he had always got the better of his temper, as a person ought.

The sylphs, the while, had been engaged in furious consultation afresh, for half wished to stop Tambul up with the dragon, and the other half objected. What, were they to lock up everyone who came into the Mixery, possibly for days together? And anyone who came looking for Jessamine, too? Such a scheme lacked longevity; better to have done with it now.

The former prevailed, and a stout silver key drifted down into Tambul's hands.

Out came Jessamine, bristling.

'Right,' she said. 'I'll sort you lot out later.'

With which smoke-wreathed threat she was gone, scurrying out of the Mixery at a pace frantic enough to evade even the speediest sylph.

In no mood to brook any delay, the dragon dispensed with subtleties. 'I want the Wizard!' she roared as she blazed down the corridors. 'The Wizard Garstang! Where! Is he!' Astonished dogs-bodies hastened out of her way as she passed; a Court Lady, sneaking down to the kitchens for a snack belike, almost came a-cropper, her drifting train tangling up with the Familiar's briskly-clacking claws.

Tambul trotted, out of breath, in her wake, determined on what intervention he couldn't have said. 'Wait!' he called weakly after her, and wasn't heeded.

'GAAAARSTANG!' screamed Jessamine at last, out of patience and near out of breath (like Tambul).

'Upstairs,' came an answer at last, and a pointing finger: skyward. Jessamine knew not the name, recognised not the face, cared for neither: a glimpse of a nondescript countenance, featureless attire, a servant of some sort.

'THANK YOU,' she roared, without slowing down.

A few more such individuals directed Jessamine higher still, and higher, until her steps turned at last to the tallest staircase in the Castle: the one up to the tallest tower. The Wizard's name, bellowed as she went, echoed off the winding stone walls, and reached the Wizard's own ears at last.

He appeared at the top of the stairs, his dark hair all blown about by the wind, his eyes wide. 'What? What is it?'

'It's the sylphs!' she screamed at him. 'They're the reason the Castle flies, and it's their mischief as is taking us wander-about. You've to give them a piece of your mind, if you please, and perhaps it's not too late.'

'They won't listen to me.'

'I call that poor-spirited,' Jessamine informed him, zooming between his feet and out into the air. 'Here have I been all over the Castle at your bidding, brought out my best manners for the *last* Wizard, faced down the sylphs in *your* stead, and been locked up in a linen cupboard for my trouble! And you won't stir so much as a finger!'

'It's too late, anyway,' Garstang offered, walking to a wall, and leaning on it. 'We are almost there.'

Jessamine turned, fair bursting with rage. 'You mean to tell me you've worked out where we are going and *didn't tell me?*'

Garstang, unmoved, merely stared down into the beclouded landscape below, in too bleak a humour to respond.

Tambul, catching up to her at last, appeared at the top of the stairs, wheezing. 'Looks like to be Durchem to me.'

'Yes,' concurred Garstang, morosely.

'And why should you both be so long-faced about that?' Jessamine demanded.

Tambul merely shrugged, gesturing vaguely at the Wizard. *Tambul* cared nothing for their destination, that gesture said: but the Wizard patently did, and *they* had to bear with the Wizard.

Jessamine scurried over, and bit the Wizard's toe. Not very hard: only hard enough to squeeze a slight hole in the curl of his shoe. 'Enough of your Wizardly secrets. Out with it.'

'I have been to Durchem before,' answered Garstang heavily.

'And?'

Garstang made no answer. Jessamine, her reserves of patience long exhausted, contemplated a vicious bite to the ankle to make him talk, but fresh disaster saved him.

The castle landed.

Not neatly, all at once, like a dove alighting upon a branch. First, the castle descended — dropped — *plummeted* from the heavens at such a rate as to knock the breath out of Jessamine, Garstang and Tambul alike. Two ended up painted across the floor; Jessamine, already at ground-level, left a few gouges in the stone with the urgent pressure of her claws. There was screaming.

The clouds vanished upwards, there to regain their proper position over a building: lofty.

After that, there came such a tumult of noise, such a barrage of juddering and shaking and the grinding of rock on rock, as to leave Jessamine convinced of her — and everyone else's

— imminent demise. The sylphs had flown into a fit of some sort, and resolved upon dashing the castle to pieces against some mountainside. There could be no other explanation — there — *there*, that terrible, tortured groaning of stressed stone on the point of flying apart, a rumbling and tumbling —

Well, in point of fact there was no tumbling. Mercifully, miraculously, the terrible motion ceased. The grumbling of the castle halted, and so did they.

Nobody moved for some time.

It was Tambul who first unwound himself from the floor, and hauled himself upright. He stood a while, dazed, blinking, his hair more of a fright even than usual.

Jessamine watched him from one, partially opened eye, half expecting some fresh calamity to sail out of the skies and flatten him for his temerity. But nothing occurred. Tambul tottered to the nearest (and notably intact) wall, and stretched himself up until he could peer over it.

'Oh, we are atop something mighty tall,' said he. 'A mountain.'

'In Durchem.' These two words, groaned in protest, came from Garstang, who had yet to move so much as a finger. He lay supine and sulking, a performance so enraging as to set Jessamine's feet to scuttling again at last.

'Come on,' she said, butting his hip with her snout. 'Up.' Her teeth snapped; a shred of his velvet cloak snipped free and wafted away on the wind.

Still Garstang did not move. 'The mountain,' he went on, 'is known as Snow Peak in the tongue of my people.'

'How imaginative a name,' grumbled Jessamine, before the full import of all his words had penetrated her brain. Once it did, she added: 'A moment. *Your* people?'

'I have heard it said that Snow Peak would make a particularly pleasant spot for a castle.'

'By whom?' demanded Jessamine, a pertinent question, for whoever had set their heart on such an adornment for the hill-top might well have something to do with the sylphs' having blithely sailed Castle Chansany hither, and plonked it down.

Garstang was getting up. The process took him some time, for he battled against a reluctance so extreme as to keep him prone for some time yet. He got to his knees first, then got one foot under him, and then finally the other — and he was up, his long bones swaying a little on unsteady feet. The glance he threw over the wall was sour, and beneath the sourness: something else. Something bleak.

Jessamine began, at last, to understand that something truly untoward was occurring. For *this* was no Garstang she knew. Ablaze with energy was her Wizard; self-willed and self-involved, blithe when he should be cautious, eager when he ought to be grave. But here he stood blank-faced, shaded around the edges with woe. Or worse: a slow, creeping fear. He, who feared nothing.

'If I mistake not, you'll find out soon enough,' said he at last in answer. He went to the stairs and started down, slowly, listlessly.

They were late, the three of them, and slow. Doubtless the rest of the Court were gathered already below, issuing eagerly forth from the castle's firmly-planted walls to see where it was they had got to. Jessamine made no attempt to hurry her master. She plodded after him, Tambul beside her, all silent with disquiet. What manner of threat could so disturb the Wizard? Nothing he seemed in any hurry to encounter.

'Is it that we are in peril?' she enquired at last. 'The castle, I mean, and the Court.'

'Possibly,' came the answer, dully.

Halfway down the third staircase, Garstang stopped a moment. 'Jess-o-mine,' uttered he. 'Tambul. Have I your loyalty?'

'Of *course*,' breathed Tambul with fervour. He enjoyed Wizarding, seemingly, and was minded to carry on with it.

'I suppose,' grumbled Jessamine.

'No matter what you see or hear?'

'We are your allies in this, as in everything,' said Tambul.

Garstang met Jessamine's eye, a question in his gaze — and a hint, just a glimpse, of his old, sardonic humour. 'Do not unduly strain yourself, dragon. Tis only a minor crisis, I daresay.'

Jessamine huffed out a quantity of reeking smoke. 'I shan't betray you, unless I am offered something altogether irresistible. Will that do?'

In truth, she could not think of anything she might find irresistible enough to prompt a betrayal of her Wizard, but had no mind to tell him as much. A little doubt never hurt anybody. It might do Garstang a world of good.

'I'll take it,' he replied, and went on, downwards.

When at last they came blinking out of the great castle gates and encountered the blinding sun of a bright morning in Durchem, a fresh tumult was there to greet them. Most of the residents of Castle Chansany must already be gathered there; enough people to fill a small town, by the look of them. Their Majesties were among them, standing together at the fore; and before *them*, richly dressed and standing very tall indeed, was a woman. Just one woman, fifty summers old at least — perhaps more, her carriage proud, her chin held high. Quite the equal of all before her, to look at her, the king and queen included. But her gaze swept back and forth, examining those gathered around and behind Queen Melany and King Griffin. Searching.

When Garstang stepped forward, her deep-coloured eyes gleamed with satisfaction, and something reminiscent of a smile touched her lips. Up went her arms, up and out, an embracing, welcoming gesture. 'Darling!' she crowed. 'At last!'

Garstang halted beside King Griffin, disinclined, it seemed, to rush into those out-stretched arms. Instead, to Jessamine's utter astonishment, he bowed — very low, almost as low as he would bow to the royals themselves.

'Mother,' he declared, and smiled.

Anybody would have called it a smile who saw it, anyway. It had the right shape for it, upward-tilted lips, a flash of teeth. But Jessamine, closely observing the Wizard's face, saw something else. It lacked all the qualities that made a smile worth having; there was no joy in it, no gladness, certainly no love. His eyes gleamed like polished stones, hard and cold. Like his mother's.

The lady accepted it, however; perhaps she did not know the difference. 'How I have longed to see you!' she pronounced. 'This very *age*, I declare.'

'And is that why we are here?' Garstang enquired, mildly enough. 'Have you, by some clever method, suborned my sylphs?'

'The Castle has visited Durchem before,' answered she, unruffled. 'Your people are eager to pay their respects, your majesties.'

'So it has,' agreed the king. 'It is by no means customary, however, to force the journey upon us.'

King Griffin, mild of manner and cool by nature, rarely showed displeasure. It was the more effective, then, when he did: at least, in general.

But the freezing tone in which he uttered those words, and the cold glare of his gaze, had no effect upon the lady. 'I intended a warning by it,' she said. 'How simple it was to persuade them! Dear little creatures, sylphs, but flighty, and easy to distract. This time, it is only me that you face: another time, who could say what danger might threaten you?' She looked to her son, and smiled, an expression as empty as his had been. 'My beloved son takes *good* care of your majesties, I have no doubt. And yet.'

Jessamine bristled in her every scale, and crept closer to her Wizard, her tail coiling protectively around his ankle.

Garstang did not flinch, though she felt a faint tremor of something assail him. 'You might, perhaps, have conveyed this warning in a letter, or a visit,' he suggested. 'We were by no means out of reach.'

'Ah, but words alone cannot sufficiently express the danger. Absorbed in a moment, tossed away the next, and forgotten! Now, you see, you are *very* cognizant of the threat, and will act swiftly upon it.' She smiled a bit more. 'And I require no reward, for I see mine before me: my dear son, whom I have gravely missed.'

Tambul said, in half a whisper: 'She wants his job.'

'She *does*,' Jessamine spat, for the woman was clearly enough a Wizard: she rippled with magic, fair blazed with it. 'That's why the Wizard asked about loyalty.'

'She shan't be Court Wizard,' decided Tambul. 'Not if we have any say in the matter.'

Jessamine drooped. She did not want this interloper taking the Wizard's job, no indeed; that hardness about her eyes boded ill. But she had power, and no mistake. Power, and persuasive-ness, and not a scruple to her name, by the looks of it.

The queen spoke. 'Your intentions may have been hon-ourable,' said she—

—'*Hah!*' roared Jessamine, at Garstang's feet—

—'But your methods can only be deplored. We thank you for your warning, and take due note of it.'

Here the queen stopped, on a note of mixed gratitude and condemnation. Jessamine waited in suspense for more. *Everyone* waited in suspense for more, for not a sound was to be heard among all the gathered inhabitants of the formerly-floating castle.

The king turned his face towards Garstang. 'What is your counsel?' said he. 'This woman is better known to you than to any other here.'

That ought to be true, thought Jessamine darkly. The Wizard's own mother.

Garstang said, clearly and carefully, 'I beg you to let her go free, Majesty.'

His words came as a shock. The Wizard — *her* Wizard — begged! Pleaded! And asked clemency, for so viperish a creature! Unaccountable.

But, she was his mother. There was no saying what foolishness sentiment might betray a person into.

'I cannot,' answered the king, with some regret. 'Such an assault on our castle cannot be disregarded.'

Jessamine watched the lady, narrowly. Her face showed serenity; too much, for the circumstances. Her fate was being decided: she was to be judged, either hero or villain. And she thought nothing of it? No. She hid her feelings, whatever they may be, for reasons of her own. Only her eyes gleamed, but with what, Jessamine could not say.

'She is to be confined until we have decided her fate,' announced King Griffin.

'Majesty—' began Garstang, but halted, the rest of his words unuttered. The King was not listening. He and his lady were turning about, going inside, even as their guards intercepted the Wizard's mother, and led her away.

The castle's own Wizard followed, his face a mask as unreadable as his mother's. Jessamine hurried after, hard-pressed to keep pace with his long strides. Tambul disappeared, last glimpsed following in the lady's train.

Garstang did not speak until he had closeted himself in his own chamber, shutting the door behind him with not even a hearty slam — only a soft, but firm, *click*. He stood for a moment in the middle of the room, adrift in thought, to look at him.

'Well, Wizard?' demanded Jessamine at last. 'And why should you ask the king's mercy for a woman you patently despise?'

'There is no confining such a power as hers,' he replied. 'Even far away in Durchem, she proved herself a danger. What further mischief shall she conduct once closed inside these walls?'

'Then why did not you say that to Their Majesties?'

He sighed, and for a while she thought he would not answer.

At length he said: 'There are those with wily tongues, and the wit to twist every word said against them. Nothing can be gained by open opposition. One is forced to become as wily as they, and as false.'

'That didn't help either, though,' Jessamine pointed out. 'She's in the castle, and by Their Majesties' desire. What now can be done about it?'

'We will watch her.' Garstang did not seem disposed to act upon this grim pronouncement immediately, for he sat down in the best-of-all-chairs, and stared unhappily at nothing.

'You'll not get much watching done from there,' pointed out Jessamine, tartly.

'I shall bestir myself in a moment.' But he did not.

His dragon, torn between sympathy and scorn, sat a while at his feet with her tail wrapped around her toes. This, again, was no Garstang she knew; shirking work may be a common fancy of his, but always in aid of something he liked doing better. Inertia had never been his preference; he had far too much energy. What she witnessed here looked less like laziness and more like despair. Defeat.

How could one woman — and his mother, no less — effect such a change upon him merely by her proximity? She must have won so many battles with him in the past as to strip him of all hope of winning any in the future.

Well, Jessamine knew something about difficult mothers, hers being no basket of roses either.

'I'll watch her,' she announced.

'Take care, dragon,' he said suddenly, when she thought he would drown in his own silence. 'She will trick you, if she can. Cozen and cosset you until you'll love her in spite of yourself.'

'But you forget, Wizard,' she answered, bumping his toes with the tip of her snout. 'I haven't a heart to love with, if you'll recall.'

With which bold words she was gone, fleet of foot down the passageways, leaving a determined trail of smoke behind her as she went.

'Ah,' came the lady's soft voice as Jessamine entered the dungeon. 'I sense a visitor. A dragon, if I mistake not. Are you?'

The dungeons were no favourite spot of Jessamine's; only once before had she ever set claw in them, and that by accident. She'd scurried out again fast enough, for they were — as dungeons ought to be — dank and dark and comfortless. She shivered now as she scrambled down the last of the lengthy stairs and shot into the dim antechamber adjoining the cells. All her fires seemed banked down here, out of reach. There were magic dampeners at work.

'Of course I am,' she replied, crossly. 'You've no need to think yourself so clever for guessing that.' She sat herself down before the one occupied cell — Their Majesties were not in the habit of throwing people into gaol, much — and surveyed the Wizard's

Lady Mother with as much sourness as interest. 'I have come to keep an eye on you,' she said stoutly.

'Two eyes, I perceive, and keen they are indeed.'

'Flattery is very welcome,' smiled Jessamine, toothily. 'But it won't get you anywhere useful. I certainly shan't be letting you out.'

'I am in no need of a rescuer.'

'Hmph.' Smoke wafted up from nostrils indignantly flared. No need of a rescuer? Why, because she meant to remain quietly behind bars, like an obedient citizen? She was anything but. Or was it because she proposed to spring herself out of the cell? Perhaps she could — but she hadn't.

'What are you in need of, then?' Jessamine enquired. 'You went to a great deal of trouble to bring the lot of us here, castle and all. Only a fool would believe you meant to help us by it.'

'And is it so foolish a notion?'

'Entirely. You might have come to us, mightn't you? And petitioned Their Noble Majesties in person. They are no fools, either of them. They would have listened. Why, you might have addressed your son, at that, for he's in charge of the magical around here. Why, then, cozen the sylphs, instead?'

Her mouth quirked, in the way Garstang's sometimes did: mischief, and mirth. 'It amused me.'

'I can see that it might,' Jessamine allowed. 'You have demonstrated your Wizardly might to everybody here assembled. People will talk of it for years to come. Is that what you wanted? Fame?'

'Perhaps I wanted to see my son,' came the answer — not an answer, at all. 'And he is by no means minded to pay me visits, or to accept mine.'

'And why is that?'

'He despises me.' The words were said without inflection, without apparent feeling.

Jessamine snorted smoke: the woman spoke truly. 'Do you deserve to be despised?'

'It is no easy task, mothering,' mused the lady. 'And when one's only son turns out to be the greatest Wizard of the age — well.' Her tone, now, held a trace of scorn, though whether it were directed at herself or her son, there was no saying.

Jessamine waited, but the lady's specific thoughts on her son's magnificence were not, it seemed, forthcoming. 'It's my belief you are minded to change places with him,' she mused. '*You* wish to be seen as the greatest Wizard of the age, do not you? And this is your means of achieving it.'

The lady smiled, in a cool way. Her eyes gleamed like cold water as she stared down at the tiny dragon at her feet. 'One of us will be remembered down the long, long ages to come,' she said. 'And there is no doubt in my mind: that honour is to be my son's.' She straightened, and glanced about at the chill, half-frozen walls. 'But for all that, there are other comforts to be had.'

Jessamine opened her jaws to respond, something acidic working its way up her gullet. But that smile widened, until it full resembled Garstang's most wicked grin — 'Hah!' crowed the lady, seemingly at nothing — and then, wreathed in cold wind and starlight, she was gone.

'Oh dearie goodness,' breathed Jessamine. She sat a moment, stock-still with horror and surprise — and a little wonder. 'Say what you like about the lady, that *was* impressive,' she informed the walls.

Then, the fire of urgency hastening her scurrying claws, she shot back up the stairs, and off in search of the Wizard.

* * * * * * *

What of Garstang, while Jessamine was thus employed? Did he remain slouched in misery in his darkened room, staring at failure with weary, unseeing eyes?

No, thank the stars. Mayhap it was his dragon's courage that shamed him into motion, or perhaps some buried gumption of his own. But no sooner had the sound of her skittering claws vanished out of hearing, than he blinked, blinked again, and sat up.

'The sylphs,' declared he, mysteriously.

'I should think *so*,' answered the carpet, without specifying *what*.

'Why did the sylphs do her bidding, anyway?' he elaborated. 'Oh, they can be bought off easily enough; I've done it before.

But they can be counter-bought, in the same spirit, and this time they weren't. It is odd.' He got out of his chair, and paced. 'Very odd. I had better talk to them.'

He did not much *like* conversing with the sylphs, for they were flighty, and gigglesome, and they didn't seem to like him much. He pressed too hard for sense, paused too little for laughter.

Still, he had to try it. He'd shirked that duty before, sent the dragon after them instead; he ought to have gone himself. Not because of any lack of capability in Jessamine, but because of — as it turned out — a surfeit of it in his mother. He alone knew her ways, her wiles.

He permitted himself a sigh, for these had been unusually trying days. He was wearied with it, and suffering besides something quite unusual for him: a degree of self-doubt. Unpleasant.

Still, the only way out of any difficult predicament was to go through it, and so: off he went.

He found himself preceded to the Mixery, by Tambul. His apprentice sat cross-legged in the centre of the room, deep in argument with someone — or, more likely, several someones — insubstantial.

'But you cannot mean to leave us marooned atop this mountain forever!' he expostulated. 'Merely because some foreign Wizard asked it of you!'

The air, both cool and tumultuous, flowed around Garstang unsteadily, toying with the folds of his cloak. The sylphs were upset. 'It was asked of us!' they repeated. 'And we obey!'

'Why,' interrupted Garstang, 'is that?'

Tambul and the sylphs all fell silent, and stared at him — Tambul, at least, though he imagined the airy and imperceptible glances of the sylphs were also turned his way.

'Why do you obey?' Garstang repeated. 'What did she offer you?'

'Nothing,' answered a small voice, sullenly.

Garstang's brows rose quite into his hair. 'You hauled this entire castle, and all its contents, hundreds of miles over several days, and for nothing? I don't believe it.' In the ordinary way of things, the sylphs had to be bribed into every duty, however small: lemonade, and ginger beer, and ribbons, being their preferred currency. Perhaps cakes. He had attempted, in the confines of his own mind, to guess at what might have been offered them in exchange for so enormous a favour, and could not imagine.

'It is our duty,' said one or two sylphs, feebly.

'You owe her no duty,' said Garstang, not sternly, but bemused, frowning in puzzlement. They could owe Hortentia nothing whatsoever — unless, somehow, they did.

Oh, mother, thought he, and inwardly, sighed.

'Let us come at this conversation from another direction altogether,' he proposed, before the sylphs, growing more unsettled by the moment, could descend into frenzy. 'Of whom are we speaking? The person who asked you to bring the castle here: who is she to you?'

They did not appear to answer. 'We promised Her Majesty,' whispered one, in a flutter.

Tambul interjected. 'You did no such thing! Her Majesty gave no such orders.'

'Peace, Tambul,' said Garstang. 'I do not believe they are speaking of *our* Majesty, Queen Mellany. Are you?'

'Her Majesty,' they answered, all of them, in a confused jumble of woe.

Garstang, in spite of himself, had to laugh. 'Hortentia, Queen of the Sylphs,' he told Tambul. 'My respected parent, by some method unimaginable, has installed herself as their monarch — or at least, she has persuaded this lot that she is.'

'*She is, she is,*' cried they, indignant.

'Very well then, she is their queen. This would produce a difficult conflict of loyalties, would not it?'

'I suppose,' said Tambul, darkly.

'Still!' Garstang cracked his knuckles, stood a little straighter. 'That's easily mended.'

'Is it, indeed?' queried a new voice. In a haze of whirling winds (very sylphish, those) and winter-white light, there appeared: his mother, their queen. Sort of.

In fact, she did not, precisely, *appear*, not in the sense of her becoming visible to the naked eye. There manifested only a hazy shape, something whirling and elegant and ineffably queenly. With, of course, the voice: not her usual tones either, but measured, with a slight but perceptible echo to them.

'Oh, very clever,' admired Garstang. Really, anyone would have taken her for a sylph of unusual status.

He felt his mother's pleasure; her glee, even, at having out-witted him. At having tricked them all. 'My subjects have ex-pressed a desire to return with me to *my* Court,' she informed her son, and Tambul. 'I continue to deliberate as to whether it might not be best to leave them where they are. My sister and brother monarchs find their services of use, I understand.'

In other words: blackmail was to be the order of business, next. Garstang produced a smile. 'Oh, I would not say that we need them so very much as all that.'

There came a flutter of distress, from some of the sylphs, though whether it was the prospect of staying that troubled them, or of going, remained unclear.

Tambul, horrified, stared at his master. The sylphs, Garstang well knew, were more useful than they weren't, even with all their mischief. Without their assistance, the Mixing and Dis-pensing of Potions would grind to a halt, and there would likely be more than an occasional accident occurring in the process of it all.

But the slightest of winks from Garstang's merry eye reas-sured him; he cottoned on. 'Oh!' he said, heartily — a little too heartily. 'To be sure. If the sylphs would like to go with Her Majesty, we shall do very well here without them.'

Someone murmured in the Wizard's ear, and he did not think it was one of the sylphs. This was a strong voice, and low. ''Tis only an illusion,' whispered they. 'The so-called queen.'

'I know it,' Garstang replied.

'You could have it off her in the blink of an eye,' the mysterious Someone went on. 'Mandron's Revealing Cantrip ought to do it.'

A tumult was unfurling in the Mixery, the while, for the sylphs were taking umbrage. As well they might; Garstang knew he would have to make it all up to them, soon enough, for delivering such an insult (and an untruth, besides). But it was aimed not at them (well — not more than a little bit; they deserved a moment's discomfort to pay them out for their tricks) — but at the Wizard, the other Wizard, the interloper Hortentia. Well her son knew that she had no Court to take them to; what would she do if her bluff was called?

'I knew the Sylphish Queen, of a time,' the mysterious voice mused in Garstang's ear. 'Not a bad semblance of her, this one, much as I'd like to say otherwise.'

Garstang had questions, chief amongst them: who *was* the clandestine whisperer of musings and opinions unsought? If he had been forced to hazard a guess as to *where* the voice was coming from, he would have said: it emanated from a large mixing jar sitting at his elbow upon a counter-top, half-full, presently, with something blue and fizzing.

Somebody else spoke, then, a voice he knew as well as he knew his own. 'I see you've found the Wizard,' said Jessamine tartly, from the vicinity of his toes.

He blinked down at her, befuddled. To whom did she speak, and to which Wizard did she refer? The Mixery being unusually replete with them of late. 'Hello, dragon,' he said, a trifle severely. 'You are just in time for the resolution to this little parade.'

The dragon, in her cheek, rolled an eye at him. 'I daresay I am. Baldringa? Shall we?'

'Baldr—' began Garstang, but there was not time for the various parts of the complicated truth to seep through into his consciousness. The mixing jar and his Familiar were already well away, halfway through Mandron's Revealing Cantrip, and unstoppable. Tambul, comprehending the trick rather sooner than his master, joined in, leaving Garstang only to gape. 'W-wait—' he tried, for he had not yet done with his own plan, not by half.

But they were far too fast for him, or perhaps he was too slow. The Cantrip was uttered, the magic was done, and the so-called Queen of the Sylphs lost her breezes and stars in a flurry of cold wind. She stood revealed indeed, in all her non-sylphly glory: an ageing Wizard, a depth of knowledge and secrets to her gaze, but nothing either fae or queenly about her at all.

'Oh!' cried a sylph, and another. 'Oh! A trick!'

Then, being sylphs, they fell into uproarious laughter. 'A fine trick! A very fine trick indeed.'

Hortentia, with cheek to outdo even Jessamine's, bowed to her appreciative audience. 'We *have* served them a magnificent trick, have not we?'

'Yes,' said Garstang. 'And since you seem intent on evading punishment for it, I shall have to be quite direct.'

His mother, curse her bones, laughed at him. 'Oh? And what shall you find to do to me, in your wisdom?'

Garstang hardly heard; he was already halfway through his own little piece of brilliance. 'Garstang's Banishing Charm,' he informed her, at the perfect moment: just before she vanished, banished to who-knew-where.

'And where's she gone?' demanded Jessamine, still tucked up with his toes.

'I haven't a notion, except that it is somewhere viciously cold.' He beamed down at her, and at Tambul, and lastly at the mixing jar.

'And what if she pops back again?' Jessamine fretted. 'She whisked herself out of that cell easy as you please, and it was magic-warded.'

'She cannot.'

'Why cannot she?'

'Because of Garstang's Wondrous Warding. I made one or two changes to it, while I was pacing about up there over the clouds. No one will be vanishing themselves into the castle for some time to come.'

'That's why you wanted her to be let go,' Jessamine realised. 'So she would end up on the other side of the walls, and therefore the wards.'

'Exactly so.' He beamed. 'How delightful to have one's castle to one's self again.'

'*Your* castle, is it?' tutted the mixing jar.

'I am its steward,' he returned, with dignity. 'And I may have done a poor job of it lately, but I mean to do better.'

Jessamine straightened, uncoiling her tail from his ankles. 'The sylphs ought to be disciplined,' she announced. 'It's scrubbing the Mixery from top to bottom, and then all over again, I vote. *And* the Potionery, *and* the Dispensary.'

'There certainly ought to be some renegotiation undertaken,' said Garstang. 'A discussion as to whose authority they're to follow, precisely, while they are residents of Castle Chansany. But that's for Their Majesties and I to deal with. Later.' He yawned. 'I am wretchedly tired.'

* . * * * * * . *

It was no easy matter, peeling the dumped and slumping stonework off the mountaintop again. Castles are not made to be airborne; they do not altogether like it. This one, having tasted the stationary state once more (however briefly), proved reluctant to take up flying for a second time.

There was no help for it, however; Their Majesties hadn't the slightest interest in ruling their kingdom from atop a mountain in Durchem. The combined might of Garstang, Baldringa, Jessamine, Tambul, and all the sylphs got it into the air at last, where it hung, groaning in complaint.

'There,' panted Garstang, at the moment of victory. 'Have you got it now?'

He addressed the sylphs, who may have whisked it skywards once upon a time without aid, but professed themselves unable to do so again. Not after days and days of propelling it westwards.

'*We've got it!*' answered they, this confident pronouncement preceding a sudden and precipitate drop in the castle's altitude. They giggled, caught it, and hefted it higher.

Garstang wiped sweat from his brow. 'Yes, well, very good. Pray try not to dash us to pieces below.' He stalked off, overcome, and took refuge in his study.

Jessamine found him there, shortly afterwards. 'What a *week*,' she sighed. It was not her custom — indeed, it was unprecedented — but she clambered up the arm of his favourite chair, and reposed herself in his lap. Her bright little eyes looked up at him with some anxiety. 'And are you well again, Wizard?'

'I should say so. Why do you ask?'

'For a while there, you were sagging rather.'

'Sagging!'

'Drooping like a wilting rose. Your mother isn't good for you, I perceive.'

'Yes, well. We shan't be seeing her again for some time.'

'You think she will give up her plans?'

'Oh, never.' Garstang yawned violently, and rested a hand atop Jessamine's warm flank. 'But I shall be better prepared, next time.'

Jessamine snorted something that might have been sceptical, but gave up the point. She was growing sleepy. 'What's to become of Baldringa?' she murmured around a yawn of her own.

'Oh, like as not she'll go back to sleep,' said Garstang carelessly. 'I should think we've seen the last of *her* for a time, too.'

Nobody contested the point. Though, if anyone had been paying attention, they might have thought that a certain astrolabe with brass fittings, resting atop a corner desk under a window, was looking just a little bit smug.

ROSEWATER AND WINE

There are, as one might imagine, drawbacks to holding one's Court in a flying castle, a long, long way above the ground.

There are advantages, too: have not most of the great castles in the land taken up their grand posts atop tall hills—perhaps even a mountain, were it a trifle on the smaller side? The enemy, if enemy there are, are like to find themselves at a severe disadvantage for it. How much more so, then, if the king one would like to depose by right of arms is habitually situated a mile or two over one's head, with naught but empty air in between.

Doubtless every king or queen in the land would take to the skies, had they the wizards to accomplish it. But there is one, rather severe difficulty associated with an otherwise delightful situation, and that is: the king and queen are as remote to their subjects as they are to their enemies. And, of course, to their fellow rulers.

Solutions exist. There is the King's and Queen's Progress, when King Griffin and Queen Mellany condescend to venture down, and show themselves to the peasantry (and the nobility, which is important, for tis the latter who'll foot the bill). These are grand undertakings, and expensive: I don't suppose you have ever attempted to move a castle full of monarchs and aristocrats, wizards and courtiers, jongleurs and scriveners, maids and grooms, tutors and cooks and dressers and ladies-in-waiting and knights and apprentices and a prince or two across many leagues of distance, in an organised parade, and then take them all back again at the end of it? Minus only some one or two hapless souls fallen down some of those hills, perhaps, or plummeted off horseback, or otherwise removed from the roster in ignominious style. Their Majesties' Chamberlain would not recommend it.

If one merely wishes to hobnob with one's royal neighbours for a little while, there is a better way: that of temporary import.

Such is the occasion. The Queen of a nearby kingdom approaches as we speak, her daughter with her. Their retainers being as numerous as their consequence is high, their progress is necessarily slow; even so. If we are to go looking for Jessamine today, we find her: not atop the castle walls practicing her fire-spitting; not with Tambul in the Mixery, or the Potionery, contributing to some fresh disaster there; not with her beloved Wizard in his study, perusing the second-favourite spell book; but down in the vast kitchens, side-by-side with Chef, breathing smoke all over a tray of comfits slowly forming under her talons. It will, we are told, develop the flavour.

The tray might have come together sooner, if there hadn't been so many disappearing into Jessamine's mouth; 'Stop that,' barked Paglar. 'There'll be none left.'

Jessamine scoffed. No fewer than four trays of sugar-coated almonds had already emerged from her worktable, mostly intact: more than enough for several banquets. 'It's for my stomach,' she said. 'I've got indigestion.' She absorbed another one, surreptitiously, and received a rap over her knuckles with a spoon.

'Those are the prince's favourites,' said Paglar severely.

'You said that about the marmalet,' Jessamine retorted. 'And the pepper cakes, not to mention those pearl-coated rosewater wotsits.'

Chef had on her usual black gown, with a cloth over her dark hair: yet she was turned half white with dustings of sugar, and flour, and other powdery comestibles. 'So they all are,' said she. 'And his highness deserves a treat. He's had a hard year.'

'I don't know as he has, particularly,' Jessamine disagreed, handing off her tray to a passing maid for drying, and beginning another. Dipping caraway seeds in syrup, she mused: 'Must be a peaceful life, being turned into a dish. I don't know as I wouldn't like to try it myself, come to think of it.'

Chef Paglar looked ready to return a sharp answer, but her glance took in the state of the kitchens: black-clad kitchen maids everywhere underfoot, turning out cakes and tarts and comfits by the hundreds, and more than just Jessamine pressed into temporary service. 'Perhaps it would, at that,' she sighed, turning a ball of dough into a neat, pressed circle with a few waves of her rolling-pin. 'You ask the Wizard about it, next time you've set fire to one of his scrolls or some such. I daresay as he'd agree fast enough.'

A smoky snicker answered her, but Jessamine made no other reply. The prince *had* undergone quite the adventure, and he seemed in merry spirits enough, if you asked him. But he hadn't been seen much about the place, since he was rescued, and brought home, and the last time Jessamine had bumped into him there had been something funny about his manner. He kept tittering. It wasn't like him.

His royal parents had announced a feast, to be followed by a banquet, and there were royal guests on the way to attend it—all the way from Far Below. But the prince loved sweets: everyone knew that. The banquet was as much to tempt his appetite, and lift his spirits, as it was to impress any strangers: everyone knew that, too.

In the midst of the marchpane, and the condimacke, and the lemony sucket, there was building a fine subtlety: ethereal spun sugar, stiffened with gum, and made into the shape of a sinuous dragon. Jessamine slipped off her high stool, and waddled over to it, tasting the air near it with a flick of her tongue. It was floral, roses and cinnamon and other such things, and it resembled Jessamine, a little.

'Away with you,' ordered its creator, the Lady Alvan. She stood in cook's blacks like the rest of them, only hers were finer: a real lady, a Court lady, with a taste for sweets and a deft hand. Ladies had time for hobbies; this one crafted gingerbreads and sugar-coated fancies for the pure joy of it. Her ladyship was dusting gold leaf over the dragon's eyebrows, a delicate process.

Jessamine scuttled away.

No mystery as to when the royals and their entourage arrived: a fanfare sounded, castle-wide. Twelve stout and hearty footmen stood atop the walls with silver-chased horns in their large hands and blew upon them fit to burst; everyone heard it.

Jessamine, tired of comfits, dozed in a sunlit spot in one of the corner turrets, plenty high enough to see all that unfolded below. The fanfare woke her; up she leapt, and stared beadily down into the Far-Below.

A town approached, or, at least, half of one.

Walking was beneath royalty, Jessamine knew, they were too important for that. These royals eschewed riding as well, for near the front of the long train of gaudily-dressed courtiers there bobbed a handsome palanquin, enclosed in gold-threaded silk. A quartet of horn-blowers walked beside it, heralding their approach: a fine idea, but Jessamine heard not a note of it.

Garstang was down there, being wizardly. Somebody had to convey their honoured guests from the Far-Below into the High-Above, and wouldn't he be in a foul mood later: nobody had expected quite so many attendants. The foreign queen had a wizard or two of her own, at least: two courtiers, draped in spangled velvets, had presence to rival Garstang's.

'Seems they'd like to impress us,' she muttered, to nobody in particular. The nearest of the footman eyed her sideways, still intent upon his horn: she thought she heard a muffled snort.

Jessamine stayed to watch the palanquin begin to rise, gently, as suited a party of important ladies: a wisp of cloud wafted it upwards. The rest would follow soon enough, Garstang with them.

By the time the royal ladies stepped into the castle, Jessamine had hurtled down and down the stairs and taken up a hiding-place: behind the heavy carven legs of one of the great, throne-like chairs that crouched at the back of the great hall. Nobody could see her under there, shadowy as it was, though her view consisted largely of the ladies' swirling skirts, and a great many booted and slippered feet.

The foreign queen's weren't hard to spot, for her slippers shone with seed pearls and gold thread, and her skirts were purple velvet. She had a queen's posture, too, feet firmly planted right in the centre of the hall. Her courtiers—and her daughter—fluttered around her, like bees circling a rose—and there were Garstang's curly-toed shoes, crimson today, and threaded with silver. His face appeared, briefly, stooping: his bright eyes smiled at her, and withdrew.

Curses.

Jessamine slithered out, in time to catch a glimpse of Her Majesty's face: she was stout, round-cheeked and smiling, with a crown of greying dark hair. At her side, her daughter: a near copy, only taller.

The hall groaned at the seams, overfull of richly dressed idlers. Despite the tumult, the queen's eye fell on Jessamine soon enough, skewered her like a chunk of meat: Jessamine froze.

'Why, a dragon, and out of its cage!' cried she, smiling. 'How lovely.'

A pause answered her; then Garstang managed a little laugh. 'Your Majesty is very droll. Naturally I would not dream of confining my Familiar in any sort of cage.'

The queen continued to smile, but something hard came into her eyes: the skewer twisted.

Jessamine fled through the nearest open door, and ran straight into yet another pair of legs: muscular ones, clad in excellent green cloth, with silver trimmings. She looked up, and up: the eyes of Prince Armael, when they met hers, held a lurking horror.

'This way,' she hissed, for her quick brain was stringing facts together like beads on a necklace: *why* all the fanfare, why the entourage, why the silks and velvets and jewels? Why the grand feast, and the banquet, and all the prince's favourite sweets? Here was an unmarried, wayward prince: out there was an unattached, suitable princess.

Jessamine scarpered down the passageways and stairs until she reached the sanctuary of the kitchen. Prince Armael thundered along behind her.

They arrived, winded and panting, into a different kind of tumult: the kind that smelled of spices and butter and pastry; and here was another tyrant, Chef, tsking away as she battered toffee into bits with her rolling-pin.

'Mind where you go!' Paglar shouted, for a small, alarmed dragon underfoot could many a disaster wreak (as Jessamine had previously discovered). If Chef took much note of Prince Armael, or realised his identity, she gave no sign of it, except to thrust a mixing-bowl into his hands, and a spoon. 'Stir,' she instructed, and he did.

Lady Alvan remained at her post by the subtlety, a glitter of stray gold leaf caught in her sunny hair. She looked up. 'Oh,' she murmured, and returned to her work.

Jessamine slunk that way, sat at the feet of the sugar dragon with her tail around her toes: she stared at it, her eyes huge. 'Not sure as Her Majesty will like it, after all,' she muttered. 'Best build a cage round it, ladyship.'

'A cage,' echoed Lady Alvan, lips pursed. 'No, that would entirely ruin the effect.'

'You're telling me,' Jessamine muttered.

Prince Armael had drifted over, lazily stirring his aniseed-scented bowl. 'How magnificent a creation,' he declared, with his slightly jittered smile. 'A pity to eat it, even.'

'All her ladyship's work,' Jessamine said, beaming toothily, and added, 'It's modelled after me.'

The prince accepted this without a blink, as did Lady Alvan. Chef came to take the bowl off him, but he stayed after: stayed to watch her ladyship painting talons with silver powder, and tying bunches of ribbons about its delicate legs.

Jessamine slithered away, and left them to it.

No able courtier herself, Jessamine's experience of castle feasts usually consisted of a dish full of tidbits, assembled for her by Paglar, and left in the Wizard's study. She was too small to help getting under the dancers' feet, and too waspish to let it slide by unchallenged when she did.

This feast, though: this one was different.

The ceaseless roar of chattering voices assailed her ears, even from a vantage point tucked under the prince's chair (rather than Garstang's, to the latter's bemusement). Ladies sat on either side of his highness, their skirts falling in folds of scarlet or sapphire silk to screen Jessamine's hideaway: almost a tent they made of it, if unduly sumptuous. On his right sat Lady Alvan; on his left, the foreign princess, Isadora.

The queen, her mother, occupied the other side of the table—both queens, in fact, Mellany as well, and King Griffin: a central phalanx of monarchs surrounded by lesser nobles.

They hadn't got to the sweet things, yet, that was later. Everything stank of meat, a pungent medley of aromas which *might*—if anything were going to—bring Jessamine out from under the prince's chair, in search of something sustaining. But she'd not like to come under the foreign queen's eye again, so she stayed; stayed, and listened.

'Do tell me about your home,' Prince Armael had said, a little while ago: a game enough question, to get the princess talking.

Talk she did, forthrightly enough: of troubadours and jousting, of fine horses and falcons and hunting parties, of grand displays of magic performed for the ladies' amusement.

'Rampant nonsense,' Jessamine muttered to herself. Did they do nothing at this foreign court that wasn't loud, savage or absurd?

'And when you come to pay us a visit, your highness, I do trust you will bring your little dragon with you.'

Jessamine, startled, bumped her head on the underside of his highness's chair.

'Oh!' roared her mother, the queen. 'Yes, it did have a ferocious look about it. I should like to see how it flies.'

'Flies, your majesty?' echoed the prince, politely.

'Yes: do not you hunt them? Like hawks after rabbits. It is the greatest amusement.'

A short pause: then the princess added, 'I am sure your dragon will acquit itself creditably, your highness; it really had a sporting look about it. There is no need to feel dismayed.'

It was sorely tempted to take up ankle-biting as the greatest amusement. Jessamine contented herself with a few smoky, fuming breaths instead; and, aware of a tension in his poor highness, wrapped her tail around his toes by way of comfort.

The prince continued in a silence Jessamine interpreted as stony; it was Lady Alvan who responded. 'I am afraid Jessamine could not possibly be spared from her duties with our Court Wizard,' said she smoothly.

'She doesn't fly,' managed the prince, chokingly.

'Cannot fly?' Her foreign majesty uttered an airy laugh. 'Why, whatever is the use in a dragon that cannot fly?'

'Right,' said Jessamine, and erupted from under the table. She made a lot of noise about it, clawing her way up the back of the prince's chair amid wreathing smoke; when she reached the table-top, she encountered several pairs of staring eyes.

'Oh, Jess-o-mine,' said the Wizard Garstang, eyes twinkling. 'There you are.'

King Griffin and Queen Mellany merely watched her in silence, both displaying an unusual stillness, even for monarchs on display. They were, she thought, experiencing feelings that could not be permitted to show on their royal faces: she wondered what those might be.

Their guests felt no such restraint. Princess Isadora uttered a little shriek, and flapped uselessly at her gown, to which tendrils of draconic smoke still clung. 'Oh, hush,' said Jessamine irritably. 'I haven't hurt it.'

To the queen she said, with a semblance of dignity: 'His Highness said that I *don't* fly, your majesty. Not that I can't. I daresay I can at that, if I thought it worth my while, but I won't do it for the sake of chasing after rabbits.'

Garstang was grinning. 'Jessamine prefers her rabbits roasted, and served in a silver bowl,' he declared.

'Well,' Jessamine amended. 'It doesn't *have* to be silver.' She slunk down the table towards her wizardly master, who had, as she'd hoped, saved a bit of his dinner for her. Curled up at his elbow, she settled down to enjoy her nuggets of succulent venison, pigeon-pie, and crispy potatoes with palpable unconcern. She hunched herself up with her back to the foreign queen and her daughter, so did not see how they were pleased to take this reproof.

She saw when dinner ended, though, and the dancing started: Prince Armael led the Princess out first, as he must. They made a handsome enough couple, she supposed, with her hand laid on his satin sleeve, looking up at him so prettily. Someone had put

His Highness in blue, the better to match her sapphire skirts: hmph.

She was still watching sometime later, when Garstang relieved his future liege of the lady. Prince Armael led Lady Alvan out; a clashing medley of silks they made, bright-red and royal-blue; Jessamine, full and contented, smiled.

* * * * *

Later, much later, after the feasting and the dancing and the music were over, and most of the Court had retired to their repose: now, at last, came the banqueting hour.

Jessamine had slunk away some time before, pattered on soft feet down the corridors and up the stairs into the banquet-house: no small thing, a sugar-feast, and full worthy of its own, special chamber. The old queen had caused it to be built, and handsome it was: octagonal in structure, each of its eight sides set with twinkling panes of glass. The moon and stars shone silvery through them, largely uncontested, for a sparse scattering of candles set up only a dim glow within.

An eight-sided table in two tiers stood tall and proud in the centre, exhibiting its succulent dainties for the delectation of these most-favoured few. Jessamine's smoked-scented almonds teased her nostrils from a silver-chased bowl; beside them, sugar-soaked nuts and spices heaped upon carven platters, dried and sun-hardened and sweet; fragrant musk and ambergris and rosewater hung heavy upon the air, amid a pervasive, thick sweetness.

Jessamine, arrived upon an empty room, had sneaked and sampled as she liked, lingering over sour orange sucket glistening with sugar. Later, with a sated smile and an ache in her belly and her teeth, she'd curled herself in the centre of the topmost tier, and waited.

In twos and threes, they'd entered: Queen Mellany and King Griffin and Prince Armael; the foreign queen and her daughter; Lady Alvan, and eight or ten nobles and ladies, bright as birds, chattering like starlings. Something checked their tongues as they crossed the threshold, some innate respect for the sanctity of sugar; came midnight, and a hush prevailed, a velvet silence, muted as the slow-shifting moonlight creeping across the floor.

Ornate boxes lay upon every silk-cushioned divan: carved ebony, silver-inlaid, and fragrant. Inside, moulded gingerbreads awaited the guests' delight, heavily spiced and gilded in gold; nestled beside them, nuggets of marmalet, quince-scented and splendid. Tall-stemmed goblets bore fruits simmered in hyppocras, redolent of cinnamon, and red wine; none of these were for dragons; Jessamine, with a pleasing sense of martyrdom, had left them alone. They enchanted the Court: many a soft, awed cry went up; Jessamine would carry those down to the kitchens tomorrow, to gladden Paglar's ears.

For a time, all ate and sipped and enjoyed with hearty delight, alike in elegant gluttony.

It couldn't last. The prince, weary, perhaps, or entranced, was forgetful of his duty; had wandered after Alvan and sat by her before a long window, their shadowed locks silvered by the same moonlight. He offered her marmalet, jellied rosewater, cinnamon comfits; she offered him smiles and wit and spiced wine. Their several majesties looked on, defeated: some with a mild and fond regret, others with a glittering, hard-eyed stare.

Jessamine pitied only the Princess Isadora, offered up like an ornate treat, gilded and scented and sweet, yet powerless to attract. She slipped at last off her perch and sidled to the princess: there, smelling of smoke and rosewater and wine, she sat by the silk-slippered feet, and wrapped her tail around a silk-clad ankle.

A hand came gently down, and touched her head, softly. 'It's all right,' said the princess Isadora. 'We would not have suited, and anyway, there's someone else.'

'Then why are you here?' Jessamine asked.

Isadora hesitated. Then, splintering that brief silence came a hard, glittering laugh; it matched the smile in her mother's eyes.

'Oh,' said Jessamine.

Isadora said, on a faint sigh, 'I wish—'

She never said what it was that she wished, for a dulcet fanfare sounded, a tinkling melody of bells; the door opened.

In came the subtlety, with Paglar behind it. They'd mounted it on wheels, for it had grown to near monstrous size: bigger than Jessamine, far too big to carry. The dragon, sugar-spun, fragile, bared its teeth at the courtiers, its tail standing high.

What an entrance. Jessamine, struck with sudden inspiration, scurried out from behind Isadora's legs, and ran beside it, puffing smoke out of her jaws. The candlelight caught it, gleaming like moon on the mist: a wyrm bathed in the fires of its own making, as it should be. Someone gasped; Jessamine snickered.

A fearsome sight it made, at that, unlike Jessamine: larger, prouder, grander, stouter, for all that its limbs were wrought from brittle sweetness, would snap like twigs. No cringing, captured thing, this: its wings spread above and behind it, flared, ready to fly. Dignity, strength, and pride: what a sight it made, what a joy; had Alvan *known*, somehow, had she heard, had she made it so by intent?

It was serving its purpose, Jessamine felt, for a foreign queen sat stiff with indignation; a foreign princess radiated delight. And here came Alvan, a goblet of hyppocras in hand: she gave it to Isadora with a curtsey; to Jessamine, she winked.

'I trust your highness is pleased with the subtlety?' she enquired.

'Lady Alvan made it,' hissed Jessamine, beaming.

Isadora sat a little taller, straightened her shoulders: if she'd had wings, they would have flared and flown, framed her little figure in majesty. 'It's perfect,' said she, and toasted the lady and Prince Armael with the wine. 'Everything is just perfect.'

A FIT OF THE SULLENS

The first-favourite spell book lay inert, entirely inert, atop the Wizard Garstang's own writing-desk, and though you may (with some justice) be disposed to observe that a book is *supposed* to be a stationary sort of object, this is a grimoire; the rules are different, in that there aren't any.

It lay like a block of wood just felled from its tree, as though not so much of a particle of it had been pressed and processed into paper, with powerful words scribed upon it.

Jessamine, perched atop the tall back of the Wizard's own, personal chair, stared down upon it in appalled silence.

'I think it's dead,' she uttered, in a sepulchral whisper.

'It can't be dead,' said the carpet, mossily.

'It can't be dead,' Jessamine repeated, stoutly, as though she might, with a little firmness, ward off the terrible truth.

Came then a slight, staccato rustling, dusty and dry. The book's covers twitched.

'It coughed!' Jessamine scurried down the chair's mightily tall arm and slithered onto the desk, getting her fierce little eyes up close to the patient. She peered, and prodded.

The bookish cough came again, a little louder.

'It isn't dead. But there's something wrong.'

Being the Wizard's favourite, the spell-book was a proud, peacockish thing, ordinarily. It wore its preferred colour, sapphire-blue, most of the time, properly adorned with intricate gilding (of course). But, being a Wizard's personal favourite spell-book, it was much more marvellous than that.

Those ornate covers were chiefly for the eyes of the uninitiated—or merely unsuspecting. A glamour, of a sort. Look past the reassuring seeming of (relative) ordinariness, and underneath there's another book entirely. A mighty grimoire, clad in enchanted glass stained in every hue; its cover was a window into distant worlds and far-off lands (or into the kitchen, if Jessamine was particularly hungry, with a bird's eye view of Paglar's freshest batch of spiced cakes).

'Come on, now. What's the matter?' Jessamine crooned to it, and tapped it gently with a claw. 'It can't be jealousy, can it? Not again?'

She did not often trouble herself to look past its glamour, its contents being more the material thing. It took a moment or two, for her eyes to remember how. Then the gold-and-sapphire gleam of its dressing-gown (so to speak) fell away, and beneath that: nothing. The glass (if glass it was; something like, at least) was cold and dead, all misted over, like thick fog. A palpable chill came off it, freezing Jessamine's claws.

It was unwise, no doubt, but a tendril of panic being just then unfurling in the dragon's innards, she made a tactical error. Her long lizardly tongue flicked out, and tasted—and, for a moment, stuck.

She wrenched it back, and spat. 'Tastes like mould,' she said to the carpet, and the shelves, not to mention the chair.

'Oh,' answered the chair. 'That's bad.'

'Very,' confirmed the carpet, mostly asleep.

Jessamine sat up straight, and addressed the shelves in tones of ringing authority. 'Right. Nobody's got into the Library as shouldn't have, I suppose?'

The shelves returned a decided negative. 'Safe and sound in here, the lot of them. Only the Wizard's been in. But that one,' —they meant the first-favourite spell-book— 'has been lying out there a while.'

'Forgot it, did he, and wandered off?' Jessamine spat again, either with disgust at her absent-minded master's habits, or on account of the mouldy taste, lingering; perhaps both. 'Right. I don't like to say it, but this is an emergency.'

The furniture, anticipating brilliance, waited.

'We'd better take it to the Book Room.'

Castle Chansany being a topsy-turvy sort of place, it perhaps makes more sense than it doesn't: that "The Library" should refer to a scant handful of volumes (priceless though they were) hidden in a secret shelf in Wizard Garstang's Study; while Their Majesties' grand and ancient collection of learning, some several thousand volumes strong, should be known simply as the Book Room.

An apt enough term, however humble. Successive generations of monarchs and wizards and librarians having added and added to it, the several vaulted chambers of the Royal Library struggled to contain the ocean of knowledge and literature crammed into it. Scarcely was there a surface visible that didn't have a book on it, or more likely several. The grand, gilded shelves, twenty feet high, being long since filled, a great many books—bound in leather or cloth, painted and inscribed and engraved, wrought from vellum and paper and linen and everything besides—had spilled over onto the writing-desks, where they lay in towering stacks; onto the carved oaken chairs, some of them, hauled from seat to seat as necessary by scholars too accustomed to the chaos (and too attached to the volumes) to object. They were stacked on the floor in places, though never too close to the long, light windows.

Whether it was the chaos, or the grandeur, or simply the sheer weight of untold ages of learning and imagination, Jessamine found the Book Room repellent.

If the truth were to be told, though, it was not disgust or dislike or impatience that tugged at her guts as she entered, but something much nearer fear. Not a bookish dragon, this: in a Wizard's Study or a busy kitchen or a sun-drenched balcony she could be comfortable, but here was an ocean of paper to drown her in.

Still. This was an emergency.

A small dragon, then, slunk stealthily into the vaulted halls of the Book Room and hovered by the door, tongue nervously darting. 'Twas chaos within, as always, albeit a hushed sort of madness: several Court Ladies and Gentlemen had arrayed themselves attractively across straight, tall-backed chairs, and sat paging ponderously through stout (or slender) volumes; poetry, belike, or biographies of some sensational personality, now deceased. These were quiet enough, as were the two or three librarians (distinguishable by the royal-green robes they wore, and rather harried expressions, besides). The books, though, were in something of a flap.

'Sorry,' uttered Jessamine, as a green robe went sailing past, a thunderous librarian inside it. 'Could I just—'

'No, no, no!' bawled the librarian, ringingly. 'We do *not* shelve histories of the Thousand Isles adjacent to the philosophies of the Tanglid Empire! Why, it could cause a diplomatic incident!'

Chastened, a tall shelf of books emptied itself again in a hurry.

'It's just that—' Jessamine tried again, addressing another.

'I have but *just* settled the natural sciences on the *lower* shelves,' barked she, sweeping past Jessamine in a flurry of dust and wool. 'The ladies like them, and I'd like to see *you* climb a twenty-foot ladder in a Court gown!'

A book tittered, or was it a sylph?

Jessamine scuttled under a large writing-desk, and peeped out. The Book Room would be reorganising itself for some time yet, she judged: the tomes and scrolls and grimoires were all in uproar.

She'd not brought the first-favourite spell-book, after all: a fat volume, and growing fatter by the year, it was too heavy to carry down all the winding passages, and up and down the spiralling staircases, of Castle Chansany.

She'd come on a fetching errand, then, and at this rate she'd be at it all afternoon.

Jessamine exited the sanctuary of the writing-desk, and drew herself up to her full and terrible height in the centre of the Book Room's mosaic-tiled floor. She inhaled a vast and hearty breath, opened her maw, and bawled: 'I NEED TO SEE THE BOOKBINDER.'

The words came up out of the fiery depths of her belly, swelled, perhaps, with the force of a mild but growing panic; if the Wizard were to come back from wherever he'd gone and find his first-favourite spell-book ailing—fading—*dead*, even, what then? She'd be for it. Besides, she rather liked the book, her own self. It had some of her favourite cantrips in it.

At any rate, her cry rattled the shelves, and sent a choking cloud of dust up out of all the forgotten corners. Somebody coughed; a book tittered, again.

'He's in his room,' said one of the librarians, and pointed.

'I thank you,' said Jessamine, with a courtly bow. A pair of ladies stared; a book, curious, trailed after her as she scurried out again.

The Bindery clung to the edges of the Book Room like a mollusc, a humble shell of a chamber alive with a hive of industry. Jessamine hurried through a low-lintelled and unprepossessing doorway, and found, on the other side, a collection of tall tables, each with an absorbed person working at it. A promising litter of objects cluttered the table-tops: freshly-cut sheaves of paper; lengths of soft leather, ready for shaping; wood sawn into thin sheets, for covers, and spools of thick thread; metal tools of every shape and purpose; three mighty book-presses; and at least five tomes halfway built. Jessamine sniffed, sneezed on a curl of sawdust, and the thick, heavy scents of leather and wood and glue.

She needed to find the important one; an apprentice couldn't be tasked with mending the Wizard Garstang's first-favourite spell-book, oh no. Her keen eyes travelled past two, three, four young faces, with nothing much to recommend them; working competently enough, but with no aura of authority, no air of certainty and skill—ah, there. An older gentleman, promisingly white-haired and bespectacled, handling a volume of great antiquity with exquisite care. The Bookbinder.

Jessamine scuttled nearer, coughed. 'Hello, Bookbinder, sir. I have a pressing problem on my hands and I'd hoped you might help me.'

He didn't hear, or he chose not to answer. He was, to be fair, engaged in a delicate operation: something to do with the crumbling spine of his delicate charge.

And this book doubtless deserved the master's tender care, but nonetheless:

'SIR!' thundered Jessamine. 'THE COURT WIZARD'S PERSONAL FAVOURITE GRIMOIRE IS ABOUT TO SNUFF IT.'

His head came up, at that. So did everyone else's. A thick silence fell.

'Oh, dear,' said the Bookbinder, and set his tome down (carefully). 'You'd better show me.'

His Eminence the Bookbinder bent in silent scrutiny over the Wizard Garstang's writing desk and remained there for some time. The spell-book, pale and mute, bore patiently with a succession of peerings and proddings, conducted with the gentle, expert hands of a physician. Whatever might be the Bookbinder's thoughts as he conducted this examination, he was not disposed to air them. Jessamine and the furniture waited in silent dread for the verdict.

At last, the great man straightened. 'I believe I understand the problem,' said he.

'Yes?' said Jessamine, trying, without success, to read the nature of the awful truth from the man's composed countenance. Just how bad was it?

'It's suffering from a Fit of the Sullens,' said the Bookbinder.

Jessamine, cautious, said: 'Well. That doesn't sound too bad?'

'I'm afraid it is very serious. Many books never recover from it.'

'Oh,' said Jessamine, quietly. 'And what becomes of them, after?'

'We pack them up, and send them away to… other libraries.'

Lesser libraries, he meant: his tone declared it. 'You banish them?' translated Jessamine, with a gasp: a more awful fate than being sent away from Castle Chansany, forever, she could scarcely imagine.

'It is really much better for them,' said the Bookbinder. 'Elsewhere, they will not be expected to do anything very much, except store a pre-determined collection of characters on their various pages, and produce them upon request. Quite restful, one would think.'

'A convalescent home,' said the carpet, thoughtfully. 'I might like that.'

'You aren't expected to do anything very much already,' retorted Jessamine. 'Just lie there like a—' She'd got distracted; she stopped. 'That can't be allowed to happen to the first-favourite spell-book,' she said instead. 'How do you treat a Fit of the Sullens, Master Bookbinder? We'll do anything.'

'It chiefly occurs when a book is neglected for too long,' answered he. 'Or fancies itself so. The treatment, then, involves a reversal of that effect.'

Oh, dear. Neglect, was it? The Wizard *had* left it lying about, open to the elements, on his writing-desk while he jaunted off doing who-knew-what. That wasn't a caring way to treat your favourite grimoire, was it?

And he *had* been consulting the second and third-favourite spell-books rather often, of late. She gulped. Perhaps this wasn't the first-favourite spell-book anymore. Perhaps it was the second, or even the third—and it *knew*.

'We'll lavish attention upon it,' Jessamine promised. 'Polish its covers daily. Read every word of its pages, and cast all the cantrips three times each. Would that do?'

The Bookbinder looked down upon her with something like pity. 'Noble efforts, I am sure,' he said. 'But it is the Wizard's spell-book, isn't it?'

Deflated, Jessamine could only watch as he quietly excused himself, and left. He couldn't do anything for the book, and neither could she. It didn't care if *she* cradled its binding in reverential hands, and exclaimed in delight over the contents of its pages. It wouldn't care if she cast every one of its cantrips seven times each, for she wasn't the Wizard.

Scowling, she kicked vaguely at the carpet, ignoring its muf-fled squeak of protest. That Wizard. Whatever trouble he was off getting himself into lately, she'd be hauling him out of it—and back into his Study, to treat his faithful friend the way it deserved.

* * * * *

Jessamine conducted a frenzied search of the castle, beginning, of course, with all the places she'd most likely expect to find an errant Court Wizard. Hiding somewhere in the Study, disguised as a candle-holder, say, or a tapestry, just to amuse himself; (no).

Seated at the long table in the great dining room, surrounded by a litter of tea pots and cake-crumbs and absorbed in the composition of some new cantrip; (no). Wandering the walls in a fog of reflection, soaking up sunshine and inspiration and accomplishing, probably, nothing at all; (no). Tucked up in the private parlour of some Court Lady, engaged in flirting (she) and obliviously pontificating (he); no.

Administering Her Majesty's personal philtre, with an accompanying round of refined conversation; no.

He was not in His Majesty's rose garden, or in the north-west turret, or in the Book Room; he was not in the banqueting-house, or in the Potionery, or in the kitchens. He was not in the castle at all, perhaps, appalling thought; if he was gone down Far-Below, who knew when he might be back? And the first-favourite spell-book languished away to nothingness in his absence.

Well then: she would be needing help, and if she couldn't have the Wizard, it'd have to be the Wizard's Apprentice. 'Tambul,' she barked, barrelling into the Mixery in a cloud of agitated smoke. 'There's a thorny problem afoot, and—oh!'

For there, after all that, was the Wizard: in the Mixery, of all places, and bless her stars if he wasn't *working*, at that. He was at the great stone sink, his arms sunk up to the elbows in some pungent and luridly-coloured mixture. He wasn't even wearing his Wizardly finery: he had on just a plain tunic, velvet, to be sure, but that was all.

'Ah! Jess-o-mine,' sang he, blithely; but there had been a momentary discomfort crossing that darkly handsome face; she'd seen it. Embarrassment, to be caught out of his fancy things and up to his elbows in muck, as though he were any old person, and not a Court Wizard at all.

'What's that?' said Jessamine, curiosity briefly overpowering her wits.

'It's a liniment,' answered Tambul shortly.

'An Extraordinary Embrocation,' declared the Wizard, more fulsomely. 'For the treating of Beleaguered Books.'

'Oh! Then you *know*.' The tip of Jessamine's tail began to tap, and smoke leaked from her nostrils.

'Doubtless you have observed the unhappy state of my precious grimoire, Jess-o-mine, and come in haste to inform me of it,' the Wizard went on. 'I commend you, indeed, but we have the matter well in hand.'

'And what, precisely, is your Extraordinary Embrocation supposed to do?'

It was Tambul who answered again, a little sourly: 'Imparts suppleness. To the leather, and what-not.'

'I hope that isn't all it does,' Jessamine retorted. 'And what exactly are *you* doing up to your very eyebrows in the stuff?' This to the Wizard, who smiled.

'I am imbuing it with my essence,' he answered, mysteriously.

'Essence of Garstang,' said Jessamine dubiously. 'Who wouldn't benefit from a liberal application of such, indeed?'

'Quite!' agreed the Wizard. 'A fulsome dose of my esteem, rubbed tenderly into its covers with my own hands; a treatment I have bestowed upon none of my grimoires, until today.'

'After which, I hope you propose to read from it, and cast spells out of it, and take it about with you a bit,' Jessamine said. 'The Bookbinder says as it's got a Fit of the Sullens, a proper one.'

'I suppose I could,' said the Wizard, paused in the act of stirring the muck. 'Do you think that would help?'

Jessamine rolled her eyes; she couldn't help it. Wizards. They'd come up with six complicated, exaggerated, lordly-sounding solutions when one simple one would do. 'Yes,' she said, with admirable patience, though the smoke was getting thicker.

'Right,' said the Wizard, lifting his arms out of the Extraordinary Embrocation. They were stained lurid blue up to the elbows. 'Bring it along when it's finished, will you?' said he to Tambul, who grunted assent.

*　.*　*　＊　*　.*　.*

Whether it helped, in some mysterious fashion, to croon lullabies to the spell-book in some language Jessamine didn't know—an ornate language, lyrical and curly and with an air of antiquity about it—well, that was the Wizard's business. Perhaps he simply liked having an excuse to employ so strange a tongue, for the rest of the castle certainly never did.

At any rate, the book liked it. Liked the Extraordinary Embrocation, too, despite the stench of it. Its gilded covers came up a brighter sapphire than ever, and the mist cleared out of its glassish bits, and showed the kitchens again (to Jessamine), and who-knew-what to the Wizard.

He handled it like an ailing child, did the Wizard, gentler by far than Jessamine knew he had it in him to be. He leafed tenderly through page after page, uttering cantrips and spells in that same peculiar language (they were patently spells, for all that they were incomprehensible; the carpet turned purple and began to float, and after that the shelves sang a round of *Ten Wondrous Wizards* in three-part harmony).

Jessamine waited by the Wizard's chair, an attentive Familiar, with her tail curled around her talons and her nose up to sniff the air (a mistake, that; she sneezed, seven times). The Wizard had no attention to spare, not for her: everything was for the spell-book, the first-favourite, the most precious of tomes.

She began to comprehend how a body might fancy itself neglected, around here; sniffed in disgust (and sneezed), and wandered off to the kitchens, to fetch herself a butter-cake.

The Wizard's voice followed her, just as she slithered out the door. 'You know that you are the very best of all dragons, Jess-o-mine?'

She paused. 'Am I, then?'

'And the best of Familiars, too.'

She sneezed again in a puff of smoke. 'I am, at that,' she agreed, and scuttled off.

SUMPTUARY

I t had a strange smell to it, cloth of gold. A metallic tang, sour, acrid; it split the air, tickled Jessamine's nostrils until she couldn't help but sneeze, and sneeze, and sneeze.

Strange, then, that she should creep back, day after day, to the Great Wardrobe, tuck herself into some nook or cranny, unobserved, and stare with round eyes at the Keeper of the Robes at work.

'Deep breath in, your ladyship,' uttered the Keeper, stationed behind the silk-wreathed figure of Lady Alvan, with her mouth full of pins (the Keeper, that is), and a knotted measuring-tape hung about her neck. The words emerged oddly, around the bristling points of silver clamped between her lips, but they were clear enough: her ladyship inhaled.

The future princess made a handsome sight at that, being blessed with hair like sunshine, and a pretty face. They were dressing her suitably, in purple cloth of gold; purple for royalty, gold for splendour, and jewels to match.

Jessamine saw her chiefly in simple blacks, down in the kitchens spinning subtleties out of sugar, and dreams. With rosewater stains on all of her clothes, and pearl-powder streaks on her face and her hair, she was a dishevelled pixie, a sylph of a wizard, her culinary artistry a magic all its own.

They were making a great lady of her, now. This statuesque creature bore little resemblance to Alvan, all grandeur and pomp and sparkle—but a pin stabbed her, and she wriggled and winced, and there was Alvan again, for a moment.

'And must I indeed appear so—so—*diminished*?' gasped she, swaddled in gold.

The Keeper tsked, in her matronly fashion. ''Tis not *diminishment*, my lady. The narrow waist is very much the fashion, at present.'

'I do not *have* a narrow waist,' protested her ladyship, tightly. 'And what's more, I do not want one.'

'That is why we are making shaping garments, milady,' said the Keeper, unperturbed. 'When you appear before the people, you shall be a true visionary of sartorial style.'

'I should like to be that, certainly,' said Lady Alvan. 'But I do not see why a narrow waist should be an indispensable accessory.'

Jessamine, crouched in a corner beneath six layers of silk tissue, sneezed. She couldn't help it. The cloth of gold had got into her nose, and caused a spasm.

A wisp of smoke wafted out.

'Who's under there?' called the Keeper, sharply. 'Come out, before you set the Wardrobe aflame.'

Shame-faced, Jessamine emerged, and swallowed her smoke. 'It was the velvets that got me,' she explained. 'They're so soft.'

'Are not they?' concurred Lady Alvan. 'What think you to a gown of purple velvet, Keeper?'

'It would become you delightfully, ma'am,' came the answer, and it was followed by a flurry of other thoughts, on the shape of the gown, and the trimmings. Jessamine lingered, listening.

Her eye strayed. There on the floor, a bright scrap of something against the dark stone. A thingummy. A *velvet*.

She swooped, and snatched, and it was hers: a shred of velvet, soft as butter, and tinted pink and pretty as the King's own roses. She lifted it to her face, rubbed her scaled cheek over it: ahh.

'Off I go,' said she, hastily. 'Urgent errand.' Her talons clacked and clicked in a rapid staccato as she fled, most unsubtle, but nobody was taking her thingummy if she could help it.

The prince's finery, richer still: gold and gold and gold again, or cloth of silver; purple damask, or richest of red velvet; trimmings of fur, lavish with embroidery.

'Tis rather heavy,' observed Prince Armael, marooned in the midst of the Great Wardrobe with his royal person all swathed in the shimmers. The chamber bid fair to disappear under a thousand bolts of cloth in a hundred colours: the silk-store was overflowing.

'Course it is,' Jessamine observed from her nest in the corner. 'There's enough metal in it to stop a sword strike.'

'A prince goes armoured to his wedding,' murmured the prince in question, tugging futilely at a gold-draping sleeve.

'And you've to match her ladyship,' continued the dragon, applying her rough little tongue to the blissful nap of her velvet thingummy. The fur was coming off it.

'A prince must look like a prince,' said the Keeper, firmly, and there ended the objections. His highness drooped, but protested no more; a good thing, too, for he'd not get away with it when he was king, oh no.

Jessamine dozed in her corner, cushioned on silk-fluff and scraps, and dreamed. She could wear cloth-of-gold, couldn't she, if you didn't mind the sneezing. Cloth of silver, too, and all in red. Not purple, that was for kings and queens, but red—red like roses, red like wine, red like the lip-colour the Court Ladies wore...

She came awake with a start, for a something had dropped on her head.

'Sorry!' called the prince, still swamped in silk. A button had popped off, and flown away. It glittered, all pearly, and it didn't stink; Jessamine licked it. Cool, and smooth.

She waited for the Keeper to reclaim it, but she didn't: stood there oblivious, stout and competent, faffing with some detail on the prince's collar.

Silently, Jessamine swallowed it. She'd fetch it up again later, safe in the Wizard's Study.

The hoard came together quickly, after that. From the queen's mantle came a slim curl of brocade, woven in green, like emeralds, and stitched in silver. From the king's glaudekin, a scrap of damask, and a snippet of silvery fur. From the wizard, oh! Everything in blue, rich or pale: velvet from his doublet, silver tissue from his sleeves, and three shades of silken thread, from his hosiery. No one questioned her presence at the Wardrobe, and they'd stopped sweeping up the plush scrappets of her nest, too. She was a fixture.

She was growing over-bold.

'This brooch will not do. No, it won't do at all,' said the Keeper to Lady Alvan, one day. She plucked at the indigo folds of her ladyship's mantle, and the ruby-studded brooch that hung there, securing it. 'It's the sapphire that goes with this article, milady, or the jet.'

'Well, I cannot find them,' said Lady Alvan, laughing. 'My finery will have to clash, a little.'

The Keeper tsked, doubtless minded to take her ladyship to task for such carelessness as that; but it wasn't her place.

Jessamine held still in her corner, in frantic thought. A brooch, a bluish one—or black. She had four such, in her lair, one of them pinned to a lone, discarded shoe: which was it? She slunk away, scuttled in harried haste down corridors and stairs, and slithered under the floorboard behind the wizard's bookcase. There they all were, and the shoe as well, a lady's dancing slipper. There were her velvet thingummies, too, and her bits and bobs of damask, and brocade. She had a length of leather in a fetching peach, a half-spool of golden thread, a ring wrought from silver and with a green stone in it, a silk-tissue sash the colour of moonlight, a lady's handkerchief with a violet stitched on it, three leather belts with bronze or copper buckles, one of the wizard's own curly-toed shoes, a jewelled pin that smelt somehow of roses, a pouch of crinkled silk tied with a red ribbon, myriad scrappets and snippets of cloth from the silk-stores, her pearly button, and a tiny bell that tinkled charmingly when she licked it.

She licked it now, and it soothed her, a bit. A blueish brooch, or a black one, and she had four. Which one was it?

Which? Which? She couldn't take all four, and ask the new princess to choose. She'd have to explain where they'd come from, all four of them.

'They came from the floor of the Great Wardrobe,' she'd say, 'Under all the discarded cloaks and dresses, the tossed-away hairpieces and capes; mixed up with the off-cuts and the thread-spools and the what-not. Nobody else wanted them.' Except, they did, in this case: a brooch was wanted, and Jessamine had it.

She sighed, and curled up on all four of them, her nose resting on the dancing-slipper. She was a princess, Lady Alvan, or close enough: there would be other brooches for her, other finery, never a shortage of satins and slashed sleeves.

For a Jessamine, there was only detritus, and other people's leavings, and if some of them chanced to sparkle, well, she was keeping them.

'No!' thundered the Wizard, on another day. 'I will *not* wear a codpiece! The thing is perfectly absurd.'

Jessamine, skulking, tittered.

The Keeper remonstrated. 'They are very much admired at present,' said she, 'and we will set it with jewels to match your—'

'Is the prince wearing one?' interrupted the Wizard.

'His Highness preferred an alternative—'

'And the king?'

'No, but some of the lords—'

'Then I won't be wearing one.'

'How recalcitrant,' sniffed Jessamine. 'And with the wedding so near. You'll give the poor Keeper a headache.'

'A headache from a wizard is highly sought-after,' said Garstang, his chin worn rather high. 'I consider it my specialty.'

'Wear the codpiece,' said Jessamine.

'I shan't.'

'Well then, I will.' She dove, and snatched the rejected article out of the Keeper's grip. It was embroidered cloth-of-silver, appealingly bulbous, and it squished when she grabbed it: there was padding inside.

'You can have no need of a codpiece, Jess-o-mine; you lack the requisite anatomical feature—Jessamine!'

She was gone, scorching down the corridor with the codpiece clamped between her sharp dragon teeth, and into the hoard it went.

The next one followed, and a third after that: the Keeper did not give up lightly, when she got hold of an idea.

'You wouldn't catch me decking myself in jewels,' announced the carpet, after. 'Or dashing off to weddings, either. What do you want with all those thingummies?'

What *did* she want with them? True, that a ribbon had always charmed her humble little heart, back when she was the Wizard's Apprentice, and a failure. She would have worn such in her drab locks with pride, at least in private.

She wanted more than a ribbon, now. She wanted a cloth-of-gold doublet lined in silk, and not to sneeze when she wore it. She wanted a glaudekin all made of brocade, like the king's, with a design of pomegranates on it. She wanted a purple velvet gown trimmed in sable, and a circlet of garnets and pearls, with hair to wear it on. She wanted curly-toed slippers and cloaks clasped with brooches; mantles and capes made of damask and satin; velvet hats with feathers in them; and yes, codpieces, even those.

But there was no sense in explaining, not to a carpet. What did it know of finery? Or of weddings? What did it know of castle life, beyond the threshold of the Wizard's Study? Give it a warm fire to lie beside and a firm brushing now and then, and content it would be.

So Jessamine said: 'It's a dragon thing,' and the carpet subsided, sleepishly.

*   *   *

It was the shoes that did it, Jessamine was later to conclude. The fancy shoes with the curly toes, that the wizard wore for dancing. She had one; she wanted another.

Why she had need of a matched pair, when she could wear neither, even Jessamine could not have explained. But her soul hungered, and must be appeased. She hatched a plan, and followed it.

The clock struck one-after-midnight, the night before the wedding, and all the castle was alive with celebration. The nobles drank and danced, the wizard with them; the Keeper stitched last-minute lace to ladies' gowns, her seamstresses beside her. The kitchens were in uproar, serving comfits and washing dishes.

Jessamine left the Wizard's Study on the softest of feet, stepping stealthily so her talons didn't clack on the flagged stone floors.

Stealthily she hurtled, along passages and up staircases, her route plotted to its last detail as she dozed in her velveted nest. Past the bedchambers of the Court Ladies, and the queen's solar; past the prince's reading-room and His Majesty's morning parlour; *down* a dark corridor lit by solitary sconces; and there, the Wizard's own door, behind which lay his suite of handsome rooms.

She had a cantrip ready, uttered it in smokish tones: the first-favourite spell-book had given it to her (she had saved its life, after all). Smoke wafted, light flared, a lock clunked—she was in.

He had his own Great Wardrobe, a whole room full of garments in every fabric and hue. She hadn't far to seek for her second shoe, however: its partner missing, it lay forgotten in a corner. He'd thrown it there, and failed to recollect it since: what cared he for a shoe by itself?

Jessamine grabbed it in shrinking jaws, and ran. It tasted of stale silk and perspiration; she gagged, but hurtled on, perhaps she could wash it—at any rate, it was handsome, however it stank, it had gold embroidery on it—

'Did you get it?' asked the carpet, as she scurried through the door, and under her floorboard.

'Yes,' she spat, expelling the shoe from her maw in the same breath.

'Good show,' it murmured, dozily.

It *was*, wasn't it? A perfect operation, pulled off with panache. Jessamine lined the new shoe up with the old one, and feasted her eyes: what a sight! They even glittered a bit, without light to make them do so; wizards' attire. They couldn't help but soak up a bit of magic, what with the Wizard wandering about steeped in it up to the eyeballs—

'Ah,' came a familiar voice, and the roof disappeared.

Light entered, and a merry dark eye: the Wizard Garstang's. His face was with it, looming over the gap in his floor, and with her ceiling held in his great, brutish hand.

His other hand darted in, quick as a flash, and took up a brooch. A black-jewelled one.

'You cannot keep that, Jess-o-mine,' he scolded. 'The princess wants it.'

Jessamine roared. A pungent cloud of acrid smoke arrowed towards the wizard, and he coughed. 'You *dare* steal from a dragon!' cried she, in her most terrible voice.

'Yes,' said he.

Jessamine deflated. 'But it's my first hoard.'

Wizard Garstang set down the floorboard. 'On account of which,' he said, 'I brought you these.'

He opened his great, brutish hand, and a fistful of ribbons rained down.

'Don't wear them all at once,' he chided. 'They'll clash.'

Jessamine grabbed three—periwinkle, violet and grass-green—and bit them. 'There. Now you can't take them back.'

He laughed, and replaced her ceiling. 'You can keep the shoes,' he called, and went back to the dancing.

The dragon skulked, pondering.

'Carpet,' said she, after a while.

'Mm?'

'I'm a member of the Royal Court, aren't I?'

'Mm.'

'A proper one. Fully-fledged.'

The carpet stirred, rustling. 'You're the Wizard's Familiar. It's an important role.'

'That's what I thought.' The matter decided, Jessamine emerged, and scarpered.

She ran, this time, for if it was one o'clock before it was past two now, and the Keeper must sleep, sometime... she thundered along in a clatter of claws, and arrived at the Great Wardrobe, panting.

'I'd like a fitting!' she gasped, and all but fell through the doorway.

The keeper, mercifully, remained, her hands full of sky-blue silk tissue. 'A fitting? For what?'

'Court attire for the wedding. Something befitting a dragon of status.' Jessamine drew herself up as she spoke, attempting a regal mien.

The Keeper looked her up and down, noting the slender, lithe physique of her, the burnished scales, and the claws. 'Cloth of gold, shall it be?'

'I'd sneeze all through the vows,' answered Jessamine, with some regret. Though she might, anyway, what with half the Court wearing it. 'Can it be velvet?'

'Assuredly. Goldish, I think, and black-trimmed.'

Jessamine beamed. 'And if you could put a ribbon on it—'

'Several,' came the answer, and Jessamine gave a dulcet, satisfied sigh.

· .* ₊ ✳ ₊*. ·

The wedding went off in splendour, even the sun seeming delighted to attend. There were not many foreign royals present; some stayed away out of offence (the prince having declined to wed their daughters). Others shied away from the journey, the castle being situated rather too high in the air for the taste (or the vertigo) of some.

They were not much missed, for the Court mustered such a display as scarcely needed augmenting. A riot of colour and grandeur welcomed the new princess to her family; and it was said afterwards, in some circles (by those who hadn't seen it), that one of my lady's train-bearers had been a dragon, with polished scales and claws, a jacket of gold-stitched velvet wrapped about her slender torso, and bunches of ribbons trailing from her shoulders, and fluttering in the wind.

HURDY GURDY

Harken: there's a bustle about the castle. A clamour, a cacophony, a veritable swarm of busy bodies engaged in diverse errandry. It's not so unusual for the castle to be busy, and noisy, and bustlesome, of course, but this is something else, something greater, grander, messier; there goes the King's Chamberlain, with hat askew and a feverish light in her eye; in her wake, a quartet of footmen, and a maid, scurrying like ducklings, their arms full of sundries.

There, for that matter, goes the Court Wizard, Garstang, striding to somewhere, talking without cease to someone—or himself. There goes Paglar with a list in her hands, scratching off entries in a spray of ink. There go the seamsters, and the scullery maids; the jongleurs, and the Wizard's Apprentice; the Court Ladies and the boot-blackers, the wizard's hearth rug (airborne) and the wine merchants, the scribes and the sylphs, even his majesty himself, King Griffin, looking harried. It's the King's Progress, for there's a new princess to display, and besides, it's been a dozen years since the last time.

Jessamine is hiding under a chair. It's not the best-of-all-chairs, since the wizard's study is being turned upside down by a legion of dogsbodies pressed into service. It isn't her own chair, either, for much the same reason. It's a broken chair, all of three legs to its name (formerly four), a thing cast into a corner thick with dust in a chamber nobody cares about. It's the only place that's quiet in the whole of Castle Chansany, and Wizard Garstang's dragon Familiar has been there all day.

She was downstairs half the night. In the kitchens, helping the cooks; in the Potionery, helping Tambul, and the sylphs; in Garstang's Study, helping the carpet, and the shelves. To pack up and move a castle full of people and things and yes, even, furniture; a vast, dizzying, unthinkable task, requiring every pair of hands—even the clawed ones belonging to a Court dragon. And now her head spun and her ears buzzed with fading echoes of tumult; silence, or close to it, bathed her in peace.

A tower chamber, this room, about halfway up; the door slammed open. Dust whirled in spirals.

Someone swore. 'It's not *here*—'

Jessamine opened a resentful eye. 'Whatever it is,' said she, 'it most certainly isn't here, and I would prefer it if you weren't either.'

Footsteps wandered in: speaking had perhaps been a mistake. The owner of the voice stooped, directed a querying eye at the coiled, scaled, sleepish thing curled under a half-broken chair. 'It's my hurdy-gurdy,' explained this person, an aged being, with grey hair everywhere and a green jerkin. 'I can't find it.'

'Then you must manage without it,' Jessamine decreed, and shut her eye again.

'I can't. I've to play a ditty for Their Majesties, when the Progress goes out, and without my hurdy-gurdy—'

'Well,' Jessamine interrupted. 'That's as maybe, but it isn't here.'

'No,' said the hurdy-gurdy player mournfully. 'It isn't.' The face withdrew.

'Tis uncommonly careless, to misplace an instrument,' Jessamine grumbled. 'They aren't cheap.'

'No more they are,' the voice agreed from beyond the doorway, lugubrious.

'If you can't keep track of your hurdy-gurdy I'd say you shouldn't keep one.'

'Nor shall I, it seems.' The hurdy-gurdy player reappeared, disconsolate, and sat down in the middle of the floor. 'I've searched everywhere,' they said. 'This was the last place to look, and it isn't here.'

The lips wobbled; words trembled on the edge of tears. 'Oh, no,' sighed Jessamine, and slithered resentfully out from under her chair. 'If you're going to *cry*—'

'I never cry,' sobbed the hurdy-gurdy player.

'So I see,' grumbled Jessamine.

'It's just that this is a disaster—' Words failed the speaker, subsumed by sobs.

Jessamine sat by their left knee, patting it in awkward comfort. She set the tip of her tail in her mouth and, meditatively, bit. 'Like as not it's been put into one of the wagons,' she said, indistinctly. 'Half the castle's packed.'

'But *which*?' howled the hurdy-gurdy player, on the way to hysterics.

Jessamine studied her unlooked-for companion. The grey hair had given her a false idea of their age: their face was more youthful than she'd imagined, nicely rounded, with full lips and rather bulging eyes. They were haphazardly dressed, even rather scruffy, though the clothes were of fine enough quality. A Court Bard, or a troubadour. She didn't run into those, very often.

Jessamine spat out her tail. 'I'm Jessamine,' she offered. 'Do not call me Jess.'

The tears slowed; a round face registering hope turned towards the dragon. 'I'm Basling,' they said. 'Do call me Bas.'

'I suppose it is imperative that we find your hurdy-gurdy?' Jessamine tried, without much hope. 'Another wouldn't do?'

Bas's eyes brightened further at the word "we". 'This one's been Wizarded,' they said, shaking further disorder into their flyaway hair. 'The Court Wizard did it himself.'

Jessamine scratched her head. 'You've seen it since, I suppose?'

'No, I was meant to get it back yesterday. The Wizard said it would be sent to my quarters, but I didn't find it there, and now my room is packed, and I can't find the Wizard, *or* my hurdy-gurdy—'

Jessamine snarled something smoky and reeking. 'Like as not he Wizarded it, all right,' she said. 'Turned it into a moth, or a jug of wine, or a butter dish, and forgot about it.'

'But I have to—'

'Play for Their Majesties, and you can't play a tune on a butter dish. I know.' The tip of Jessamine's tail beat a tune of her own against the floor: something with a whiff of war about it. 'We'd better find the Wizard, then,' she decided, and she was off as she spoke, leaving Bas to hasten after.

He wasn't in his study, of course; when is a Wizard ever where he's supposed to be? Jessamine tore through the Mixery, next, then the Potionery—and paused. If not the Wizard, there was at least the Wizard's Apprentice, packing slim glass bottles into a cloth-lined crate.

'You haven't seen a hurdy-gurdy, have you?' Jessamine barked.

'A what?' said Tambul, absently.

'Or the Wizard?' said Basling.

'I've seen *him*. Eighteen times since breakfast. No—' Tambul thought. 'Eighteen and a half. I saw the back of him an hour ago.'

'And what was he doing?' said Basling.

'Running away.'

Nobody bothered to ask what had sent the Wizard fleeing: a Potionery in chaos was eloquent enough. 'If I haven't got my hurdy-gurdy by the time the Progress leaves—' began Basling, and halted: they'd heard something.

Jessamine heard it, too: a buzzing, wailing, twanging sound, half a melody, perhaps, and the rest a drone; just on the right side of discordancy, and eerie.

In came a hurdy-gurdy, the Wizard with it. He was playing a jaunt, and humming along.

'*There* he is,' sighed Jessamine, and 'There it is!' said Basling, together.

The Wizard's mind was somewhere else: he gazed upon them, unseeing. 'Hmm?'

'You've stolen a thing,' Jessamine told him.

'What thing?'

'That.' She pointed her snout at the instrument. 'The Bard wants it back.'

The Wizard Garstang took in the presence of Basling, forlorn. 'I'll give you any money for it,' he offered, smiling, and played a trill.

'I've need of it,' said Basling, not smiling at all.

'Any potion, then. A cantrip?'

Jessamine crawled under a cabinet, and left them to it. At least the noise had ceased: the Wizard couldn't make bargains and music both together. Her head throbbed.

The altercation continued, grew rather heated. At the back of it, Tambul's potions clink-clinked and clattered into their crates. The hurdy-gurdy started up in a blast of noise, and cut off abruptly; Jessamine contemplated murder.

So did Basling, judging from the noise, but then there came footsteps stomping away, and the door slammed.

Quiet at last—or nearly. Some glassy things clinked, softly.

Then: a tuneful note, and a buzzing.

Jessamine peeped out, saw a wizard and apprentice but no bard. The hurdy-gurdy's crank was turning itself; the wizard tested a key.

'You can't just go around pinching people's things,' Jessamine informed him. 'If you want a noisemaker so badly, get your own.'

'I have,' he told her, with a glittering smile. 'I gave three potions for it.'

Not much to Basling's satisfaction, but what matter that? You got away with things, when you were Garstang.

Jessamine left him to it, and slunk away.

She was wanted, later. They were sending people down, Garstang and the king's chamberlain, in groups of ten or twenty: down from the clouds into the Far-Below, to wait under the oaks. Quite the crowd was gathering, above and below, and what a ruckus.

The wizard needed his Familiar, though there wasn't much for her to do: she was there to admire the figure he cut as he wafted magic about, that was all. Baldringa, a wizard retired, had turned out to join the revelry; bodiless, still, and in the guise of a velvet hat.

She interfered. 'They're sideways,' said Baldringa to Garstang, from three inches to his left. 'They'll be dizzy by the time they get all the way down there. Better keep them straight, that's what I'd suggest.'

She wasn't wrong; the gaggle of Court Ladies canted sharply, liable to invert, and people never liked being turned upon their heads, as a rule.

Garstang swatted the hat away. 'It's not easy,' he said, with ice in the words. 'You try hauling three hundred people a mile up, or down. They'd be inside out, by the end of it.'

Unwise words. Baldringa was the Court Wizard for many a year herself; she'd done her fair share of Progress, like as not. But the hat only grinned—somehow, without the teeth to smile with—and wandered off after a jongleur.

The next group assembled, mostly Wardrobe folk. They drifted off in a blare of music, buzzing merrily in time; Basling's disputed hurdy-gurdy followed the wizard like a hound, blasting noise on cue. He'd got a lute to join it, to some troubadour's disgust; the pair were playing in the round.

'I suppose the music helps?' said Jessamine, rather tart.

'Immeasurably,' was the answer, if absently: he was busy.

'A Court Wizard requires a fanfare, if he's to get any work done.'

'Yes, and if I could just get a pipe from somewhere—there's a three-part melody from Dandry's Chorals and it'd be just the thing—' He turned abruptly, marched off, leaving a seamstress and a broiderer stranded fifty feet down.

'Don't worry,' Jessamine called after them. 'There's a hat handy, it'll soon sort you out,' which it did, fortunately, for Garstang was half an hour coming back.

When he did, he had three pipes along, trailing and trilling like a row of cygnets. Someone brought him a drum, most unwise; he had it pounding a beat all by itself, louder than a drum (or anything else) had much right to be. Chatter died away: there wasn't much point, when you couldn't hear your-self think.

Came time for Their Majesties to waft away on a tide of wizardry, musicians going fore and aft, to play the fanfare. Three grand pavilions hovered before the gates, draped in silks: two small ones for the players, and the King's, all over velvet, in the centre.

Basling, looking mulish: 'We aren't going.' They had a piper with them, a drummer, a lutist, all empty of hand; diverse oth-ers, their instruments retained, but packed and buttoned in cloths and cases. All were thunderous.

The music stopped abruptly, with a squawk. 'Not going?' said Garstang, looking thunderous himself, all dark of brow. 'But it's the Progress. Everyone's going.'

'We don't seem to be needed,' answered Basling, arms folded.

They weren't wrong. There hung the hurdy-gurdy, just be-hind the wizard, with no hands to play it; beside it the drum, and the pipes, and a pair of lutes, now, worse and worse.

'Of course you are,' snapped the Wizard, beckoning. 'Come along. Their Majesties cannot go, 'til you do.'

'Then Their Majesties aren't going either,' said Basling.

Later, past sunset. The Progress hadn't progressed, Their Majesties hadn't gone. A Royal Procession's no good without the royals; they had music, if no musicians, and might have gone regardless, but they wouldn't. The Progress being a harmonious business, Queen Mellany explained, in music as much as mood, the dispute must be resolved.

There was no mending it, not today. Basling and their cohort went away, the Wizard too: separately to quiet spaces, marvelling at each other's conduct.

Jessamine knew her duty, and went with Garstang. The Court remained Far-Below, much of it, and the halls rang hollow without them. An eerie place, the castle, with no people in it; Jessamine, shivering, kept close to the wizard.

His chair had gone Below, hers too. They sat, then, on the polished floor of an empty Study, the walls ringing with their voices.

'I don't understand it,' Garstang said. 'Why shouldn't I play music, if I've a mind to?'

'Playing music's well enough,' answered his Familiar, sleepily. 'But the same's true of others, mind.'

'Nobody said they weren't allowed to play.'

Jessamine yawned, maw gaping like a cave. 'You wandered off with their instruments,' she pointed out. 'And their purpose, too. What was left?'

'Why, plenty!' sputtered Garstang, without saying what.

'How long does it take,' murmured Jessamine, half asleep, 'to learn to play, I wonder?'

'To play what?'

'A hurdy-gurdy. Or a pipe, a lute, a drum.'

'Oh, five minutes,' said the wizard, waving this off.

'Without magic,' said Jessamine.

Garstang's eyes went wide: he hadn't a clue. He was quiet, after that; his mind was quick enough, when he grasped an idea.

At great length, he sighed. 'I liked it,' he offered. 'Playing music.'

'So does Basling, and the rest.' She paused to let this settle, and added, 'They might teach you, if you asked.'

*   *   *

It rained, the following morning, in flurried squalls of water: no fair weather for a Progress, but the day dispatched one nonetheless.

The pipers' pavilion went down first, with all the pipers in it. The silk drapes sulked in sodden swags and the wind sang louder than the pipes—but a tendril or two of wizardry set the latter to rights, and the air rang, clarion-bright, with melody.

Then followed Their Majesties, face-first into the storm. They'd weathered worse in bygone times, and smiled despite it: most likely, the music helped. The prince and the new princess were with them, spangled with jewels, and rain-splattered.

It was the wizard's job, if anything, to keep the weather out. He forgot, and kept forgetting (except occasionally); he was in the pavilion behind, the last one, with all the troubadours in it. His hurdy-gurdy smelled, still, of paint, for he'd daubed it there himself: it squeaked with newness.

He was awful with it. Jessamine, despairing, stuffed her head under a pillow: it didn't help. Half his notes were wrong, and the rest wonky, clumsy-fingered. But he cranked and plucked and played with hands alone, no magic; and Basling, music's master, played beside him.

PETTY WIZARDRY

'It wasn't me,' said Jessamine.

'I know, dragon.'

'I don't say as I wouldn't pilfer a thing, if the fancy took me. Not often, of course.'

Garstang nodded along. 'Of course.'

'But if I were to pilfer a thing, it wouldn't be crockery. What use have I for dishes?'

'Well,' said Garstang. 'It isn't precisely crockery—'

'If a spate of ribbon-theft were to break out across the Progress, now, *then* you might look to me for an explanation. But I've no use for dishes, be they shiny as you like.'

'Thank you,' said Garstang gravely. 'In fact, you weren't a suspect.'

'Oh,' said the dragon, a trifle crestfallen (possibly).

'Not that I shouldn't imagine you capable of banditry, of course, should you turn your scintillating brains to it.'

'I detect satire,' answered his Familiar.

'But on this occasion—'

'*Oh,*' interrupted Jessamine, who couldn't help it. Enthusiasm took her that way, sometimes. 'You don't mean there's detecting to be done?'

'I mean exactly that.'

Jessamine sat bolt upright. 'I'll find Their Majesties' sceptre, you see if I don't,' she declared. 'And their orb, too.'

'Now, wait a moment, Jess-o-mine,' began the Wizard, but needn't have bothered: she was off.

It's hard to say precisely where they were, at the time. The Progress had been underway for a week and more, a castle's worth of folk had trudged and straggled their way down many a winding road. At that moment they were halfway down a field, the dragon and the Court Wizard. It had just been planted, and the earth lay in rich brown folds, smelling of green and gold. The column was trudging, without much liking to be, the ground being all over mud. The remnants of what had once been a path, or even a road, could still be discerned, faintly at least; Jessamine ran down it.

She passed Tambul, flanked, no doubt, by a quantity of sylphs (not visible). She passed Paglar toiling along in a cluster of kitchen maids, all of whom Jessamine waved to, though without stopping. She passed even a Court Lady or two mounted on palfreys, on their way to tease the Wizard Garstang—or perhaps to cadge a ride on the sweep of his floating carpet (small chance).

She hurtled past all these, and many more, threading her nimble way through a forest of boots, and arrived at last where the chamberlain rode, a ways behind Their Majesties' pavilion.

'Lord Chamberlain Sir,' she said, slightly short of breath. 'You must tell me. Which fancy box did you pack the goldest things in?'

The Lord Chamberlain ought by rights to be a venerable fellow, one would think, his beard white with wisdom and a frown line between his brows. This one was none of those things. 'Fancy boxes?' said Myrtle, a youngish lady in fact, with a high forehead, a long nose, and a tendency to look down the latter at small dragons. Perhaps it was only that she happened to be so tall. 'Gold things in boxes? What?'

'Their Majesties' Orb and Sceptre,' Jessamine elaborated. 'I've a fancy to polish them up a bit, and what with one thing and another they seem to have got into the wrong boxes.'

This was her prevailing theory. Never mind the high drama of missing valuables; that was hysterical wizarding nonsense. Things got into the wrong places when you moved a castle's contents across the country, that was a fact. They'd turn up in the middle of His Majesty's ceremonial robes, belike, or tucked into Paglar's fine copper cooking pots. A search they must have, and a fine, rousing one at that; there would the grand articles be, and all well again.

The Lord Chamberlain regarded Jessamine all the way down her very long nose, and frowned. 'They were kept in my personal possession, in fact, since they are priceless.'

'Oh, dear,' said Jessamine.

'A stout, steel chest, with two locks on it. I hold one key, and the king himself holds the other. So you see it is quite impossible for them to have been mispacked.'

'Right,' said the dragon. 'It is your expert opinion that they cannot have been packed wrongly, and yet they are still missing.'

'Precisely,' said Myrtle.

'Then there's only one possible explanation.'

Myrtle sighed. 'Yes.'

'They've been spirited away. By magic.'

Doubtless the steel receptacle had been protected by spellwork as well as locks. But the thief, whoever it was, had chosen a perfect time to go spiriting things away. What with all the chaos, the absence of two objects (however priceless) might not have been discovered for weeks.

For that matter...

'Who discovered they were missing?' she asked, as the Lord Chamberlain was turning away.

'The Wizard. He had some faffing about to do.' Myrtle illustrated her point with some vague hand waving.

'Faffing,' said Jessamine.

'We're arriving at Dolons tomorrow.' That was all Myrtle was inclined to say, for she swept off, doubtless with a hundred tasks to get on with; Jessamine let her go. She needed no further explanation, really. They were going to Dolons: of course the Wizard had faffing to do.

Jessamine could almost feel the smoke steaming out of her ears, a sensation of warmly bubbling rage.

It took her some time to retrace her steps back to where she'd left her Wizard, but her mood had not noticeably altered by the time she got there.

He was seated tailor-style atop his silly carpet, with a Court Lady at his elbow, one of the ones riding a palfrey. They were talking.

'It's based on Tamworth's seventh principle, but with a twist,' Garstang was saying earnestly, while the lady did a marvellous job of appearing interested. 'It's carefully balanced, you do have to watch that the core doesn't—'

'Garstang,' Jessamine barked.

'Oh, dragon! I was just telling, er, this lady about our—'

Jessamine hurled herself skyward and clawed aboard the carpet. A bit of it got rather shredded. 'What were you planning to do with the crockery?' she demanded.

'I take it you are still applying the ignominious term "crockery" to the ancient and highly valuable items in question?'

Jessamine smiled at the lady whose name Garstang had forgotten, showing every one of her teeth. 'I hope you were not planning to employ these ancient and highly valuable items in some manner of grand and magical display?'

The lady discovered a pressing need to withdraw, and did so, with a squeak.

'That was rude, dragon,' said Garstang, chidingly.

'I reserve the right to be rude, when I wish to.'

'There hasn't been a royal visit to Dolons in twenty years. I thought the occasion deserved a little pizzazz.'

'Having the Sovereign's Orb and Sceptres perform tricks for the amusement of the crowds is not—not dignified!'

'Nonsense. It's only crockery.'

Jessamine glowered.

The Wizard laughed, to her great irritation, and only narrowly avoided a savage mauling. 'No tricks. I only thought it might be—elegant—if they were to...float a bit. Perhaps a slow rotation, nicely catching the light as the Progress approaches. That sort of thing.'

'Very artistic.'

Garstang bowed from the waist, still managing to make a graceful, flourishing business of it.

'Was that to make Their Majesties appear impressive, or yourself?' Jessamine said tartly.

Garstang smiled glintingly. 'Why not both?'

Jessamine began to regret climbing aboard the carpet. It bumped and rolled most disconcertingly. 'You're nervous about Dolons. Is that it?'

'I am,' Garstang admitted.

'And the faffing helps.'

'Immeasurably.'

Jessamine knew better than to ask how it helped, or why. He would tell her, at great length, and in extraordinary detail. She hopped down instead, landing in squelching mud. 'Bother.'

'And where are you going?' the Wizard called.

'I suppose I'd better find your crockery, hadn't I?'

'It'll turn up.'

'What if it doesn't?'

To that, there came no answer: the idea was a new one, most like, and he was consternated. No matter. Jessamine could save her Wizard's sanity with or without his help; it wouldn't even be the first time she'd done so.

* * * * * * *

'Right,' said Jessamine a little later, to her assistant (a small dog). 'There's only two possible ways those sparklesome things have gone missing. One of them's theft.'

The dog, a delicate creature smaller even than Jessamine, grinned in a teeth-bearing fashion she thought rather encouraging.

'But if there was any sign they'd been stolen—with or without using magic to do it—surely even the Wizard would be a bit more concerned. Not to mention the Lord Chamberlain.'

The dog said nothing, pantingly. It had wandered away from one of the Court Ladies, most like, and would soon be reclaimed from the clinging mud.

'That leaves the second thing,' Jessamine continued. 'Magic, of course, but not the thieving kind. In other words, the crockery's spirited itself away.'

And why would it? She had little doubt that it had been sumptuously housed; this double-locked box would be velvet-lined, insulated against the heat and the cold, nice and quiet—really, everything you'd think a set of fancy dishware would want by way of abode.

Either it had somewhere even more luxurious to wander off to, or—it had something very important to do.

An idea occurred.

'Oh,' said Jessamine, and beamed, toothily, at the dog. 'Thank you, you were a tremendous help,' said she, and darted off, towards the head of the column again: Their Majesties' Pavilion. A streak of muddied white thundered along at her heels: her faithful assistant, giving chase.

It was not actually Their Majesties' grandest of pavilions she was looking for, but the one directly behind it. The king and queen's equipage was easy to locate, on account of the glittering flags flying from tall poles at each corner. Not merely a matter of pomp and display, though that was part of it: the flags could be seen from miles away, giving due notice of the Progress's imminent arrival. Thus it was that they were greeted, whenever they stopped, both with sufficient fanfare and—far more important—ample comforts. Food, rest, baths.

That had been Myrtle's notion, Jessamine knew. The Wardrobe had spent a week making all the flags.

Pennants flew from the other grand pavilion, too, equally fine: this one carried Prince Armael, and his new bride. Heavy brocade curtains hung all about it, keeping off the rain and the wind; by the Wizard's pleasure, the thing itself floated a foot or so above the ground, drifted along as serenely as you'd like. Jessamine had no difficulty in boarding it, despite its altitude; a great leap, and a flurry of her webbed wings: in she went.

The prince and new princess were enjoying a beverage, served in painted glasses. The prince was looking better, assuredly: his sweep of blond hair properly groomed, his garments rich enough, and neat, his pale eyes less given to wildness around the edges.

The Princess Alvan's doing, at least in part. She, of course, was perfection: as much at ease in Court regalia as she'd been in the kitchens, up to her delicate eyebrows in sugar, and gold paint. She smiled at Jessamine.

'Sorry,' said the dragon, 'to bother you, but I wondered if you've seen a golden orb anywhere about?'

'With jewels on it,' said the prince. 'Blue?'

'Sapphires,' supplied his wife. 'And a pair of sceptres, all over filigree, and pearls. They're here.' A cushion of purple silk lay behind her: she gestured at it. Jessamine crept near.

A fat, weighty globe of solid gold lay in the middle of it, bristling with sapphires, and on each side of it a thin, ornate rod dozed in apparent tranquillity: the sceptres. 'Well,' said Jessamine severely. 'And what have you got to say for yourselves? You've given me a deal of trouble.'

The crockery went on minding its own business, whatever that was, without remark. Jessamine scowled.

'It was my fault,' admitted the prince. 'I was musing.'

'Making a joke of them, I suppose,' Jessamine guessed, knowing his highness to possess a peculiar notion of humour. She supposed his wife found it charming.

'Well, yes,' said the prince. 'Though I don't know how they could come to hear of it.'

A good question: Jessamine eyed them. 'Baldringa?' she guessed. 'Come out of there.'

'I shan't,' answered the orb, petulantly.

'The Wizard wants to faff, and I doubt you'd want to be lurking when he does.'

'Tell him to faff with some other golden orb. I'm using this one.'

'Some other Orb of Sovereignty? A thousand years old, enchanted with unfathomable power, and invested with all the royal pomp and whatnot?' Jessamine tapped the orb with a talon, *click click*. 'You find another golden orb. Go on.'

'No.'

'Don't make me use my Curse of Banishment. You won't like it.'

A sulking silence followed. The orb did not speak again, nor did the sceptres, but a slinking something whisked out of the air, and vanished: an old wizard, chastened.

'I'd better take these back, then,' said Jessamine, and did so.

* .*. * *. .

The towers of Dolons appeared first, in much the same way as the flags on the royal pavilion. Towers protrude, as a rule, and these more than most: as they drew nearer, Jessamine realised they were floating.

There were three, all differing in size: a wide, pale one, a narrow, dark one, and one so shining and delicate it had no business calling itself a structure. The building to which they were not quite attached had more glass in it than wall, and Jessamine understood at once why the Wizard had bothered with all the faffery. The Dolons Academy of Wizardry was that sort of place, no doubt: you wanted to put your big boots on, if you were going in.

Which they were, some of them. A small forest of coloured tents lay spread out across an expansive front lawn, ready to house the greater part of the Progress. A trio of Great Wizards—you could tell from the height and grandeur of their hats—stood waiting to welcome the rest, posed before the grand double doors like a collection of fanciful statues, still and smiling.

Garstang had got himself a hat. It wasn't especially impressive, a mere velvet bag of a thing, but that, too, made sense: there was no competing with these. He was right at the front on his flying carpet, and Jessamine with him; only the two royal pavilions went ahead of them.

'Now that we come to it,' Jessamine said, as the pavilions came to a halt and somebody started a speech, 'I think I am a bit nervous about Dolons, too.'

'It's wise to be,' answered the Wizard, her Wizard, and patently the best of them, regardless of hats.

Jessamine waited with titupping tail, wreathed in agitated smoke. Garstang had never talked of Dolons, in any regular way, but the name had often crossed his lips: whenever he completed some thorny cantrip or challenging spell, one that would stymy any ordinary wizard, he had a way of laughing—a great, hearty HAH! with an odd echo behind it—and then he'd say, to no one in particular, 'Take that, Dolons!'

The results of his magical labours made a fine show, Jessamine had to admit. The orb and sceptres seemed quite pleased with themselves, all lit up and slowly spinning, with nothing but wizardry to make them do it. The flags and pennants were playing music, she thought—something was, at any rate, and it sounded like nothing she'd ever heard before. And the grand pavilions, elevated as they were, wafting along despite their weight like leaves on the wind—really, the Court Wizard had made a creditable display of himself, for those who valued such things.

These people assuredly did. When the speeches were over (Jessamine, being wholly uninterested, heard not a word), the royalty had disembarked, and the rest of the Progress were dismissed to arrange their comforts as they liked, at last it was time for the Wizard Garstang to step forward—with Jessamine.

The three grand wizards expected something very fine indeed, for they were alert, all anticipation. Two of them were old men with white beards, as one might expect of a great magician, but the third was a woman, not a great deal older than Garstang. She was rotund, red-cheeked and dark-haired, with a glimmer of something about her—magic, or humour, or both. When the words "Castle Chansany's Court Wizard" were uttered (by the Lord Chamberlain, Myrtle, doing a fine job of fanfare), Garstang bowed.

The faces of two grand wizards fell in tandem, then two sets of overgrown eyebrows rose skywards. 'You?' said one of them. 'You are the Court Wizard?'

Garstang only smiled, though there might have been a bit of venom in it.

'Hello, Gar,' said the third, with a twinkle. 'Welcome back.'

Garstang grinned. 'Milady Roswin,' he returned, and bowed more floridly than ever.

The grand wizard Roswin wasn't the sort you would expect your Court magician to fall in love with. Surrounded as he was by the kingdom's finest ladies, a flower garden of rare and delicate blooms carefully cultivated to please; why this one, then?

She was a wizard, that must be a point in her favour. But her hair was untidy, she had a loud, uncouth sort of laugh, and she had patently spilled tea, or something like it, down the front of her ceremonial robe. She smelled like a human woman, too, which Jessamine gathered was undesirable; the fine ladies of the Court wore so many scents between them, she was like to sneeze for a week, if she got too close.

The two had fallen into conversation the moment the royals had been escorted away. Where the pair were wandering to, Jessamine did not know; neither did they, she suspected. They had a lot to say to each other, and Jessamine pattered quietly along behind them, trying her best not to overhear. She had never seen Garstang so spellbound—not with a *person*, at least. They smiled at each other, teased each other with a cosy familiarity, and, when they arrived (by accident or design) at the chamber marked for Garstang's use, they parted from each other with—with a hug, he got his arms all the way around her and everything. It wasn't the perfunctory sort, either: the hug went on for a while.

Jessamine crept in after Garstang and crouched by the door, her eyes very wide, and her heart palpitating in a very odd way.

Garstang did not notice, at first. He contented himself with wandering the handsome suite of rooms: a bedchamber hung with tapestries, and sapphire-coloured bed curtains; a study, with his own best-of-all-chairs already set down in it; a little room just for his clothes. He was humming.

He came out of his fog at last, and grinned in Jessamine's general direction. 'Come in, dragon. Have you seen the nest they've made for you? It's in the wardrobe-closet. I asked for some extra ribbons.'

This soothed, a little. Jessamine slunk thitherwards, and found a large basket there, filled to overflowing with fine, fancy fabrics (and, yes, ribbons). This ought to have pleased her; well, it did, in a distant way. But something hung heavy about her heart, and she tucked her face into a length of purple velvet, resolved to sleep the strange feelings away.

A demonstration of wizardry was taking place when Jessamine awoke, and trailed down to the great hall. Every wizard and student in the Academy must be assembled outside, not to mention the many folk of the Royal Progress. Jessamine could hear them, a roar of chatter and laughter and cheering, as well as diverse, less identifiable sounds: swooshes and thumps, bangs and pops; the sorts of things that filled her Wizard's study, from time to time, when he was restless.

Jessamine had often been lonely, in the days when she'd been a human (partly), and ugly, and not much use. She hadn't felt it since; not until today. The hall with its stone walls and mullioned windows seemed larger than before, a sea of emptiness: she could suffocate in it.

Hurriedly she scarpered, down the steps and out into the crowd.

Garstang was in the thick of it, of course. She could hear his deep voice, unusually amplified, booming; she wove her way through hundreds of legs until the forest of people ended, and there he was. He had the orb and the sceptres, again, was sporting with them; Their Majesties sat in splendour, a little raised above the masses, endeavouring to appear very much amused.

They probably were, at that. Garstang knew well how to amuse, though she didn't think it was his royal masters he was trying to impress—nor the grand wizards who had, once upon a time, most likely taught him his trade. It was Milady Roswin's good opinion he sought—had sought from the beginning, most like, with all the faffing.

They were staging a duel, pretending to battle one another. It hardly seemed right to employ priceless articles of crown property in such antics, but he was roguishly irreverent, always. It was one of the things she loved about him.

There was no sign of the other grand wizards. The bearded ones, who'd laughed at the idea of Garstang as a great wizard himself. And why not? Shouldn't they be presiding over the revelry, when its purpose must be to display the talents of Dolons' Masters? Hmm.

She spotted them at last, out on the edges of the crowd. One in a dark red robe, the other in green, and like enough, otherwise, to be brothers. They had their heads together, talking, and though their faces wore genial smiles as they watched Garstang and Roswin's display, Jessamine knew a thinly-disguised grimace when she saw one.

She left the circle, just as Garstang executed an especially impressive feat of wizardry: he'd fired an illusory wall of flame at his opponent, and it had (after a roar of approval from the audience) dissolved into a gentle rain of stars. And hearts, she noted gloomily. The crowd sighed gladly.

She didn't wait to see how Milady Roswin took the gesture, for the scowlsome wizards were on the move. Their gait seemed, to her, stealthy, prowling, and that aroused her suspicions. She slunk in behind them, kept herself close. She could wish the crowds quieter, the roar of noise lesser; there was no picking out more than a few words of her quarries' conversation.

'—bound to employ Hade's Second Manoeuvre—pure arrogance—'

'—volatile, extremely volatile—'

'—if we were to—effects quite startling—'

'—rid of her, at least—even both—'

Jessamine, rigid with horror, missed whatever they said next altogether, and had to scramble to catch up. Rid of them both? What! Sabotage, was it? Extremely volatile—whatever Hade's Second Manoeuvre might be, there was danger to it; something that could go wrong. In Garstang's hands (who else could they be referring to when they spoke of "pure arrogance"), it would be safe enough, but with malicious interference—

Jessamine abandoned the scheming pair, and bolted for the circle at the centre of the crowd. The quantity of legs seemed to have quadrupled, and they were bent on her destruction, every one of them; thrice she was almost stamped upon, and she ran full-tilt into someone's foot, bumping her head smartly.

At last, the clearing: she hurtled into blank space, halted in momentary befuddlement.

There were Garstang's shoes: the toes curled over. She ran at them. 'Wizard!' she hissed. 'Do not perform Hade's Second Manoeuvre!'

'Cannot talk just at present,' Garstang answered, sounding rather strained: he hadn't heard her.

What was he doing, and by the by the Lady Roswin's feet, the trailing hems of her robe, were absent—Jessamine looked up.

She was flying. Of course she was, what a fine display it made; no chair or carpet under her to facilitate her flight, just a stray wisp of cloud, with stars in it. All of Garstang's focus was fixed on her, and well it might be: to levitate a carpet with himself on it was one thing, but to send a woman soaring through the skies like a swan, at least ten feet up— quite another.

Extremely volatile. 'Bring her down,' Jessamine barked. 'Now! If you drop her—'

'I would never drop her,' answered Garstang, through shut teeth.

'I know *you* wouldn't, but *they* might.' The interfering wizards were beyond Jessamine's sight, but they were out there, and plotting.

'I have this under perfect control,' Garstang insisted, though he was sweating with the strain of it.

'Pure arrogance is right,' Jessamine spat. 'If you love this lady, get her down from there, now.'

That got his attention: he threw her a startled glance—as though his feelings hadn't been evident from the beginning—and said, 'What? Oh.'

Whatever he saw in Jessamine—palpable panic, perhaps—galvanised him at last. He was almost in time, too; his attention snapped back to the levitated lady, and she sank, slowly, two or three feet down.

Then the threads of mist holding her up there dissolved to nothingness, and she fell like a stone.

Garstang saw it coming, as did Jessamine: they were both moving her way at a run, an instinctive response; what did Jessamine think she was going to do if she got there first? She'd only be squashed flat.

And she was, a bit. Garstang didn't so much catch Roswin as collide with her falling body. They went down, Jessamine all a-tangle with them, and lay, for a moment, in a three-way stupor.

'I'm not dead,' Jessamine uttered after a moment, with not a little surprise. She lay with most of Garstang's considerable weight crushing her, and could barely breathe.

'I am,' Garstang croaked. 'I think.' For his part, he had all of Roswin's not inconsiderable weight to bear: she seemed stunned.

Jessamine heaved and wriggled her way free. The crowds were swarming around the downed trio, with much concerned chatter and commentary; rising over the medley of remarks came somebody's booming great voice. '—deeply irresponsible display—shocking misuse of power—unthinkable in a graduate of Dolon's—'

Jessamine made her way—slightly pained—to the feet of the loud person in question. He had shoes with curly toes, like Garstang's; a final insult. She readied her teeth.

'—immediate review into the circumstances—could have been killed—suspension from the faculty—ouch!'

A pair of cold grey eyes scowled down at her. Jessamine grinned, broadly.

'A dragon! This is all that was needed. And quite wild in its habits—not at all domesticated—'

'I heard you,' Jessamine interrupted. 'Plotting.'

The wizard—it was the one in the green robe—stopped talking.

'If Milady Roswin had died, it would've been you that killed her. I know it. And if you try to hurt either of them again, I will make sure everybody else knows it, too.'

His steely eyes glinted, mouth curled up in a scornful smile. 'And who would believe you, dragon?'

'I'm the Court Dragon of Castle Chansany. The Wizard Garstang's Familiar. I have tea with Her Majesty Queen Mellany every week. You decide.'

She left him then, rather hurriedly, in case he had any dark thoughts of disposing of her, too. She scarpered back to her own, dear Wizard, finding him on his feet again, with Roswin leaning on his arm.

'You're the greatest fool there ever was,' she informed him. 'And insufferably pompous, to boot.'

'That is true,' allowed Garstang, unsmiling.

Roswin sighed. 'No harm is done, however.'

'Not for lack of trying,' Jessamine muttered darkly.

Roswin gazed at Jessamine's Wizard with an odd sort of smile: a gentle, fluffy, moonish face. 'Garstang would never hurt me.'

'I didn't say it was him that was trying,' Jessamine snapped. She was growling, without meaning to, even snarling a bit. The events of the day had stretched her patience in too many ways, and shattered it. She briefly considered awarding both the maddening pair a bite to the ankles, and thought better of it.

Instead she scuttled away, back to her wardrobe nest, and went grumblishly to sleep.

*   *   *   *   *

'I suppose they didn't like you much,' she said the next day, from a place of honour atop a floating carpet all her own. The Progress had moved out, leaving Dolons—and the Lady Roswin—behind.

Jessamine had been briefly afraid that Garstang meant to stay behind with her; he was tempted. But he hadn't.

'My tutors?' Garstang answered. 'Not a bit.' In a better mood, he would have smiled at that—grinned, even, half sheepish, half amused. 'I was... erratic,' he allowed.

'And arrogant.'

'Always that, yes.' Garstang rode tailor-style on his favoured mossy rug, the curled toes of his shoes sticking up, along with his hair. His personal grooming suffered when his heart did, she noticed.

'They're dangerous. The grand wizards.'

Garstang's expression darkened. 'One of them, especially.'

'I don't mean dangerous to the heart.' Jessamine spat in disgust. 'I mean dangerous to everything else. They could have killed your lady-me-love.'

'She isn't that,' Garstang said. 'And there's no proof they were hoping to murder her, dragon. Or me, either.'

'What else is like to happen when you drop a woman from a height of ten feet?'

Garstang sighed. 'The error was mine. I should not have been performing Hade's Second Manoeuvre at all, and never upon Roswin.'

'You're arrogant, but not without cause,' Jessamine said. 'If anyone can perform volatile magical manoeuvres without risk or flaw, it's you. All would have been well, if those two hadn't meddled.'

'She wasn't supposed to be elected to the Council. No one thought she would win.' Garstang smiled: he was proud. 'For that, they dislike her even more than they dislike me, I believe.'

'She'll be all right, won't she?' Jessamine asked. 'Back there with them?'

'Roswin is the most brilliant wizard I ever knew, and I am including myself.' Garstang gave a little sigh. 'And the most brilliant woman, too. She beat me at everything.'

Love was certainly strange. Ordinarily, her eccentric, top-lofty Wizard would despise such a person. 'She'll say yes, next time,' Jessamine said, around a mouthful of something—yes—just a little bitter.

Garstang gave her a sharp look. 'How did you know that I'd—?'

'You're transparent as a pane of Dolons glass.'

He laughed, at that. 'I think she will never marry. She has too much to do.' He patted her head, though, gently, and added, 'Until then, you are woman enough for me, Jess-o-mine.'

He jested, of course. Jessamine would have to be contented with that; and, for the most part, she was.

DREAMSTUFF

Something was off. The Wizard Garstang, chief magician to the Court of Castle Chansany, knew it the moment he opened his eyes, stretched hard enough to crack all the bones in his long spine. He lay abed a while, blinking hazily at an unfamiliar ceiling, and thinking.

Nothing hurt, at least. His head, limbs, heart all felt sound enough—what had they *done* to the ceiling, honestly, did it require quite so many curlicues? —The Court, on Progress, had been for several days the guests of the Baron Trent, a frail fellow, with a young wife who liked *things*—

—Perhaps his head did hurt, come to think of it. The curls and flourishes across the ceiling didn't help, busy and glaring, like the rest of Trentwood. He liked a bold colour himself, would not have objected to the emerald paint, but all the flowers—

He turned his face to the window, where sunlight filtered through diamond-paned glass. Something was off, but he couldn't say what—his mouth tasted foul, what in the world had he eaten at last night's feast? Or drunk, more likely, the wine had been excellent and copious, that explained the headache, but there was nothing in any of that to much disturb him; it would soon pass.

He searched his mind, groping through sleep-fog like a man blinded, finding nothing...

Nothing. That was it, that was *it*. Ten minutes awake, and scant thoughts rattling about a brain hollow as a blown egg. Where was the riot? The messy mass of mirage, strange visions and mad ideas; he hadn't dreamed. Not a scrap, not so much as a flicker of dreamstuff.

'This is terrible,' he said, heart thudding. He hurled himself out of bed, dressed in velvet and silk, brushed the tangles out of his hair; ran at last out of his bedchamber and clattered down the stairs, as though he might run away from the silence in his mind. Alas, it went with him.

He talked overmuch at breakfast, merry to the point of fever. Ladies flocked about him like sparrows, chattering and flapping— 'The best wizard in the kingdom, I daresay he shall do something magical presently—Oh! Oh! Turn us a trick, Lord Wizard! Can you make my hair curl?' (A woman sallow, hair as limp as wet paper) 'Can you alter the hue of this gown? I never did like red above half (a woman roseate, her face flaming as bright as her velvets) 'O! Would it not be the dearest thing if Peachblossom were to talk? How I should like to know what the sweet creature thinks! (A woman stout and vapid, dandling a ball of canine fluff upon her knee like 'twere a child).

The Garstang of yesterday would have obliged—had, in fact, made a dish spin atop the brocade tablecloth, caused a gold-chased pot of tea to pour itself out for a lady.

But today he hadn't dreamed, and he dared not cast—not even a mellow little cantrip. Not here, in front of everyone; that must wait. 'Patience, good ladies, patience,' said he with a wink, and a wizardly flourish. 'You shall see magic aplenty tonight, and I must save my strength for it.' There was revelry planned, the sort to make a showman of him: music and mischief.

They tittered, and let him be. He daubed sweat from his brow with a surreptitious swipe of his napkin, and wished for Jessamine. Where at Trentwood was she like to be?

*　.　*　.　✳　*　.　*

The dragon in question avoided the dining-rooms at meal-times, as a fixed and unbreakable rule. The tumult bothered her ears, and the way the courtiers had of flirting with all and sundry—especially Garstang—set her sharp teeth on edge. Coy glances, witty sallies and ripples of laughter; goodness, no. Not even the choicest morsels could tempt her.

Besides, she had made a friend of the cook below-stairs, and half the kitchen maids, too. They kept her well-supplied.

She was down there even as her master formed his wish for her, having slept curled around a chair-leg before the dying fire. She was on hand to receive a plump duck's egg, fresh out of the poaching water; the crusts of the fine white bread a maid, Sally, was toasting; the skins, pungent and slippery, from a pile of kippers, rich with smoke.

Following which repast, she felt equal to anything—which was fortunate, as it was going to be the sort of day when anything could happen.

'You're wanted,' said Sally, just as Jessamine curled up by the hearth again, to sleep off her rich breakfast. 'They're asking all over the castle for you.'

'They?' she queried, without opening either eye.

Sally shrugged, slicing with her great knife into a crisp onion: *snick*. 'Cannot say as to who, or why. Seems pressing, though.'

Grudgingly, Jessamine uncurled, and stretched out her thin red tail to its furthest inch. 'Doubtless a disaster brewing. They've got wizards for that sort of thing, you would think.'

'Aren't you a wizard?' Sally's knife made short work of another onion, flashing in the firelight.

'Only when I can't avoid it.' She was the Wizard's Familiar, or so he called her, and she had been known to help with a cantrip or two, on occasion. But not if she could help it. 'I suppose I'd better—'

She was interrupted by the entry of a page in green livery, his young face flushed with exertion, or excitement, or both. 'Is the Wizard's Dragon here?' bawled he, the words falling all over each other with his haste.

'Yes,' sighed Jessamine, resigning herself.

'Oh! Well then, milady, I'm to tell you you're wanted upstairs, very quickly, that is to say immediately, ma'am, if you please, for there's an emergency afoot.'

He had hair the colour of Sally's onion-skins, Jessamine noted idly. 'And who is it as wants me?'

'The Wizard, milady, if you please.'

No one had called Jessamine "Milady" before, that she could recall. It was not unpleasing, except that he was patently doing so in hopes of softening the impact of these peremptory summons. She flicked her tongue over the points of her teeth: yes, nice and sharp. Ready for biting.

'I come,' she assured him. 'There's no use asking you where the Wizard is, of course. He's like a moth, always flitting off, just when you want him.'

'He was in the music room last I saw, milady ma'am,' said the page, and bowed.

The music room was the last place she was likely to find him now, then. Jessamine stifled a groan, and hauled her overloaded belly towards the door. 'Sally,' she said as she slunk into the passage. 'Pray save me an onion tart, for later. I'll need reviving.'

'That I will,' answered the maid, and off went Jessamine.

The Wizard being a creature of the purest chaos, Jessamine found him entirely by accident, and when she least expected to do so. Which is to say she found him the moment she stepped into the great hall, and by means of being—almost—stomped to pieces as he stormed through.

'Ah!' ejaculated he, coming to a sudden stop, and beaming down at her. She didn't like that smile at all; he was in one of his mad moods. 'Dragon, I am all to pieces.'

Jessamine surveyed him. He looked ordinary enough, dressed in his fancy garb and with a soft velvet bag of a hat over his dark hair. His curly-toed shoes were a little scuffed, to be sure, but not much, and her nose informed her he hadn't forgotten to wash recently. 'What seems to be the problem?' she ventured to enquire.

'Well!' said he, with gusto. He did not elaborate, save by making a series of mysterious gestures with his expressive hands: magic in progress. He uttered a cantrip, too, in a rolling, booming voice, and Jessamine awaited the results. A great bang, and a shower of coloured sparks; all the heavy oak chairs and silver chalices turned into butterflies, and flown away; the tapestries brought down off the walls, and reciting poetry. Anything of the sort.

None of these things happened, nor did anything else: the hall, empty apart from their two selves, rang with a quality of silence that could not but strike dread deep into Jessamine's soul.

The Wizard Garstang was never silent. He didn't know how to do silence, or rest; he was a whirlwind of a man, a hurricane of madness and magic and merriment.

Jessamine stared up at him. His eyes were wide and wild, and he was sweating.

'You've...' began Jessamine, and couldn't go on.

'Yes,' said Garstang, heavily.

'You've lost your magic.'

The Wizard (erstwhile) held up both hands, palm out, in a helpless gesture: nothing, it said. Nothing here.

'Oh, dear,' said Jessamine, and sat down on the cold stone floor. 'This is very bad indeed.'

'Terrible,' groaned Garstang. 'I'd as soon die, Jess-o-mine.'

'Come, now, less of that. Most of us live magicless lives, and are none the worse for it.'

'Yes, but I cannot.'

She couldn't argue with him, not really. Garstang without his wizardry, who was he? A mere courtier in fine shoes, a being of shallow wit and hollow courtesies. And, she thought, a mad-man. The magic and the chaos of him were one and the same: deprived of the one, he could never tolerate the other.

'How did it happen?' she asked.

'I woke up empty. Naught in my head but a thought of breakfast, Jess-o-mine, that was all!'

'I don't follow that.'

'I didn't dream, dragon. Not so much as a flicker.'

'Perhaps you just…forgot,' Jessamine suggested. 'It's the common way with dreams, isn't it? Nobody remembers all the peculiar things that go on in our heads in the night…' She trailed off, for Garstang was wearing a face that said: *Oh, don't I?*

'I,' he answered with dignity, 'never forget.'

'And if you don't dream, there's no magic either.'

'What is magic, but the stuff of dreams?' A fine sentiment, she thought, but in this case meant more literally than she might otherwise assume. Not a metaphor: the truth.

'Have you ever gone a night without dreaming before? Perhaps it was just the one.'

'Never,' said he, dashing that hope.

Jessamine nodded. 'Right. Well, then you must see a healer.'

'An apothecary?' He scoffed. 'What manner of concoction are they like to give me, that I cannot make myself—and better?'

'Or that Tambul cannot make for you,' Jessamine said tartly. 'You being shy of actual labour.'

He waved this off. 'Believe me, if we had anything in the dispensary that could remedy a dream-drought, I'd have taken it already.'

The entire contents of Castle Chansany's Potionery had been brought along on the Progress, Jessamine knew, at fantastic cost. Garstang had insisted; 'And what if I'm called upon to perform some important wizardry, and without the tools to do it?' he'd said, with enough justice to sway Her Majesty (and the Lord Chamberlain).

'Then what's the cause?' Jessamine said. 'Who or what could have the power to bleed your brain dry of dreaming?'

'I don't know, dragon, but we need to find out.'

'Of course. *We* need to find out,' she muttered. 'Cannot you manage a little emergency yourself, once in a while?' She'd been trying to have a holiday. Catch up on her napping, eat too much confectionery, that sort of thing.

Garstang said nothing, but his face changed. There was real anguish there, when you stopped and really looked at him. Fear, too. She'd never seen him afraid before, not really, and now he was petrified.

'Right,' she said, her mood shifting as mercurially as her Wizard's did, most days. 'Right,' she said again. 'Don't worry. We will have this sorted by the end of the day, and you'll be chock-full of dreams again by the morning.'

'But there's to be a feast tonight,' Garstang reminded her. 'With music, and dancing, and a banquet, and Trentwood's Magician is presiding.'

The Magician of Trentwood was a man of Garstang's own age, and full of vim and vigour. He had patently identified the Court Wizard as a chief rival, and set himself to outdo him at every opportunity. His name was Lord Silverton (a title granted on account of his wizardry rather than his lineage, Garstang had said, with a proper contempt at the presumption), and he would delight in humiliating Garstang—and, by extension, the Court of Castle Chansany.

'Well. Then this is all very urgent indeed, isn't it? Best get started.' Jessamine bit his ankle, just gently, to shock him out of his stupor. 'Garstang. To the library. If there's a book about this then you must find it.'

'Yes,' he said, shaking himself. 'I'll take the scriveners with me.'

'I'm going to talk to Tambul,' Jessamine decided, and without waiting for either answer or interference, she scurried off.

Wizard Garstang got on better with delegating studious tasks, in the general way of things. It wasn't that he didn't like reading, or that he had no diligence. It was only that his mind had a way of flying away from the subject at hand, and the less interest he felt in a topic, the sooner his butterfly brain was like to wander off.

Well. He had a strong motive to pursue a greater understanding of dreaming, and magic, and the links between the two—not to mention the nefarious possibilities inherent in the business. That didn't make him interested, quite.

The library at Trentwood would never compete with that of Castle Chansany, but that was no fair standard. It was a very respectable book room, for a provincial mansion house:

sizeable, with polished walnut shelves up to the ceilings, most of them stuffed full of leather-bound volumes. Three tall windows let very little light through their thick mullioned panes; the housekeeper, or perhaps the maids, had set several beeswax candles out to counteract the gloom, each enclosed in a glass surround. The drapes, heavy crimson things, stirred in a pervasive draught: the wind keened outside, and rain beat hard against the windows.

A drearier morning's work Garstang could not, at that moment, imagine.

'The matter's rather important,' Garstang informed the three scriveners he had hauled out of a frigid annex off the great hall (where they were copying royal proclamations), and swept along with him, like a row of ducklings. 'By what means might a person—a wizard, say—cause another person—also, perhaps, a wizard—to cease dreaming? If you can have an answer for me before sundown—' He broke off, for it struck him that a long patch of gloom in one corner might be occupied. It was, it absolutely was; a man sat there, not even reading, merely silent.

A glimmer of long, silvery hair revealed his identity, even if his face lay in shadow. Lord Silverton. The hair was an affectation, of course; the man wasn't old. It matched the rings on his long fingers, paired beautifully with his elegant name; Garstang scowled.

The Wizard of Trentwood was watching him.

'Yes, well, hurry along,' Garstang snapped, dismissing the scriveners. They scattered towards the shelves. Garstang hesitated, minded to get out of the library post-haste, and find some other, more interesting occupation. But Silverton's cool stare piqued his interest—and his irritation. Had he no manners?

'Something seems to have caught your attention,' Garstang observed, having placed himself near enough to watch the other wizard's face.

A faint smile answered him. 'You are having trouble with your magic, are you?'

'Who told you that?'

Silverton shrugged. 'No one. But if you've lost your dreaming—'

'I haven't lost it. It is merely—temporarily compromised.'

'How inconvenient.'

'Given that I have revelry to host tonight, it is thoroughly inconvenient. I don't suppose you know of a solution?'

Silverton turned his sleekly elegant head, and stared out at the flashing silver rain. 'I really couldn't say.'

The man was probably delighted about it; no Court Wizard showing off his superior craft at Trentwood, most desirable.

Perhaps he was even responsible for Garstang's plight. His pose of bland unconcern certainly suggested it.

'Never mind,' he said, his tone as bland as Silverton's expression. 'I'll have my magic back by nightfall.'

'I do hope so,' said Silverton, distantly.

Garstang abandoned him to his patent daydreaming—insult to injury, that—and stalked off.

Tambul, the Wizard's Apprentice, rarely left the Mixery, when the Court resided at Castle Chansany. If he wasn't there, he would be in the Potionery, or—very occasionally—in the Dispensary (the latter not particularly preferred, since it threatened him with the appalling prospect of having to talk to the recipients of his potions).

Trentwood had no such rooms. As such, Jessamine was at a loss to imagine what the irascible wizard-in-training might have found to do with himself, and where. He had no interest in food, save as sustenance, so she ruled out the dining rooms and banqueting houses. He probably wasn't in the library or the reading-rooms, preferring the company of his own notebooks (or the Wizard Garstang's spell books, of course). He certainly wouldn't be anywhere the courtiers were gathering, or the residents of Trentwood, either. He'd be tucked away in a quiet corner, and the crowded mansion didn't have many of those left.

She found him at last in the music room, of all places. No quiet spot, that, one would think, save that most of the instruments had been taken out of it, and carried off; Jessamine had heard the results in snatches, as she'd scuttled about the house looking for Tambul.

He—small, dishevelled and glowering—had tidied himself away into a window-seat, with an old lute tucked into his lap. The battered thing had only two strings left to it, one of which Tambul sat desultorily plucking. It twanged discordantly.

'Tambul,' barked Jessamine, rushing across the room, and screeching to a stop at his feet. 'What have you got in your potion chests? We need a dream-draught.'

Tambul roused abruptly, like a man surfacing out of deep water. 'A dream-draught? As though I might have such a thing. That's ridiculous.'

'The Wizard needs it.'

'What?' Tambul set the lute down, sat up straighter. 'Nonsense. He's got a head full of dreams. Thousands. Or he wouldn't be the Wizard, now would he?'

'Exactly,' said Jessamine, and waited for this to sink in.

Tambul was no slow-wit. His eyes opened wide; 'Oh,' he said, the word layered with shades of dismay.

'If you haven't got a dream-draught, then we need to make one.'

'Make a—' Tambul spluttered, silenced (for a moment) by sheer incredulity. 'You cannot just make a dream-draught, Jessamine.'

'Why not? We need one, and by sundown, too.'

'Where do you propose to get the dreams to mix into it?'

'I beg your pardon?' Jessamine's tail began to tap with irritation. Really, the man had no grasp of the concept of an emergency.

'We can't mix up good, useful dream-stuff out of nothing. Visions, possibly, hallucinations— but not dreams. They've got to be the proper sort.'

'What's the difference?'

Tambul sighed and picked up his lute again. There was an aggravated quality to his subsequent twanging. 'A vision can be anything. It doesn't matter, provided it's not meant to be the prophetic sort. But a dream is something else. They're personal. They come from the heart and the soul. They are made from wishes, hopes, and terror. They speak to you of all the things you cannot admit to yourself when you're wakeful. Do you see?'

'Yes,' said Jessamine grimly. Here was a problem indeed. Who knew what secret terrors haunted the Wizard Garstang's soul? Or covert wishes, either? None but he, provided that he dreamed, and that was precisely what he was no longer doing.

Tambul plucked a discordant chord. 'If he'd kept any old ones about, I suppose he would have mentioned it.'

'He didn't. Mind you, he was in a panic. I don't suppose he was thinking clearly.'

Tambul stared. 'Wizard Garstang, in a panic?'

'I know. I never saw such a thing before, either.'

Tambul set the lute down again, hard; it met the windowsill with a sharp *thunk*. 'Well, that changes things.'

'How?'

'This is an emergency. A real one.'

'I know.'

Tambul flexed his short, thick fingers, a workman readying his tools. 'We can try for a dream-draught. We'll need dream-catchers and some sleepy volunteers.'

'I volunteer!' said Jessamine, sitting up straight.

'I don't know, Jessamine. You don't look at all sleepy.'

This was true. She was far too lively, a mix of hope and interest and an obscure fear setting her wits to jumping.

'Besides,' Tambul went on. 'To do it by sundown? I doubt it.'

'Then what,' Jessamine snarled. 'Honestly, Tambul, you're no help.'

'We can try to mend the Wizard.'

'Mend—? What, is he broken?'

'Not broken. Cracked a bit down the middle, perhaps. Something's become of his wishes and fears, and maybe we could find out what.'

'As if he would ever tell.'

'Well, he'll have to, won't he? Because you won't like the third option, and neither will he.'

Jessamine attempted to resign herself, which was hard. It felt like hanging a dead weight from her heart. 'What's that?'

'We accept that he can't wizard, at this time, and get someone else to do it.'

'Oh.'

'Yes.'

'Meaning you.'

'And you. You aren't the Wizard's Apprentice now, but you were, not so long ago.'

'ME?' The syllable broke from Jessamine's maw like a wave, a surge of horror. 'But I was terrible at it.'

'So I heard.'

'And what's more, I didn't like it.'

'Then who else do you suggest? Because I'm not up to all his tricks, not at a Court Revel.'

'There's another one about. Silverton.'

Tambul snorted. 'You try telling the Wizard that. He'll eat his own hat rather than ask the Wizard of Trentwood to cover for him.'

*　.　*　*　＊　*　*.　*

This, alas, was all too true. It wasn't a matter of arrogance, despite appearances. The Wizard of Castle Chansany had one fear left to his name, at least, and it was presently fuelling all his uncharacteristic panic—and his stubbornness, too. But who among us likes to feel that we can be easily outdone by our peers and rivals—or, worse yet, replaced?

If anyone had thought to ask, he might have admitted to some unusual feelings (or, perhaps, a lack thereof). A dead weight around his heart, as Jessamine might have put it.

Then again, perhaps he would not. Self-knowledge is enough of a challenge, let alone performing it upon demand.

Either way, when the Wizard Garstang took himself off to his chamber, and lay down upon the bed, and tried, at least, to daydream, nothing came of it.

He lay like a shadow of himself, stripped of colour. Visions had he aplenty, of the things he had used to want, but they had faded somehow, worn thin. Power, of course, always that; great and terrible magics, and influence at Court. Well, he'd had both, and for some years, too. The dreams of yesteryear had worn out at last, like an old pair of shoes, and what had taken their place instead—well. No one knows save the Wizard, and he isn't saying—not even to himself.

He gave up on the daydreaming at last, and hurtled to his feet again. It wasn't energy fuelling this surge of activity, more a kind of feverish restlessness. He'd felt it before, though never so strongly, nor so often, as of late.

A thought struck him like a thunderbolt, stopped him halfway down the twisting stairs to the library. Was that it? Was that what had turned off his dreams and his magic, like the spigot on a keg of beer? Was he bored?

'Stars alive,' he swore, for he had a quick, sharp, darting sort of mind; he had hit upon the truth.

And what a truth, the very heights of inconvenience! To decide now, halfway through the Royal Progress, that he wanted none of it, he'd had enough. Their Majesties would kill him, he was sure of it, take off his head, defenestrate him with the greatest relish—

Well, no. *They* would not. Jessamine might.

Narrative irony being what it is—inevitable—it *would* be at this moment that the dragon herself came skittering up the stairs, wings flaring, and ran into him.

'Ouch,' she said to his shins, and looked up. 'Oh. There you are.'

She sounded cross, but this was often the case. 'Hello, Jess-o-mine,' he said, attempting joviality.

He received suspicion by way of reply. 'Your eyes look strange,' she said, squinting her own at him.

He blinked them. 'I feel strange,' he admitted.

She sighed. 'Tambul says you're half cracked. I suppose that means something's amiss.'

Tambul had the right of it, on the whole; Garstang felt cracked, fractured down the middle, half his heart still wedded to the Castle and all its ways, the other aching for freedom.

'There is something amiss.'

She sat down on the stone step, and wrapped the curve of her tail around his ankle. 'Better air it, if I were you. It'll only fester, otherwise.'

Garstang sat down too, and put his head in his hands. 'I'm afraid you'll be angry.'

'I often am,' she said calmly.

Well. Nothing for it. Garstang hauled the awful truth out of his soul and held it up for her to look at.

She was silent, perhaps with dismay. Perhaps with disgust. He was half disgusted with himself; how could he grow bored with prestige, power, and privilege?

At last, she sighed, a long and smoky exhalation. 'This is since Dolons, isn't it?'

'Yes.'

'Is it the Lady Roswin?'

'Partly.' He thought about it. It was partly the lady; he had taken the piece of his heart that missed her (most of it) and locked it up somewhere, but it was beating against the doors, now.

It was partly Dolons itself. An academy of powerful, creative wizards—even if some of the old masters despised him, well, that was mutual. The company of his peers, the challenge of new magic, old powers, ideas! A heady mix, energising.

'You'd better go back, then,' offered Jessamine.

Garstang surfaced from his own thoughts long enough to detect a note of sadness in her tone. She was profoundly sad, he thought, but trying to be brave about it. As he debated what to say, her scaled head came to rest against his knee, and stayed there.

He laid a hand upon it. 'Shall you come with me, Jess-o-mine?'

He felt her still; for a moment, she wasn't even breathing. 'Shall I, though?' she said, half a gasp.

'I hope you would. I hope you will.' He meant it; the prospect of a new life lost much of its shine, if there was to be no Jessamine in it.

Her tail began to tap. 'I'd miss the Castle something terrible,' she said, but it didn't sound like a no.

'Me, too,' he admitted. 'We would visit, of course.'

'Of course, we would visit,' she agreed.

'And Baldringa could return as the Court Wizard. There's no getting rid of her anyway.' She was probably lurking within earshot at that moment, the gauzy mist of her dissolved into his belt-buckle, say, or the jewels on his shoes.

'I'd suggest Tambul, but I think he would hate it. He's a Potioner.'

'A superb one,' Garstang agreed.

They fell silent, for a time, both lost in thought: new horizons, new adventures. New dreams.

At last Garstang said, 'Well, Jess-o-mine, have you decided? What's it to be?'

Jessamine beamed at him, a real smile, with all her teeth in it. 'I'll go with you,' she said, and his heart eased.

When the Royal Progress left Trentwood three days later, it took the old wizard, Baldringa, with it, and the new wizard, Silverton. It took Tambul, the Potioner (promoted from the post of Wizard's Apprentice). It took Moggat, once of the kitchens, now an Apprentice Wizard (replacing Tambul). It took the king and queen, the prince and princess, the Lord Chamberlain Myrtle, the bards, the jongleurs, the Wardrobe, Chef Paglar and all the cooks, the scriveners, the scholars and, of course, the furniture.

The Wizard Garstang, once of the Court, now of Dolons (maybe) went another way, and Jessamine with him. He'd got his dreaming back, his magic with it; and truth be told, so had she. With his spell books and his carpet and his dragon to go with him, Garstang flew off into the mists of the future with the lightest of hearts, and the brightest of smiles.

With her hoard of silk ribbons, her butter cakes, and her wizard to go with her, Jessamine bared her teeth at the wind and the future, half a grimace, half a grin. There was a strange fizzing in her blood, a racing of her heart, a jumping of her wits and her nerves. It was fear, it was excitement, it was possibility. 'There's one question I perhaps ought to have asked,' she said, as the turrets of Trentwood blended into the clouds behind them, and disappeared. 'What am I going to do at Dolons?'

Garstang had a lute with him, he was playing a lively tune. 'Anything you like, Jess-o-mine,' he decided, strumming. 'Anything in all the world.'

WITH GRATITUDE

The Castle Chansany tales appeared first on Patreon. My thanks and appreciation to all my wonderful patrons for supporting, reading and loving the adventures of Jessamine, Garstang, and all the rest of the Castle Chansany cast.

https://www.patreon.com/charlottenglish

Also by Charlotte E. English

House of Werth

Wyrde and Wayward

Wyrde and Wicked

Wyrde and Wild

Wyrde and Wondrous

Wonder Tales

Faerie Fruit

Gloaming

Sands and Starlight

Summertide

Ravensby Od

www.charlotteenglish.com